WE ARE THE KINGS

WE ARE THE THE KINGS

A NOVEL

ARIANE TORRES

BOLD STORY PRESS

Washington, DC

Bold Story Press, Washington, DC 20016
www.boldstorypress.com

This is a work of fiction. Names, characters, places, and incidents either are the product of the author's imagination or are
used fictitiously. Any resemblance to actual persons, living or
dead, events, or locales is entirely coincidental.

First edition published March 2022

Library of Congress Control Number: 2021919583

ISBN: 978-1-954805-13-2 (paperback)
ISBN: 978-1-954805-14-9 (e-book)

Text and cover design by Laurie Entringer
Cover photo by William Porter Davisson, France circa 1960

Printed in the United States of America
10 9 8 7 6 5 4 3 2 1

For JMT

CHAPTER ONE

'll admit that I didn't handle it well, falling to pieces that way after seeing a woman I somehow knew from the window of a train somewhere outside of Johannesburg. Keith had shifted in his seat, annoyed and embarrassed, quickly scanning the train car, I think to determine if other passengers were as appalled by my behavior as he was. I didn't try to explain my reaction, what the woman, who I of course couldn't really have known, evoked for me. Because it wouldn't have made sense, particularly to Keith, that a strange woman's familiar face made me think of my childhood, my grandmother Adele, the suffering of the displaced, a multitude of other things. That would have been too much for him. He was a literal, vanilla wafer of a man, and he'd already been through enough. And this was supposed to have been a romantic trip.

Our relationship, though new, hadn't been smooth. There had been the requisite incompatibilities. I was too liberal; he lacked the proper reverence for Liz Phair and T.L.C. I like to eat while reclining; he prefers to be upright and equipped with proper utensils. There had been our first weekend getaway that I'd promptly ruined by having my personality, huffing off in the middle of dinner after a wine-fueled tirade about I-can't-remember-what. But Keith had held on, and I respected the hell out of him for it.

We'd met at a bar a few weeks after I'd adopted my pit bull Roo, a beautiful block-headed darling of a dog who was in desperate need of my Jewish mothering. Though I'd undertaken dog-ownership on a whim, tending to Roo's

1

needs became me, which is to say that despite being a bit weary from trudging to and from dog parks, I was also palpably, magnetically aglow with the satisfaction that comes from raising a child alone. I'd pranced into the bar wearing a tasteful but understated vintage sundress and ordered a Scotch. Keith was seated on a stool sipping a reasonable pale ale. He was wearing Dad Nikes without any evidence of shame, and I was inexplicably drawn to him. After I'd fallen hopelessly close to love, I described him to Adele on the telephone. This man is different from the others, I told her. He owns numerous pairs of unwrinkled khakis that he hangs in his closet on actual hangers. He takes vitamins almost every day. He has the wherewithal to purchase things like batteries and light bulbs and socks. She was decidedly moved. My goodness, she said. Is he a homosexual?

It was because of my aunt Joan, my father's sister, that we ended up in South Africa in the first place. I'd called her sometime last spring from Adele's house in Newport, Rhode Island, a stately old cedar shake mansion, perched high on a craggy bluff that overlooks the ocean. I'd sat in the kitchen, cross-legged in a Windsor chair, the receiver of the rotary phone resting on my shoulder, its coils stretched taut by years of women sitting and talking just as I was. I'd fled New York for one of many long weekends, after taking a leave of absence from my job, for no real reason, or a multitude of them, none of which made sense to Joan. Well, then you should at least see something of the world, she told me. After all, her life hadn't even really begun until she moved to Cape Town the autumn after she turned forty-three, she said, which made her sound like Adele, which I didn't mention because she doesn't like being told that she's at all like her mother. Which for the most part she isn't.

I'd left work at a high point, having just successfully managed a project that involved implementing small in- and outdoor garden-farms at a few medium-security prisons upstate. My boss Leon referred to our operation as an environmental advocacy think tank, which it wasn't at all.

We simply aided other projects already underway, providing research assistance, embarrassingly unsubstantial manpower, and money, to causes that supported our outlined ethics. My first role had been as a researcher for the virtues of compostable toilets. Then I was tasked with speaking publicly at two events about reusable tampons, which are less unpleasant than you might think. My coworkers had shunned me initially, I think because they assumed that a woman like me, no stranger to an indulgent facial, rarely without a designer handbag carelessly flung over a suntanned shoulder, could not be a true believer. But I am and I have been for as long as I can remember, at least since I was a child standing on my tiptoes in the hall at Adele's house with my chin resting on the windowsill, transfixed by a storm that sent massive, frothing waves crashing towards the shore. I had assumed that what I was seeing was the manifestation of God, because I could think of nothing on earth more powerful, knew of nothing else that could wreak that much havoc, without warning or provocation, at least that I could see, and then disappear again, or change form completely, becoming something beautiful and soothing. After I'd explained this, while passing out homemade granola in mason jars with thoughtfully mismatched lids, my colleagues and I became fast friends.

Like Keith, Adele was perplexed by my decision to stop going to work, but unlike Keith, she did not tell me that I was being silly or irresponsible or impulsive, even though I'm almost certain that she thought those things. Instead she welcomed me to her home and listened to me rant, just as she'd always done in my times of tribulation. She found my life amusing. That was the word she used, which I did not find insulting. Perhaps if she had had more going on, she would have found the minutiae of my goings-on less interesting, but luckily this was not the case. Of course, by this time she rarely left the house. She relied on all of us—me, my sisters, my mother, and my aunt Joan—to inform her of the mysterious happenings of the outside world. If there was an estate sale in town or something equally important, she would sometimes make the gestures of preparing to take a trip, folding fur blankets in case she got cold and leaving her leather driving gloves on the hall table by the door, but most of the time she didn't actually go anywhere. She drove a hunter-green convertible BMW, I think from the '60s, with a cream-colored leather interior. My grandfather Henry used to say that it ran beautifully if what you actually wanted to do was travel halfway down the driveway and then turn around and walk back to the house for a gin and tonic when it broke down, which I think was the case for her most times.

When I wasn't in the bath, or walking soulfully along the beach, or nibbling buttered toast while in repose on a sofa with a Victorian novel, I spent a good deal of time kvetching to Adele about my current predicament. The problem, simply put, is that I've yet to find a way to coexist with a man without feeling as if a part of me is dying. Early one evening Adele and I sat on the porch, a cool, airy space decorated with potted plants and wicker furniture, pieces that are hauled away during the off-season to be meticulously repainted and rewoven. The cushions are also attended to during this period, so that at the approach of spring each piece emerges bright and new-seeming, practically sparkling, like the bursts of lilacs that line the side garden, and the vibrant green tufts of moss that creep up between the stones along the pathways that surround the house. As I spoke, Adele remained impassive, even though I also told her that I'm desperately afraid that I'll die childless and alone. I was sitting with my bare feet resting, sort of curled on the edge of the coffee table, and it took every ounce of her strength, I realized after the fact, not to reprimand me as she often did for "draping myself" as opposed to sitting on the furniture. She had her legs crossed and was absentmindedly bouncing her snakeskin Ferragamo slide against the bottom of her foot. Her golden-white hair was perfectly coiffed, with gentle voluminous curls framing her

4

golden-tan, lined face. She was wearing coral lipstick, white linen pants, and a camel-colored cashmere sweater. In one hand she held her wine glass. Her long, never-chipped fingernails were painted dark red, like her toenails. She then waved her free hand as if she were swatting a fly and pointed out that from what she could gather, I am the one who both intensifies and then destroys almost all of my relationships, which she called "affairs," or "courtships," I think to give a semblance of substance or respectability to the shitshow I often described to her.

I nodded back at her. She was correct, after all. I am rather Attila the Hun-like when it comes to matters of the heart. She then padded off to the kitchen, returning with a warm, crusty baguette wrapped in a large linen napkin and a tray laden with an assortment of cheese. She set the tray down carefully on the coffee table and handed me a cocktail napkin, which I deferentially placed on my lap, and then I refilled my wine glass with the crisp white Burgundy she'd selected to accompany the cheese. She tore a small hunk of bread from the loaf and smeared it with one of the creamier cheeses. She studied it for a while—she often studied her food—and finally told me that I was being ridiculous. I was only thirty, she said. I had my whole life ahead of me. I pointed out that my oldest sister Isabella, who now has two daughters, had already had a child by my age, a point that I began to back away from as soon as I said it because Isabella is currently leaving her husband, a pompous, mop-headed dud if you ask me, although unfortunately nobody did.

Isabella and I have become quite close in the last few years. I was the first person she told that she was planning to leave, which surprised both of us. She called me from Providence on the way home from the gym at about eleven o'clock in the morning and spoke in shorthand, as if I'd been there all along and understood why she was doing what she was doing, which I didn't quite, but I never really have. To be perfectly honest, I'd written the whole thing off years before, seeing her as yet another casualty of avoidable domestic drudgery, stuck in the age-old cycle of inane cohabitation that occurs when a relatively reasonable woman couples with the kind of man who is used to immediately getting what he wants. As time went on Isabella had appeared to shrink, despite the pregnancies, and when she and Jason walked into rooms together she was always behind him, partially obscured by him. Yet miraculously, or predictably, depending on how you see things, the spirits of my nieces were bold, shockingly confident, clearly fueled by her lifeblood and not his, which of course had the effect of further depleting her. Isabella is neither passive nor dull, however, though I must admit that for too long I thought of her as a bit of a square. As the oldest of our brood, our lives separated by four long and, for the most part, formative years, her priorities, particularly when we were children, seemed to align more with the adults in our lives than with my own. She takes after our mother, not just physically but also in the sense of needing to establish a safe domestic space wherever she is, and of having the remarkable ability to determine the potential danger in practically every situation, whether it's an expedition to a sledding hill, a walk to the deli, a thoughtfully planned mushroom trip, or international travel on a meager budget.

Alessandra, roughly two years apart from us both, is quite the opposite, though they point out that I still lump the two of them together as one unit. As a child she was reckless, sarcastic, not particularly interested in my thoughts, and completely occupied with an interior life that was untouchable to me, which of course made her that much more alluring. Adele always said that Alessandra marched to the beat of her own drum, which was a polite way of acknowledging her dogmatic tendencies, like her phase of eating only one color of food at a time, say blue or orange, once going an entire week consuming only Welch's grape juice and the blue corn tortilla chips that are actually purple. During another period she ate only carrots and macaroni and cheese. Between the ages of six and eight, she took charge of her hair, obstinately fashioning it into a pomaded helmet that was part Friar Tuck and part Blanche, the sexiest Golden Girl. Then all of that got snuffed out in her teen years when she perfected a particular kind of '90s-era aloofness, which she's yet to grow out of. Despite this, or because of it, of the three of us, she is also probably the most beautiful, with dark, heavy hair, and stark, rather perfect features, though this is not to say that Isabella is anything but an absolute pleasure to look at. It's just that she keeps herself impossibly thin, which bothers me for a number of reasons but mainly because I think of it as a rejection, or a shaming of the authenticity of our Semitic blood. Because while we are delicate beings, with the refined, angular features of a noble Scottish line, our stock is also that of the practical, enduring German Jew and the hearty Russian potato farmer, which means that we have a particular heft, a sense of purpose, the ability to withstand great physical agony, that cannot or should not be stifled by a beautifully managed eating disorder. I will never, as long as I live, apologize for any space I take up.

My mother had planned to name us Susan, Rhoda, and Jinny, after the three female characters in the novel *The Waves* by Virginia Woolf, but she changed her mind at the last minute because she missed Italy, where she'd studied painting for a few months after graduating from college. That's how she explains why three half-Jewish girls from the East Side of Providence ended up with dramatic Italian names instead of introspective, Bloomsbury-esque, English prep school names, though that's only half the story. Years before her first pregnancy, she became convinced that she would have three daughters because she'd split a hash brownie with a lovely young Florentine woman who read her palm, or did her charts, I can't remember which. The woman was fluent in English because she'd spent a few years in California, and was responsible for introducing my mother and Joan to both the Grateful Dead and the enchanting perfection of the avocado, which means that she had remarkable credibility, to them at least. After combing my mother's hair with a mixture of warm water and honey, she told her that she would experience tragedy, which would make itself clear quite soon, and that she would also have three daughters. This woman, Carlotta I think her name was, also robbed most of the men she dated and sprinkled LSD on her morning eggs practically, but because only a few days later my mother learned that my father, her boyfriend of only a year or so then, had cancer, she took every word of the reading maybe a bit too seriously.

Because we were instructed not to, my sisters and I have never called Adele anything but Adele. Words like grandma and grandmother she found unflattering, tasteless, and not at all fitting with the kind of woman she was. Adele's mother named her Adele because when she was pregnant, she either saw a woman in her bedroom or dreamed that she saw a woman in her bedroom, who told her to. The woman was covering her mouth, muffling her voice, so my great-grandmother had asked her to repeat herself and the woman kept saying the same thing over and over. "My name is Adele. My name is Adele." And finally my great-grandmother, who, from what I gather, would have been fine going by great-grandma or something like it, heard that she was saying the name Adele. My name, Marcella, coincidentally, means young warrior, or warlike and strong.

The story I always tell about Adele is also the story she always told about me, though with her version, the details varied considerably. It has to do with the time she asked me and my sisters to pick the wild blackberries that grew along the edge of the field below her house, and I completely lost my shit. I can't remember if I was four or maybe five, but I do remember that I was at the beginning of a series of bold experiments involving a bowl cut and side-swept bangs. Adele had handed each of us a little gardening basket and told us that she needed enough for a tart with a crust that she'd learned to make when she and Henry rented a flat in the 6th arrondissement in postwar Paris right before my father was born, an experience that made her an avowed, lifelong Francophile. She romanticized that year or so, Joan told me, because it was the only time she experienced a world other than her own. For the first time she openly flouted conventions, embraced ideals that didn't align with the ones with which she was raised. She befriended a bohemian woman who lived in her building who taught her about art and literature, and together they took long walks around the city, pushing my newborn father in his stroller. She also dabbled in cooking, perfecting two recipes—an onion and Camembert quiche and a blackberry tart that was my father's favorite—in a kitchen that still bore the scars of the war. During the day Henry did research for his doctorate in something related to an obscure World War II resistance movement, which he never completed, and Adele became conversant in French but never learned to cook anything else.

Adele had incorrectly assumed that my blackberry tantrum was related to my father being sick. She thought that the visits to the hospital where we brought him freshly picked blackberries were too much for someone my age. What it was actually about, from what I remember, is that I don't like being told what to do. That was the day she came to understand me, she always said. That was the day that she came to really know who I was. Then she'd describe to me what had happened. Sometimes it was cool outside, one of those perfect New England summer days with a heavy breeze but not so cold that you needed a sweater. Sometimes it was so warm that she'd stopped us on the way outside and had us come back in to put on sun hats and sunscreen, something that my mother said Adele never did because no one really did that in the '80s, even if they claimed to. What I remember from that day, while sitting in Adele's lap, sobbing, with the side of my face pressed against her chest, is that I came to know who she was, too, though I didn't have the language for it then, and couldn't have articulated what it was that I felt. I had my hands wrapped around her slender arm, with my fingertips, stained lavender with blackberry juice, the color of my mother's eyelids, pressing tiny indents in the soft golden brown of her skin. I could feel Adele's chest heave, almost in unison with mine, and I was certain that despite her WASP restraint, her strange formality, and her devil-may-care attitude, that for a myriad of deep and real and unvoiced reasons, she was sad too.

My mother told me that it wasn't until she met Adele that she truly understood the importance of negative space in a painting. The thing about WASPs, she said, is that what they don't say is much more important than what they do say. Being around them is like going to another country, or speaking another language. In a silly, self-deprecating kind of way my mother describes herself, particularly in relation to my father and his family, as a good Jewish girl from Providence, which she is, very much so, but the point of this portrayal is to underscore just how foreign she found their Newport customs and mannerisms, which were so unlike those of her own family. When she was first dating my father and they'd visited Adele and Henry she'd had no idea how to interpret their conversations. Dinners were particularly confusing because she'd be sitting at the table with everyone, finding it all a little dull, and then she'd realize that all along, amidst the pedigreed commentary and knowing nods, that a lot had been said that of course hadn't been said at all. She told me, laughing, that it had been maddening. They talked about Vietnam, she said, as if it were an English country garden.

We had this conversation when I was about nine or ten while sitting at the table in our kitchen in Providence where I grew up. I was eating olive tapenade using a rye breadstick as a utensil and she was sticking toothpicks into avocado pits that she then suspended in water in little juice glasses, which is something she's done forever and because of that, for quite some time I assumed that it was something that all mothers did. I've since learned that it is only my mother, with her lavender Russian eyelids and her sarcasm and her stories that are detailed like Italian Renaissance paintings, who's been trying to grow avocados in juice glasses on the windowsill next to the coffeemaker since she was twenty-six.

When I stayed with Adele I slept at the far end of the house in a four-poster bed. The windows of my bedroom looked onto the gardens, a small patio, and the section of the lawn where Adele had once, drunkenly, gotten so angry during a croquet game that she threw her mallet into the rose bushes. Before bed I usually lingered in her dressing room, a small alcove off her bedroom that faced the water, and talked to her while she brushed her hair and toned her face with apple cider vinegar. She used small squares of cotton, which she'd brush slowly across her forehead and then down the bridge of her nose as if she were applying foundation. She'd then drink the remaining vinegar, usually about half a cup, from a green marbled glass that she'd inherited from her mother when she married my grandfather. She told me that she used to have eight of them, or maybe twelve. The one I watched her drink from so many times was the only one she hadn't broken. Sometimes she'd rest her elbow on the dressing table, leaning on her hand, looking bored, and in a leisurely way, swirl the vinegar in her mouth like Henry used to do with his Scotch. When I was little she told me she'd been toning her face with apple cider vinegar and then drinking the remains of it for over sixty years and that's why she looked as good as she did despite the cigarettes and the sunbathing and the daily pitchers of gin, which I believed until I tried it and learned that it actually makes you shit your pants.

I was in kindergarten when it happened, still learning to manage the responsibility that comes with perfect bangs. Douglass, my first real love, I knew from a playgroup organized at the Jewish Community Center. I explained the situation first to my grandfather on my mother's side, who we called Poppy, because he was a real man's man, which I knew because he used to pull his pant legs up slightly before he sat down by grabbing the material at the front of his thighs and deliberately tugging at it, which he did to prevent his pants from wrinkling. The extent of my relationship with Douglass at that point entailed his offering me the orange dinosaurs from his pouch of fruit snacks one day because he was allergic to citrus. We all knew this because his mother sent him to playgroup three days a week with a handwritten note saying so. I explained to him that fruit snacks, even the orange ones, were not citrus and that the yellow ones were lemon-flavored and presumably also contained whatever it was that his mother was so worried about so if he was really going to carry on with that stupid logic, he should refrain from eating those as well. He responded by shrugging back at me with the kind of male indifference that I still struggle to recognize as being indicative of someone who needs to be punched in the temple and not someone who's complicated and interesting.

Poppy told me that I was Goddamn ridiculous when I explained to him that in order to woo a potential mate I needed apple cider vinegar. If you drink a cup of vinegar, he told me, you'd crap yourself. That was the only reason that anyone would do that. I don't remember or I've intentionally blocked out the events that followed, but what I do know is that they began with my drinking vinegar and they culminated with my shitting my pants. Afterwards, while crying softly on the toilet, wearing only a formfitting baby-blue turtleneck, I could hear Poppy in the hallway talking to my grandmother, Anya, my mother's mother, who we call Nana. He'd warned me, he wanted Nana to know. If I drank that cup of vinegar, I was going to crap myself. But I'd gone and done it anyway, he'd said laughing. I consider that episode the crux of all my current problems.

Nana was the only person who had really opposed my going to South Africa, although I think my mother also would have if my aunt Joan hadn't lived there. Nana told me that it was too dangerous and that I was too small. Through the telephone I could hear her tapping her pen on the table, which she does when she's working on a crossword puzzle. She told me to pack tampons and Tylenol and a shower cap. I said something to her about my relationship with Keith. Don't be hasty, she cautioned me. People say that life is short, she said, but it isn't. It's very, very long. And then she reminded me about the time that I'd soiled a pair of perfectly nice Little Mermaid bikini briefs and then failed to elicit carnal feelings, or any feelings at all, in Douglass. I told her that that felt like an unnecessarily low blow, and she agreed but explained that in life, we all must suffer.

Adele, in her own way, had said much the same thing. I'd told her, over perfectly poached eggs on wheat toast, that I planned to will myself to love Keith. I'd do it while cleansing my soul through travel. I was getting older, I said, and my tolerance for my own games was wearing thin. Adele responded by telling me that what she thought would happen is that I'd come to see just how big the world is. I'd recognize my own minuteness, and the world's vastness, and I would take comfort in that. I found this line of thinking both wildly unhelpful and also typical of the kind of thing she'd say while calmly sipping her morning coffee, the papers spread out before her, her plush cashmere robe tied snugly at her waist.

Joan had been particularly insistent about the importance of rail travel, claiming that the view from the window of a train is the best way, and actually the only way, to see the back of a city. You can't really know a place, she'd said, or your own place for that matter, if you don't understand its secrets, and those secrets are usually hidden, but for the trained eye, amidst the crumbling structures that have been pushed to the outskirts. This recitation, dispensed in her laughing drawl, summarized the thesis of the book she's now famous for. Begun as an undergraduate college term paper, she disentangled the secrets of the railway and the fancy men who attempted to obscure them, by riding numerous trains and sketching the ways the cities they transected bulged at their edges. Then, in her early thirties, after toiling in secrecy for years, she produced a radical, expository reinterpretation of old accepted history, and from what I can tell, has consistently refused to apologize for doing so, despite all the chaos it caused.

When I relayed this conversation to Keith, he rolled his eyes, while still facing the television, riveted by a story line involving adult men in husky children's parkas ice fishing competitively. We were sitting on the floor in my apartment in front of the trunk I use as a coffee table, drinking gin and tonics, using old *New Yorker* magazines as coasters. When I asked him to explain his reaction he told me that a train ride from Johannesburg to Cape Town seemed like a waste of time. I somehow managed not to slap the shit out of him.

We left the following week. Roo stayed with Adele, who had grown quite fond of my Tonka-truck-shaped offspring, feeding her roast chicken and small pieces of smoked fish on the china she reserved for outdoor lunches. Adele had promised that she would email me regularly with pictures of Roo, so I wouldn't worry about her, which we both knew was a lie, as Adele was apprehensive, to say the least, about the internet, didn't have an email account, and had no plans to get one. But I let this go. Motherhood, I'd learned, is mainly about the art of the compromise.

Joan had recommended that I read Alan Paton's *Cry, the Beloved Country* and Nelson Mandela's *Long Walk to Freedom* before the trip, which I didn't get around to, but I packed them to read on the train. When I saw the woman in Johannesburg who I thought I knew but of course couldn't have, I'd just finished reading the part where Mandela talked about boxing the air in his prison cell. Even though he had barely more than a few square feet, he'd run in place or box the air every morning, which he did to stay sane. Poppy had been a boxer too. Nana had told us that he'd beaten up three guys at once because one of them called him a kike.

My sisters and I used to ask him to tell us that story when we were little and he'd refused to, so his friend Lou, who worked at Nana and Poppy's deli, would tell it to us instead. Lou had also been a boxer and when he told us the story he'd act it out, exaggerating each movement. He'd say, and then he tap-tap-tapped like this, and he'd make beautifully direct and pointed motions, making a fight look like something easy and fluid and managed, which Poppy used to say was the very thing that separated those who could fight from those who couldn't.

It was something about the woman's features that I recognized, maybe the slope of her nose or the arch of her brow. She had faint lines by the sides of her eyes that conveyed not a particular age exactly, but a particular kind of life. She wore an off-white dress that was stained at the bottom from being repeatedly dragged through the dust of Soweto, and she was standing eerily still, ghost-like, in a makeshift yard in front of a makeshift home, constructed from scraps of metal and worn pieces of wood that looked like every other house around her. Because the landscape was so flat, I could see for miles, far past the back of the city we'd left behind, and I knew that the woman was one of the people Nana talked about—a sufferer, someone who had been gathered up and removed—who were in many ways Nana's people too.

What I couldn't quite explain was that the woman had somehow brought to mind Nana's arthritic hands, tiny and knobby and overworked, and the way the top of Adele's back had begun to hunch, and my grandfather Henry as a young man fighting the Nazis in Germany, and the trains he'd described to us, trains filled with people on their way to Dachau, and my father the way he'd looked when I last saw him, corpse-like and colorless except for his veins, and my mother crying in the bathtub after he died. I don't remember what I said to Keith to account for this reaction, only that after I'd spoken, he took my hand and put it on the armrest and sort of patted it, which felt condescending and strange, but it was actually much worse than that. There aren't words or expressions for what really happened, or if there are I don't know them. But something about the combination of the face he made while he moved my hand and the loneliness of knowing that I'd been intentionally misunderstood, made it suddenly very clear to me that I didn't and wouldn't ever love him.

And so the thing that happened, what I've been getting at all along, is that Adele died. In one moment, or a short series of them, a symbol of a bygone era, a secret history of American womanhood, and a pillar of my childhood suddenly disappeared. And when I saw that woman I think a part of me must have known or could have somehow seen it coming, even though I couldn't have. Because the truth is that Adele died afterwards. When I got the call I was already back in New York and all those weeks in South Africa only lingered in smells and fading memories and stupid pictures I'd taken on my iPhone. But that doesn't matter. That's what Adele would have said, that it really doesn't matter. So that's why I remember it the way I do it now. And it's also why I let myself fall to shit that day on the train.

CHAPTER TWO

This was the third funeral to be held at Adele's house, in my lifetime at least, though in previous generations there had been plenty of others. Gravestones, in various states of decay, ranging in size and shape, and labeled with notable names and dates in austere fonts, stood in rows in the small plot not far from the house. My father, who died when I was four, broke with family tradition, however, by stipulating that his remains not be entombed with his ancestors, but cremated, and then scattered along the shore to be carried out to the ocean, which Adele thought was improper and theatrical, but she went along with it anyway, solemnly throwing her allotted handful so that the particles that remained of her son hovered briefly in front of her before drifting away. Afterwards there had been a short, relatively informal service on the back lawn that had been lined with folding chairs and a few tables. My memories of it are vague, and perhaps not even memories but recitations of the memories of my mother, my sisters, or Joan or Adele. Henry's service I do remember, mainly because of the strange man Adele had yelled at, a man my sisters insisted had been at my father's service, too, though of course I could not corroborate this.

Like Henry, who died when I was sixteen, Adele was to have a proper burial in the family plot. Her funeral, unlike the others, my sisters and I planned with a good amount of help from our mother and, somewhat unsurprisingly, very little from Joan. She was far too distracted unpacking the boxes she'd shipped before her flight that had arrived

the day after she did, the contents of which she at first refused to talk about. Instead she sat for long periods on her
bed in her childhood bedroom, the room where Alessandra
now often stays, staring at the painting on the wall that my
mother painted for her in the early '70s of a piece of salmon
resting on a bed of ice. Look at the orange, she said to me
one afternoon when I brought her iced tea, which I knew she
wouldn't drink. Only my mother, Joan pointed out, could
make orange out of every color but orange. There's blue in a
range of hues, she said. And gold. White. Even purple. And
look at how the ice sparkles. I'd looked at the ice, translu-
cent, gleaming with flecks of color, but I don't remember if
I said anything back to her.

Joan's one contribution to her mother's funeral had been
to dig in her heels, over the dinner my mother prepared of
breaded eggplant and tomatoes, when I wondered out loud
about whether Adele might actually have wanted to be scattered in the ocean too. The water had had a profound hold
on her. Late into her seventies, she went swimming every
day that she could, weather permitting, though what most
would consider temperatures far too cold to be enjoyable,
she found brisk, invigorating. She was a big believer in subjecting one's body to the elements, which is why she kept
her bedroom frigid. Fresh air, even in winter, was vital to
good health, she'd always told us. Joan recalls tiptoeing to
her room when she was unable to sleep as a child, and being met with a gust of cold air as soon as she pushed open
the door. Across the room Adele lay sleeping on her back,
her hair spread out around her on her pillowcase. Joan told
us that she'd liked seeing her mother that way, like some
glamorous Hollywood star, her mouth full and red, her nose
slightly upturned.

I'd only brought it up because Joan had spoken fondly, or
maybe not quite fondly but not without warmth, about following Adele to the water when she was a child. She'd told
us that she found the memories soothing because they allowed her a glimpse of a part of her mother that she rarely

saw, carefree Adele waking as the sun was rising, slipping on her bathing suit and tiptoeing down the stairs and out the back door. Joan would trail after her, watching her mother's tall slender form, wrapped in a bathrobe, towel in hand, as she strode down the rocky path to the beach. Then she would drape her towel on a sagging wooden lawn chair and wade into the water, stopping at chest level, and then turn to her side, swimming forcefully, her sturdiness suddenly visible, the muscles taut in her tanned arms and legs, her dirty blonde hair, wild and wet. But this vision of athleticism and confidence vanished as the day wore on. By the time Adele padded back to the house, each footstep progressively drier so that only the faintest outlines of her wet toes were visible on the stone pantry floor, she was herself again, the woman who stood too upright, who held her face too tight. Adele had likely seethed with rage for so many of the years we'd known her, Joan said, perhaps to dismiss my scattering of ashes suggestion, which felt rather melodramatic to me, though it was also probably true.

My sisters and I lingered in Adele's kitchen after dinner. Isabella was leaning against the counter, her eyes red and weary looking. Her white summer cardigan was rumpled, and she wore a knot of gold necklaces. My mother and Joan had offered to bathe my nieces, Consuelo and Vanessa, before bed. We could hear gentle splashing and faint laughter from the large claw-foot tub in the back guest bathroom. The dishes, except for the wine glasses, were drying on a rack by the farm sink. Fireflies glinted in the fading light on the patio just off the pantry. Alessandra was sitting at the kitchen table, staring out the window, one of Adele's monogrammed pads of paper and her computer in front of her. But we still didn't come up with a plan. Joan had insisted that the only reason our father hadn't been buried in the little cemetery, surrounded by the ancient stone wall, was because he'd been terrified of it. It was haunted, she told us, sounding again, to me at least, so much like her mother. Alessandra said something like, well, what do you make of that, after Joan left, but it sounded less like a question than a statement.

Though Adele had loved bagpipes, as all good Scotswomen do, after much deliberation, we decided that such a racket at her funeral was absolutely out of the question, much too strident for someone so tasteful and self-possessed. We eventually settled instead on a Czechoslovakian violinist I found online, a woman who wore combat boots and closed her eyes while speaking. Her music was soft and tranquil, the perfect backdrop to an otherwise lovely, late summer morning, still early enough that beads of dew glistened on the leaves and on the grass we stood on, mowed down to a compact, bright jade-colored carpet. That morning I'd crept down to the kitchen before anyone else was up, and sat at the trestle table, my toes curled around the rung of a wooden chair. The sun was just rising, breaking through the morning fog so that the air outside looked like yellow and orange foam, a solid, hanging high above the water and the lawn. There was a palpable stillness; all the surfaces scrubbed clean, the copper pots polished and gleaming, the wide plank floors cooled by the spurts of raw summer air that whistled through the open dampers of the fireplace.

We ended up laughing during the ceremony, which was appalling, or perfect, depending on how you see things. Though I didn't feel quite right, real grief was far from my mind, because I couldn't quite let go of the feeling of Adele, still so very present, in all of our interactions, in all of the spaces we occupied, the perfectly decorated rooms, the wild but meticulous garden, even along the rocky coastline, in each heaving, foamy wave. I could still recall, too lucidly, the way she'd looked at me the last night I saw her. I could hear her strange voice. As I'd left her dressing room she'd reminded me, as she so often did, of the fury I was able to garner at the thought of picking blackberries when I really didn't want to. Don't ever lose that, my darling, she'd said. Followed by a polite hint that of course it wouldn't hurt to temper it a bit. Then she'd spritzed some sort of lavender-infused mist on her wrists and chest, and turned back to her mirror.

At one point during the service Isabella nudged me and motioned towards a man with a pronounced Robert Redford vibe to him, older Robert Redford, weathered, worn down, but still clearly handsome, and not frail. Joan was staring at him, too, and I couldn't interpret her expression, a strange somewhat angry half-smile, which I thought Isabella saw, too, though she didn't. She'd been too focused on old Robert Redford. After the burial we nibbled on tea cakes and mingled with the various guests, family members, friends, the teenager who worked behind the counter of the cheese shop further in town, and I lost track of the man. I think we all did.

I spent a few days at Isabella's house after the funeral, a classic white 1940s colonial revival about five blocks from my mother's house, of the same era, on the East Side in Providence. My mother had recommended that I do so, assuming that because Isabella was newly separated from Jason, she likely needed my help, though it turned out that she did not. I was of course welcome, but in many ways, Isabella life's had actually gotten easier. There was an almost manic order to her kitchen, the perfectly arranged cooking utensils in their stoneware container, the coffeemaker, gleaming, next to the canister of coffee, that, like the sleek white ramekin of kosher salt, was placed just so. I couldn't help thinking of the Silverman's dog, a lanky mutt who had lived next door to Nana and Poppy when we were children. The dog used to lick her paws until they were hairless. It was an anxious behavior, Mrs. Silverman had told us, but there was nothing to be done about it.

It had begun to feel as if Isabella had been working against and not with Jason, she'd explained to me when I'd casually asked about the meticulousness of her surroundings. By simply existing, by living the way he wanted to, he'd somehow torn down all that she'd built up. He made messes in areas she'd just cleaned. He forgot the plans they'd made together to accommodate his schedule. He ate the food that she was planning to use for something else, and left gobs of toothpaste not quite in the drain of the bathroom sink but just outside it, and bottles of beer on the windowsill next to the chair where he did most of his reading. She laughed after awhile, and apologized for ranting, which she wasn't quite, explaining that it actually wasn't any of those things and it wasn't the accumulation of them either. It was Jason's obliviousness that had finally made her leave him.

When I'd arrived, Isabella brought my bag to the basement where she'd arranged a few pillows and a comforter on a sofa, but I ended up sleeping in her bedroom with her. She even permitted Roo to lie at the foot of the bed. We talked late into the night every night that I was there. One evening she told me that she couldn't help associating divorce with death, which of course made her think of our father, who loomed larger for her than he did for me because she had had four more years than I had to get to know him. My mother hates this 'divorce is death' logic, finding it patriarchal, antiquated, and perhaps a painful indictment of her own past decisions. It isn't at all the same thing, she'd declared, defensively, still, so many years after our father's death. We'd been in the backyard at her house a few weeks after Isabella announced the split, sitting on the grass next to her garden where she grows herbs, squash, tomatoes, and salad greens. Our mother had been kneeling, with her back to us, and her words came out as if she were spitting them. Alessandra was back in Providence, too, the first time in quite a while, and she'd remained silent throughout the conversation, which was unusual, even for her. One evening before bed I'd said something about my toothbrush, made entirely of recycled material, and she'd looked at me blankly, as if I were speaking another language.

Nana had a different interpretation of this exchange, which she outlined the following night at dinner. I'd explained to her our mother's reaction to Isabella's conflation of death and divorce, and Nana wondered if our mother's response had more to do with our mother and Nana than Isabella and her divorce from Jason. Nana had reacted poorly to the news of my mother's first pregnancy, so many years ago, she told us. You are saddling your daughters with avoidable suffering, Nana had warned my mother, which in some ways Nana still believed. She shook her head with small, sturdy motions as she spoke, portioning out pieces of whitefish topped with breadcrumbs, which had been Isabella's favorite dish as a child, though she barely touched it that night. The world is already too full of suffering, Nana had said to my mother. To marry a man with cancer is like willfully embracing a death sentence. In hindsight, she admitted, that was probably the last thing a newly pregnant woman wanted to hear from her mother.

My nieces find the notion of our father perplexing, this mysterious, hazy figure, a man who has touched the lives of so many of the women they currently know, but who no longer exists. Further obscuring things is that Isabella's strangest and most prominent memory of him is one she doesn't want to share with them. It's the reason she hates what she describes as the murky half-life between the middle of November and a few days after the New Year, a period of chaotic, frenzied togetherness and bitter cold. She associates it with seeing our mother crying, even though when she saw her that way, years ago, when she stood in the dark hallway after she'd been asked to go to bed, it was actually springtime. She remembers the open windows, the lilacs in the backyard, the screen door slamming open and shut. Our father had yelled at our mother, although she hadn't done anything wrong. He was angry about something else, something Isabella didn't understand, but he focused his anger on the way our mother had poured his coffee, that she'd taken the pot out before the machine had finished brewing, that the remaining coffee splattered onto the counter and the back of the machine. In a rage, he'd taken the pot from her and shoved it back into the machine, slamming it against the wall, knocking over the tiny avocado plants that she grew in juice glasses on the windowsill, so that the floor around her was covered in coffee, avocado pits, droplets of water, toothpicks and shattered glass.

In gathering energy to leave her marriage, Isabella began to see her memories differently. They started to feel profound to her, no longer requiring repression, but in need of real airtime. Her memories served as a sort of lifeline, she told us, reassuring her that if she left, if she actually did the unthinkable, that she wouldn't be alone, that the world was still full. Behind her, bolstering her up, was a collection of experiences that she'd unconsciously stopped relying on or even thinking about, almost discrediting them entirely, so that the past that had begun to feel real to her wasn't hers at all, but Jason's. It felt as if she were disappearing, she told me, and it was affecting everything, her ability to communicate, the tone of her voice, even her appearance. All of this was obvious to me, and had been for a while, though it wasn't the kind of thing we talked about. Despite the closeness in ages among my sisters and me, the geographic proximity, and the intensely female-centric and close-knit structure of our family, there were topics that felt, for reasons I can't quite explain, somehow off limits between us. I'm not the kind of woman who respects such boundaries, however, so I did, on more than one occasion, discuss this oddness I'd observed in Isabella, though I did it respectfully, behind her back with Alessandra.

Alessandra and I live only twelve and a half blocks from each other on the Upper West Side of Manhattan, a recent and surprising turn of events. She'd been planning to move, first downtown and then to Munich of all places, but then had abruptly broken up with her boyfriend and moved to West 98th Street, farther from the architectural firm where she works but closer to Columbia University's architecture library. She claims to be writing a book, an adaptation of her undergraduate thesis, some apparently extraordinary treatise on architecture and violence. Alessandra's move coincided with a period of openness with me, part of what my mother describes as Alessandra's "rhythms," though this is not to say that any of us understand what prompts the phases of intimacy or the episodes of remoteness.

I'd helped her unpack and was surprised by how little she had, the spare, almost bleak Scandinavian aesthetic of her place, so unlike any of the homes we'd spent time in as children. Her bookshelf was the only place I spotted clutter, texts of various colors and sizes, with spines warped with age, crammed together messily, though the shelf itself was basic, of cold white metal. She was baffled by Isabella, too, but her concern came from a different place, one that surprised me. She wondered how intertwined their finances were, recalling that Isabella's house had been purchased with money from a trust our father had created, that Adele had given her access to. Adele had made a bit of a show about it, telling Isabella that a woman has to have sole control of the home. She was no feminist, she'd said, but men having rights to property was downright unseemly.

My days in Providence with Isabella were filled with mom rhythms, which I found hilarious, foreign, almost anthropologically fascinating, the pickups, the drop-offs, the packing of snacks, the planning of meals and organizing of materials for crafts and sports, the cleaning of fingernails and dirt-encrusted summer feet. Before adopting Roo I'd maintained a lifestyle that put few strictures on my freedom, allowing me to leave my apartment breezily in the morning for work at no specific time and returning that night or days later, eating when it occurred to me to, and washing my hair only when it was no longer an option not to. But Isabella insisted on a schedule, and I was happy to abide by it. In her fuel-efficient hatchback, on our way to or from some fancy child's activity, Isabella yapped about her divorce in contradictory tones. She was at times sarcastic, but also frequently spoke with urgency, defensively, as if she had a case to make, I think because her female friends who'd known her since college couldn't make sense of her behavior. He is such a good man, they'd insisted. You have no idea how lucky you are. She'd had to justify her decision to leave, to women, women like her, women who knew and understood her.

The fact that she was enraged, exhausted, no longer in love, that she'd lost herself, seemed not to warrant, in their estimation, an actual response. In an almost pleading way she explained that it felt as if she were walking off the stage of an unexceptional sitcom, finally freeing herself of the pretense, the bullshit, and that they wanted her back on set, in a three-sided living room with a laugh track. But she could no longer play the part of the nagging, haggard, unfunny woman who'd become fed up, especially when the scenes justifying her mood, her appearance, her temper, are never shown. I nibbled the emergency cheddar bunny crackers she'd packed in teacup-sized Tupperware tubs and nodded in solidarity, sipping from a juice box. It was her own fault though, she said staring ahead of her at a line of similar cars filled with similar women, because she'd never shown those scenes to her friends, or to anyone really. She'd in fact hidden them, intentionally. So, in a sense, she understood why it was so baffling to everyone that she'd up and leave a good man, a liberal, open guy, someone who got it, or could at least talk as if he did.

Sitting on her sofa later that day, nestled among perfectly fluffed throw pillows, it occurred to me that I related to aspects of what she was describing much more than I was comfortable with. I'd begun to see parallels in our lives. The problems I'd watched her grapple with from a distance, astounded that she hadn't seen coming, I'd inexplicably found myself facing. She sat opposite me, curled up, compact, all sharp angles, her arms wrapped around her pointy knees, her shoulders slouched. She ran her manicured fingers through her hair, sort of smoothing it. This was not how she'd imagined things turning out, she wanted me to know. This was not where she'd seen herself ending up. And though I wanted to be present with what she was telling me, to be the force of goodness and strength that I knew she needed, I couldn't help thinking about where I'd ended up instead, jobless, in a relationship that I found draining and stupid, without much of a plan for the future.

Roo sat next to us on the floor, annoyed that she hadn't been invited onto the sofa. So I patted her distractedly and said something that I'd hoped would be uplifting, something about the limitlessness of the future, which I'd actually intended as reassurance for both of us. Isabella laughed in a biting, caustic way, and continued to take more responsibility for her situation than seemed reasonable. She became a bit melodramatic, which I loved, sighing and leaning back despondently, each movement clearly exhausting her. She was imprisoned, she said wearily, rolling her eyes, by a farce that she'd helped create. She pointed to his shoes, sensible but slightly clunky, in a dull adult male brown, I think to indicate that even when he was no longer there, she was still cleaning up after him. He was still taking up her space.

When I asked why his shoes were still there, she described their first meeting. It was as if she had to return to square one to justify—I don't know what, perhaps her inability to really let go. They'd met over ten years before at a friend's barbeque, a few blocks from her apartment, when she was in the process of extending a deadline for her doctoral research, a project that remains unfinished, on the role of women in revolutionary politics. Jason stood some distance from her, surrounded by people, balancing a plate of food, a beer, and a napkin in one hand and gesturing with the other. He was tall and handsome, she'd noticed, but not overwhelmingly so. He'd said something that she couldn't understand because she hadn't heard the beginning of the conversation, but everyone around him had laughed.

They fell in love quickly, she now believed, because they'd found things in each other that they missed about themselves, things that had been there once but that had been abandoned for one reason or another. She'd become so wrapped up in the contrivances of academia, so self-conscious and long-winded, that her sense of humor and her confidence suffered. He'd been too focused on material success, had stopped reading for fun. He hadn't travelled in years.

On their first date he said something politically incorrect, quite offensive, and also truly hilarious, in response to a complicated teaching situation she'd described, and she'd found it relieving to laugh the way she did. He was smart enough to understand the lingo, the pretentious jargon of scholars. His imitations were impeccable. He understood her world and had no patience with it, but also, at least early on, was genuinely invested in what she did every day. But the respite he'd initially provided from the tenseness of her world faded over the years, as did the value that they collectively attributed to her work, but she wasn't conscious of this change while it was happening. It had only recently occurred to her how easy it had been to put off her own work so that she could take on his, and because she hadn't sensed this transition, she had never asked for help, had never even considered that she could. So by the end she could no longer laugh at his pointed jokes about the world of academia, the brilliant and accurate and effortless soliloquies about the navel-gazing professors she had once idolized. She'd tried to for a while but ended up feeling as if she were participating in her own humiliation, so she'd stopped.

On my last night in Providence, Isabella told me that she'd realized, after falling to pieces not long ago over an argument with Jason, that she'd crumbled the way our mother had after our father slammed the coffeepot into the coffeemaker, toppling her tiny avocado plants. It hadn't occurred to her as a child that an adult might surrender that way, or that someday she'd do it too. Recognizing this was painful and a sign of defeat, of what she couldn't quite explain. Perhaps it was that Jason never sank to those levels, but could remain calm and self-possessed while she flailed. She told me that in those moments, she'd just start sobbing. She'd grow so tired of the messes, the almost willful way he ignored her, his quick, thoughtless responses, the way he humiliated her, intentionally, she was sure of it, by interrupting her in front of her colleagues. And then something seemingly innocuous would set her off.

The most recent time it was the soggy cereal he'd left in the drain of the kitchen sink. Instead of disposing of it himself and putting his bowl in the dishwasher as she'd asked him to do countless times, he'd left it half-full on its side, its contents slowly oozing into the drain, so once again she'd had to pick out each dripping clump, using her pinky finger to fish out crushed oats and nuts, dirtying her hands with whatever else had also gotten stuck in the drain, tomatoes from the previous night, oily salad dressing. Then she'd washed her hands, only to dirty them again not long after, scrubbing her own dishes and those of her daughters. The extra cleaning took up only a few more minutes of her day, but this sort of thing had become a metaphor. As did all the other instances like it, and they were all metaphors too. So she'd snap. Listen to me, she'd scream. I am more than this. I am more than a woman who fishes wet cereal from the drain. But then she'd begin to lose herself. She'd get disoriented, partly because Jason would either smile at her quizzically or stare at her blankly, making her feel irrational, because what kind of adult screams that way, about cereal of all things?

And to this question she didn't have an answer. She'd become ashamed, and start to fold back into herself, backing away from her point, conceding that she was crazy and he was reasonable. And then nothing would change, and the days went on, and she'd try to make sense of it all, how she'd become the kind of woman who fell to pieces in the kitchen that way. And just as she'd gotten past it enough to no longer cringe when it crept back into her consciousness like the memory of a bad dream, Jason would remind her of it, noting with astonishing accuracy one of her most flamboyant and desperate and ridiculous sentences. He'd smile during these recitations, suggesting that he was being playful, though he wasn't. He was making it clear that he hadn't forgotten her transgression and that she shouldn't either. Rather remarkable really, this coming from the man who couldn't remember to turn off the lights before bed, who'd never once bought toilet paper without being asked to, or voluntarily washed sheets or towels, or made sure their daughters had brushed their teeth before bed.

Obviously I could relate to my sister having had a bit of a meltdown every once in a while, which I assume would be true for most women. What I couldn't relate to was her experience afterwards, the lonely broken spiraling she'd described, as I've always found tantrums to be invigorating, a call from deep within, reminding me of my vast power, even if they are also slightly embarrassing in retrospect. And maybe in some ways Isabella did find strength in those moments, because at some point she began to tell her own stories to her daughters, cementing herself in their consciousness just as she'd observed Jason doing. It hadn't been a conscious decision, she told me, but it had a therapeutic effect. Telling her own stories provided an escape from her marriage, reminding her that she hadn't always been this way, that there had been a version of her before Jason. Consuelo loved the story about our mother deciding on our names in particular. Imagining her grandmother as a young woman, a woman who went by Leah and not Grandma, who made her own peasant dresses out of beautiful fabrics woven in Mexico, who wound up alone in a foreign land so she could learn to paint like a true master, felt thrilling and strange, so far from the woman Consuelo now knew, with her silver-brown hair, often in her kitchen, a room that smelled of tahini and garlic, half-read newspapers spread on the kitchen table and Carole King playing softly on the speakers she'd had installed throughout the house when she turned sixty.

Isabella recounted what our mother had told her, how in her early twenties, she'd boarded with a woman named Marcella, my namesake, in Florence while doing a painting fellowship with a Renaissance expert. In Marcella's living room, near a window that looked onto the square in front of Santa Maria Novella, she'd sat on two thick cushions on the floor and painted while Marcella and her best friends, Alessandra and Isabella, drank wine and told stories. My mother recalls them laughing, then crying, then laughing again, sometimes in the span of less than an hour, something they'd been doing together, they told her, for over fifty years. This kind of friendship had struck my mother as the pinnacle of female intimacy, the obvious ease they felt around each other, the respect and space and support their bond provided. My mother had always described the women to us as Italian sisters even though they weren't, something my nieces found funny. The women had actually met as teenagers. One was Albanian, and another half-Ukrainian. Isabella, the only one of them who hadn't outlived her husband, lived in the apartment building next door and every night her husband would call on the telephone to the apartment where they sat talking and laughing and crying and tell her to come home. He'd open the window in his living room and they'd open the window in the kitchen so that the husband and wife could have touched each other if they'd wanted to. They'd motion to each other while they talked but they still held their phones by their ears.

My sister Isabella had picked both of her daughters' names, but she'd had to argue for them. Consuelo after the Vanderbilt daughter who had married and divorced a Blenheim prince and who then threw herself into British politics and social causes, because she'd come across a biography of her at the university library the day after she learned that she was pregnant. And Vanessa, a few years later, for Vanessa Bell, Virginia Woolf's sister, an artist, who Isabella thought of as the sleeper. Jason believed in family names, which Jewish people approach differently from WASPs, and Isabella had had to hold her own in a way that, in retrospect, had been too exhausting, had taken too much out of her. Before he moved out, she'd heard him talking about their daughters to one of his parents on the phone, excitedly, detailing their minutiae, the inner workings of their thinking, completely lost in his admiration, but the tone of his descriptions and something about the way their names had sounded, in the affected, laudatory tone he used with his family, felt off to her. She described to us standing in the hall, within earshot of Jason but out of his line of vision. She was lurking angrily, slouched in resignation, one hand on her hip and a stack of clean towels in the other. The gulf between them then became too clear to her, her discomfort echoing off the walls crammed with family photos and the Mayan calendar Vanessa had made from glass beads and cardboard cutouts. It occurred to her later that the thing that had actually pleased him so much was that embedded in Consuelo and Vanessa's sayings, expressions, and gestures, he'd recognized a tangible, physical extension of himself. She told us that she'd been stunned by this realization, unsure if it was accurate, or mean, or a result of her own anguished envy.

My mother related to this, though she told me later that she hadn't wanted to appear overly critical of Jason in case Isabella changed her mind and went back to him. Isabella had apparently considered leaving before, which was news to me. But the fear of being seen only as a mother or a wife, and not also as a creator, or an innovator, or a contributor to the workforce, a fully individuated, nuanced person, was something my mother had wrestled with herself. She'd often felt unfairly pigeonholed: a serious painter would never have abandoned her fellowship for a man, but a woman of any worth at all wouldn't even consider putting her own ambition before playing the role of nurse to the man she loved. Complicating things further was Nana's frequent and piercing criticism of my mother's decisions back then, which my mother knew had more to do with the limitations Nana had experienced as a young woman than anything else, though that didn't blunt its pointedness. All those hours of studying and attempting to replicate the great works of the Italian Renaissance in order to understand what genius had generated them, now amounted to very little, Nana had said. My mother left Florence abruptly and had showed up bedraggled and opinionated, according to Nana, fully prepared to save my father, a goy for God's sake, whom she'd only just begun dating.

My mother had wanted to be a scientist. As a child she'd spent her free time at the deli my grandparents ran on Hope Street, teaching herself to paint by arranging cross sections of deli meat and sliced fish on ice into still-life compositions, because that was as close as she could get to real biological specimens. At home she'd bring her crayons and paints to bed, tucking them in next to her two teddy bears. She'd wait until her parents were asleep or otherwise occupied, then she'd peel back the poster she'd hung of Jackie Robinson, and draw on the wall behind it, eventually filling a perfect rectangle with tiny flowers and animals.

Painting then became an obsession. She told us often that she'd even dreamt in paint, strange fairy-tale-like images that morphed with those of castles, baseball fields, and the blocks that surrounded her house on the East Side. Though my mother had real skill, Nana worried that her decision to focus on painting in college, even with the Italian fellowship, was shortsighted, and that she should apply herself towards something more practical. My mother insists that all along she'd had much more direction than she got credit for. Back in Providence, when she was pregnant with Isabella and taking care of our father, she quickly found lucrative work illustrating medical textbooks, which was probably the only job, she pointed out, that required the skills she'd developed studying the contours of smoked salmon, whitefish salad, and images of a suffering, crucified Jesus Christ.

During much of my childhood, my mother's work was visible in almost every room of our house. Paintings of various organs and body parts on huge sheets of stretched canvas hung or leaned against the walls, ulcers, livers, lungs, cracked femurs, arterial pathways, even vaginas. But Nana still couldn't make sense of it. Even if it was a real job, there was an intangibility to this particular kind of art that felt precarious to her, and to be fair, her experiences as a young woman had allowed little room for precariousness. Nana had left New York City in her early twenties for Providence, ostensibly to help her father's cousin, whose wife was sick, but she had ended up working at a factory that produced airplane parts. Black-and-white pictures of her in the factory wearing a dark tweed, tight-fitting skirt and jacket, next to similarly dressed women, hung in frames in the hall of the house where she'd lived during my childhood. After Poppy died, she gave them to me and my sisters, saying that the memories they evoked of the place they'd met were too painful to look at every day. Nana had gotten the job a few years before the United States entered World War II, when FDR was willing to provide resources to what would become the allied powers, but before the bombing of Pearl Harbor. She worked a floor below Poppy's station doing something that he described as pulling a machine down from above, and using it to stamp the edges of sheets of perforated metal. Poppy told us that even though he wasn't Nana's supervisor he used to keep track of what she was doing, not to be rude but so that he would have something to say when he finally got up the courage to talk to her. He eventually proposed, albeit with a fake ring, because he was too head-over-heels to wait any longer but too poor to afford what he believed she deserved. This remains, in my mind at least, the most romantic thing I've ever heard, though Nana is quick to point out that for women in her position, romance had very little to do with anything. It wasn't until they'd been married for a few years that he was able to replace the fake ring with one of real value, and she had feigned ignorance when he'd handed it to her, even though she actually knew better.

My sisters and I played with both rings when we were little, taking turns wearing the real and the fake, each one representing something in our games that changed depending on our moods or current interests: invisibility, laser power, the ability to fly or grant wishes. Nana kept both rings on her dresser in a small brass box that had belonged to her mother. One of the first things we'd do when we arrived there, after flinging our jackets and sneakers in the corner in the downstairs hall, was to race to Nana and Poppy's bedroom, and wrestle, sometimes violently, over whichever ring Nana wasn't currently wearing. The victor then paraded about for a while until she was distracted by something else, the set of dominoes on the coffee table, the cookie jar, one of Poppy's cigars, or some sort of art project using jar tops, corks, small pieces of string, and wrinkled pieces of waxed paper, all items found neatly arranged in Nana's kitchen drawers, as she believed in repurposing everything.

We often cooked with Nana, too, forming a small assembly line to chop vegetables or bread pieces of fish—first dipping it in egg, then flour. Then the luckiest of us, who'd had the good fortune or physical strength to assert herself next to Nana, got to rest it delicately into the sizzling pan. If we stayed for dinner we crowded around the four-top table, often splitting a can of cold, sweet cream soda among the three of us in glasses with short stems. For dessert we ate whatever Leticia, Nana's best friend who worked with her at the deli, had left over. Leticia saved everything, so as they were closing up for the day, she'd rummage around in the back room for two small boxes, previously used for salt or napkins or ketchup packets, and line them with leftover tinfoil, on which she'd pile spiced cookies, Hamentaschen, or brownies. She'd take one box to her apartment for her son, Darren, and Nana would bring the other box to her apartment for us, which we'd then bring to the living room, where we were allowed to watch a show or two on the channel that aired reruns from the '50s and '60s, like *Bewitched* or *Perry Mason*. On weekend nights we'd watch black-and-white movies. Katherine Hepburn was a favorite of ours, particularly in *Bringing up Baby*, because she was so impossible and caused all sorts of problems while looking glamorous and unmoved in her wide-leg slacks and blouses. I remember being horrified to learn that she'd actually had freckles and that in so many of the movie roles I was familiar with, they'd been covered with thick makeup.

Nana's current apartment, also small and well organized, only blocks from the house she had shared with Poppy, has the same living room furniture arranged in the same way, though it's decorated with my mother's paintings, the very ones that caused so many arguments, that she had found so morose in the '70s and '80s when my mother painted them. Now she points out details in them, smiling—a hue she hadn't seen until that morning because of a particular angle in the sun, the way a tendon or a ligament casts a shadow on matter slightly below it. This, I've learned, is the kind of thing women of a certain age can do, this being steadfastly impossible about something one minute and then absolutely gushing about it the next. It's quite magical, really.

CHAPTER THREE

On my first night back in my apartment in New York, I dreamt that Adele was sitting in front of her vanity wearing one of her white silk nightgowns. The material was loose, hanging low on her chest, revealing sunspots and faint creases in the tanned skin of her chest. The wind in the room was oddly powerful, and the long white linen curtains waved violently, thrashing about, tangling with the bottom of her nightgown. I woke up to the din of late-night Manhattan traffic, gasping, as if it had been a nightmare.

Adele had believed that she was haunted, or at least she said as much, but never in an entirely straightforward way. She described ghosts as little Gods, or parts of God, certainly nothing to be frightened of. When we were children, she told my sisters and me that the ghost that haunted her also protected her, and that if we were good, she'd protect us too. I don't remember exactly how I interpreted the peculiarity of this notion initially, or whether I considered it in any way other than how she instructed us to. It simply became, without question, a part of our life with her. Our beloved Adele, a glamorous, old guard WASP, tall and reserved and appropriately God-fearing, was trailed by a spirit, a woman that was absolutely, undeniably real. Henry of course thought this was nonsense. He'd raise an eyebrow and smirk dismissively, or he'd say, "Oh, bollocks," whenever someone mentioned having seen her ghost near the staircase or walking on the lawn. But he also never came out and said that what we all felt but couldn't quite describe wasn't actually there.

Isabella saw the ghost once from her bedroom window, walking on the lawn, a dark figure, almost as tall as Adele. She'd stooped to pick something up from the ground before disappearing, melting into the early morning mist. Alessandra saw her in a maze Henry had mowed in the field below the house the day he tried to teach her how a compass worked. She told us that she'd gotten lost and couldn't read the coordinates on Henry's old army compass, so she'd followed a woman who was covering her mouth who led her to the edge of the garden. And I'd had the same experience that my aunt Joan had had as a child; I felt the ghost but couldn't see her the night our father died. I'd slept fitfully, then woke up choking, and for reasons I can't explain, had run towards the front stairs where I stopped and sat down on the landing, tugging at the collar of my pajamas because I couldn't breathe. I heard the window being opened behind me, though I was alone, and the hazy night air spilled into the room. My first thought was that it was God because I could suddenly breathe again, the mist cold and soothing on my throat.

Joan had told us years before about recognizing the woman's presence after a horrible fight with her brother, Luke, our father, when she was a child. My father had yanked her hair so hard that clumps of it remained in his fist after Henry had disentangled him from Joan. Adele had insisted on punishing them both, for reasons I still can't understand. So Joan had run from the room and flung herself on her bed, sobbing, until she heard someone enter her room and walk towards her, and then she felt gentle, soothing pressure on her back. Joan had wanted it to be Adele, she told us. She wanted to feel that her mother understood why she'd screamed so loudly. But when she raised her head and turned around, she saw that she was alone in her bedroom, though she didn't feel it.

Another time Joan felt the ghost when she'd been running from my father, though she can't remember why. She'd raced past the garden and into the cemetery, my father's heavy feet stamping behind her, but he'd stopped abruptly a few feet from the wrought iron gate. The wind had picked up, suddenly and dramatically, with branches swaying as if they'd snap, and leaves swirling in little cyclones on the ground. Joan had been crouched behind a taller grave marker but had stood up to see my father cowering, staring at her. You're doing that, he'd yelled at her, though at first she wasn't sure what he was referring to. Stop doing that, he'd shouted, this time more frantically. But she hadn't done a thing, she told us. She'd strained her eyes, puzzled. Stones from the walls that surrounded her had shaken loose, disrupting centuries-old configurations, and were rolling towards him. There was no explanation for it, she told us, but she was certain that what she was seeing was real. She remembers hoping that she'd developed some sort of pagan high priestess superpower, and was disappointed a few days later when she failed to conjure it again.

Whatever it was, this obscure, wraithlike presence, it had an undeniable hold on Adele and Henry's house, cutting it off from the rest of the world, so that it somehow operated by different rules, as if it were of another era. Even the weather felt different there, somehow more extreme or powerful, rains that wouldn't let up, wind that rattled the walls, snow that pummeled the house from all directions. Henry had purchased the house sixty or so years before, at Adele's insistence, soon after their marriage. He was charged an exorbitant price for it, he always said, by the stodgy textile tycoon who'd bought the place from Adele's father. Adele had insisted that the cost of the house was absolutely within reason. It had been her childhood home, and she believed that she was meant to live there. The ghostly presence that she felt there had stayed with her for her entire life, she always said, even following her to Paris, where she and Henry moved a few months before my father was born. Henry, in a rare lapse, had allowed Adele, a young woman no less, to make the final call on a financial matter, though clearly, as the cost of the house continued to be a topic of conversation throughout my childhood, the matter was far from resolved.

My sisters and I behaved differently there than we did other places. We never sat on the floor like we did at Nana and Poppy's, a piece of honey cake in one hand and a glass of whole milk in the other, our bare feet dirty, our clothes rumpled. At Adele and Henry's house we bathed before dinner and then sat politely, in dresses, during a daily cocktail hour that preceded the evening meal. We usually assembled in the smaller parlor, a large room with a mahogany bar that led to a library with floor-to-ceiling bookshelves and a carved wooden ladder that ran on a wrought iron track. Until four o'clock, the hour deemed appropriate to begin drinking, the bar and the entrance to the library were kept hidden by an elaborately carved door that was indistinguishable from the carved panels of the wall. Joan told us that she hadn't even known of the library's existence until she was six because she wasn't allowed to "idle," as Adele called it, near the bar. While Henry and Adele drank gin and tonics from crystal highball glasses, my sisters and I drank cocktails of seltzer and grenadine, and nibbled on nuts or crackers while quietly trying to dislodge the door that by then had slipped magically back into the wall. Joan told us where the spring was once during a call from South Africa. We'd sat on the floor, the receiver shared among the three of us, as she described the small knob of wood that at first glance looked like a knot, but even knowing that, we still found it difficult to operate.

Because Alessandra has always felt the need to conduct herself so that she's in direct opposition to any particular status quo she might sense, defiantly differentiating herself from everyone around her, simply for the sake of it, she often took on Joan's viewpoints, even if she couldn't understand them, only because she sensed that they often contradicted Adele's. So her stories about Adele's ghost varied, and sometimes described something uncannily similar to something Alessandra herself might have done. One morning the ghost consumed half a jar of honey in one sitting using a

wooden spoon and no napkin. Another time she left a reflection piece, an angry, curse-laden essay about bourgeois
entitlement, on the kitchen table. Alessandra revered Joan
in an almost religious way as a child, and this adoration has
dimmed only slightly over the years. Joan was a symbol to
Alessandra of contrarian badassery, proof that it's actually
quite sensible to do whatever you want, which isn't quite
what Joan has done, though it's impressively close. Alessandra always slept in Joan's childhood bedroom, waking
up early to make her own coffee, a habit she'd surreptitiously taken up at age seven. She'd sip from Joan's favorite mug
and rummage through Joan's old books. Sometimes she'd
take down our mother's painting that hung near the door
in a frame without protective glass, because she'd accidentally dropped it. Though she'd been asked not to, she often
ran her fingers along the ridges of paint, outlining chunks
of pearly ice and incandescent fish gills. In elementary
school Alessandra had kept a calendar on her nightstand
with Joan's schedule on it so that she could call her every
Sunday, adjusting the time she called to Joan's current time
zone. Joan travelled often, writing for magazines and conducting research, work she got because of her book, and
she made a point of keeping Alessandra informed about it,
talking to her as if she were an adult, which only further
inflated Alessandra's already incorrigible ego.

Just as Joan had as a child, at Adele and Henry's house,
Alessandra spent most of her time with Henry in his office, while Isabella and I wandered about with Adele as she
tended to the house and grounds. Alessandra would sit on
the hunter-green chesterfield sofa near the fireplace with a
stack of books on her lap, pretending that she was reading,
she, too, a no-bullshit scholar like Henry. If we were outside and had the misfortune of catching a glimpse of her as
she stared moodily from the window, she'd often give us the
finger or make the motion of one's throat being slit. Adele
would gasp in horror but of course carry on and we'd amble
after her, armed with one of her notepads, prepared to re-

cord such things as an overgrown shrub, out of place rocks, or branches hanging too far over a pathway. We'd then walk the rooms of the house, noting chipped dishes, wilting flowers, un-fluffed pillows, or dust behind a console table. Our reports were then given to one of the many people who worked for Adele and Henry over the years, a colorful crew of locals, students, and oddball savants who maintained our beloved magisterial WASP wonderland.

Isabella and I ate lunch with Adele in the kitchen, usually egg salad and tomato on toasted bread with tiny discs of shortbread for dessert. Alessandra took her midday meal with Henry. They'd both decide at some point that they'd done enough. She'd flipped through the requisite number of encyclopedias, examining their old maps, or images of paintings, mosaics, textile patterns, or architectural blueprints, which were her favorite, and he'd completed enough of that week's lecture—he was still teaching at that point—consolidating notes or organizing slides or reviewing something. He'd then remove his tweed jacket, the essential sartorial adornment for a history professor even if he was home on a weekend entertaining an irascible child, and stroll to the kitchen to assemble a spread that he'd describe as light though it actually wasn't. He'd then return to his study with a brass-handled wooden tray piled high with plates and napkins, a warm baguette, various cheeses, sausage or prosciutto, olives, and bowls of fruit lightly dusted with sugar. He'd sit with Alessandra on the sofa with the tray on the coffee table and she'd practice eating as slowly as he did because food was something to be savored, he said, not crammed into one's mouth without thought.

Those lunches were the times he was most talkative, I later learned. Henry was often quiet or distracted at dinner, prodding us, but rarely Adele, with questions, or gently teasing us about our grammar or misuse of a particular utensil. But in his office, he'd lean back slightly, his napkin hanging diagonally on one knee, and tell Alessandra stories that she'd later relay to us, about his Gramercy Park childhood where he'd been able to travel for seven New York City blocks through basements and over rooftops, never touching the ground, or about his experiences as a young man in Germany, recollections that terrified us, and kept us up at night. But even better than Henry's stories were his lessons, which he designed for Alessandra when he had writer's block or couldn't focus, exploring such topics as mercury and thermometers, time zones, currency, and radio frequency. The afternoon he attempted to demonstrate how a compass worked, he'd mowed a maze in the tall grass near the woods that she was to navigate her way out of. He drew it out first on paper and then fired up the lawn tractor and rode about triumphantly for a while, creating an impossible tangle, and then left Alessandra in the middle of it, holding his old army compass. He'd instructed her to look at the compass and to follow the directions that he'd call out from the garden, but after waiting for a while and hearing nothing, she grew frightened and had started yelling for him. The wind had picked up, unexpectedly, as it so often did there, and the sky had darkened, making the tall grass appear olive as opposed to a bright, emerald green. She'd become alarmed first because Henry had stopped responding to her and then because there was a strange stirring around her. The grass waved oddly, almost at a slant, which made the path she'd just walked seem unfamiliar. So she'd followed a form, a woman with her hand on her mouth, or maybe it was the wind, or something, and she was sobbing by the time she found Henry collapsed at the edge of the garden. He'd had a flashback, a result of his experience in Germany in World War II, something we'd witnessed often enough as children, though that didn't make it any easier to observe.

Alessandra fought with Henry only once, at the beginning of her sophomore year in college, which is shocking given her personality. In a particularly stern way he'd told her that she should have taken German if she were going to focus so heavily on German architecture. She was taken aback by his tone and certain that he was wrong, she told us, and she'd even attempted to say so, but he'd talked over her, not an easy feat, saying that she couldn't possibly understand a country's structures if she didn't speak its language, that already too much is lost in translation between art and intellect. She'd insisted that architecture was about something besides language, that language was a part of it, but not vital to really understanding it. But he simply couldn't understand why she chose Greek, as it wasn't remotely useful to her. She could have at least taken Latin, he'd said, his voice heavy, as if she'd really put him out. She'd gotten tears in her eyes, an uncommon occurrence, while trying to explain that the letters in the Greek alphabet are architecture. That's why she'd taken Greek. He'd stared at her, unblinking, and then nodded. Such an exchange may not sound like much, but for a man like Henry, it was about as heated as they come.

In a defeated rage Alessandra had stomped from his study, where she paced on the lawn with half a pack of Marlboro Lights and a bottle of pinot noir, inhaling and exhaling furiously, and guzzling from the bottle. Joan had told her that fighting with Henry was a rite of passage, so while swigging and smoking, Alessandra had comforted herself with images of Joan as a young woman experiencing something similar. She pictured Joan sitting on the sofa as she had so often sat, frail but bright-eyed, the way she looked in the framed photographs that sat on the back hall console table. Thinking that way, Alessandra later told us, of Joan's intensity and her own anger and confusion, made the oddness of the way we all interacted within the family in relation to academic pursuits or intellectual matters seem particularly striking. Joan was the one who'd "made it," after all. Not Henry. Henry had dropped out of his Princeton doctoral program, after years of rigorous drinking in Europe, though of course we never discussed this. It had only slipped out in a drunken moment of gregariousness when Adele had said too much, attributing it to the flashbacks, and also to his drinking, and also saying the program was actually either too lax or too restrictive, or not challenging, something. But still, he was the one we all pandered to. His was the opinion we seemed to value most.

Alessandra told us about the argument a few weeks later during a family dinner, a celebration of a birthday or something I can't quite remember, though I do recall my flared jeans and black liquid eyeliner. Isabella had arrived fashionably late, rail thin in an oversized sweater and designer boots. She made a big to-do of rearranging her linguini with clam sauce, and then nibbled at her salad. Alessandra, in understated, and likely pilfered DKNY, wound her pasta around her fork with aggressive precision while describing the argument with Henry. Our mother then told us the story she always tells about how Poppy had reacted when she'd told him as a child that she'd wanted to be a scientist. Very matter-of-factly he'd informed her that she'd have to learn to speak German. Alessandra sighed, explaining that the story didn't really seem relevant, and our mother raised her eyebrows and made the sort of face that conveys both love and exasperation and asked Alessandra if she had any fucking idea what it means for a father to have said that sort of thing to his daughter in the '50s, which she of course did not, though she obviously wouldn't acknowledge this, so she quickly became quite absorbed again with her pasta.

Henry got sick not long after that argument. Initially, his doctor thought he had Parkinson's disease, but it turned out to be ALS, a diagnosis that Adele had tried to hide from us at first because she couldn't face it herself. To avoid doing so she made up ridiculous excuses about why we couldn't visit, something she'd never done before, astrological predictions, that the neighbor's horses were getting wild and might trample one of us, that the sheets might be wrinkled, and then finally, after weeks of lies, in tearful bursts on the telephone she'd asked that we come. Alessandra and Isabella drove from their respective colleges in borrowed cars, and my mother and I came from Providence. But before we'd even settled in and been offered "a refreshment," before we'd even been hugged and told that we were "oh so lovely," as was her custom, Adele dragged us all up to her bedroom. Henry was sitting on the end of the bed in his undershirt. The bed was unmade and clothing was strewn about the room. Adele was frantic, almost crying, emoting in a way that was so unlike her that it had the effect of making me want to flee, to be as far away from her as I could get.

She yanked the curtains open so forcefully I thought she'd rip them down and then she wrung her hands self-consciously. Then very calmly, sounding artificially kind and affected, she told Henry to show us how he put on a shirt, something she clearly knew he could no longer do. By then his movements were too shaky. He'd looked at her sadly and then at us and then to the floor before standing up clumsily, bracing against the bedpost. He then reached for the navy-blue button-down shirt that hung on a hanger on the door, his breath rasping. Alessandra had started towards him, her eyes filled with tears, but Adele put her hand on her arm, not clasping, but pressing her to stay where she was. So we watched as Henry exhausted himself, forced to expose his failing body, as he tried desperately to put an arm in the sleeve of his shirt, each attempt feebler than the last. Finally my mother got up to help him, unable to bear the scene any longer, but he didn't seem relieved. He looked embarrassed, possibly even angry, but he said nothing. Then, in a quivering rage Adele told us that she couldn't bear the thought of being alone, as if Henry didn't even exist, as if he weren't in the room, clutching the bedpost and gasping for breath. That was the first and only time that I hated her.

Not long after that, Henry died. Though I wasn't as close to him as Alessandra had been, I'd adored him. He was a strange treasure, a relic from another era, sarcastic, brilliant, at times unpredictable. He once jumped into the pool fully clothed while holding his gin and tonic. He often wept quietly while reading aloud to us from *Winnie the Pooh*. It wasn't until he was gone that I began to disentangle how much of their world had been a result of his unique spirit and what had been a result of Adele's, as he'd always been so much softer, still powerful but stoic. And so it was in some ways fitting that he died so quietly. It happened while he was reading, in his favorite chair, and because we had to see it this way, we decided that that was probably the best way he could have died. He'd started seeing things at night a few days before. Moments in Germany came back to him in snippets, and there was something about his sister. Adele said that he couldn't quite understand what was happening because he was both aware that he was hallucinating and convinced that what he saw was truly there. At his funeral she recited a Scottish prayer that they'd both known as children. She stammered, became hoarse, repeated words, her face pale and stark. She seemed at the point of collapse. She told us again that she didn't want to be alone, but refused to consider moving. She went four days without eating, unintentionally. My mother called Lauran, one of the people who worked at the house, and asked her to stop by more often, to bring her food, and we all tried to visit her more frequently.

During one visit on an eerie gray fall day we took a walk along the shore and Adele began babbling incoherently, about Henry, my father's cancer, the ominous dark clouds in the distance. She described a recurring nightmare she'd had while she was in Paris. It had something to do with a woman in her childhood bedroom, and something about the front staircase, a series of moments she struggled to articulate. It became clear to me at one point that she was trying to tell me that she believed she'd made our father sick. It had to do with her past, which she didn't elaborate on, instead describing the terrible images that came to her at night. To avoid sleeping she'd paced in the narrow hallway between the bathroom and the bedroom, stepping around the little squares of light that fell into the hallway from the window. Because she was so tired, she thought about her steps and their relation to the squares of light as some sort of mathematical equation but she could never remember in the morning why thinking that way had made sense to her.

After Henry died, cocktail hour began at three o'clock in the afternoon, sometimes two. Adele took long morning swims in the ocean and often stayed in her bathing suit for hours, with a robe or an assortment of shawls wrapped around her, as she wandered from room to room, on an eternal search for the perfect book that would suit her mood but that wouldn't upset her or remind her of Henry. One evening she told me that before he died, she'd asked Henry to haunt her. We'd had dinner, just the two of us, but she'd barely touched her food. Instead, she swirled her wine glass, her eyes dull. When I asked how he'd responded she looked as if she might cry. He'd been guarded, of course, she told me. And he said that he'd try, but he'd been distracted, and didn't think he'd have any control over what happened after he died anyway. She'd pressed him, begged him really, to try as best he could to come back to her, and her voice cracked as she spoke, the memory clearly still too fraught and visceral. That night, long after I thought she'd gone to bed, I saw her walking on the lawn from my bedroom window.

Isabella and Alessandra were in college by this point. They visited Adele when they could, but the real onus fell on my mother and me, which wasn't such a bad thing. Though I missed them, I'd fought for sixteen years for my mother's undivided attention, and then suddenly she was all mine, which made the two years before I left for college particularly happy ones. Tending to Adele became a bond we shared. My mother began to rely on me in ways she hadn't when my sisters were home. I helped her to catalogue her paintings on a new, digital database. I woke up early on Saturday mornings to drive to the Italian markets with her, my travel mug full of steaming coffee and foamed milk, and then to a spot in Bristol where a few hippies had erected a makeshift farm stand. Together we watered and pruned the house-plants and folded the laundry, sometimes while sharing a glass of wine.

The first summer that my sisters were gone, my mother and I spent a few days a week at Adele's house, ostensibly to help cull Henry's extensive book collection, sorting what should be saved and what should be donated to the local library or the university where he'd taught. Isabella and Alessandra headed to Europe, spending a month or two wandering, retracing the steps my mother and Joan had travelled when they were in their early twenties, when they were brave and certain in a way that they claim they no longer are. My sisters called every once in a while, and sent postcards, which I dutifully read aloud to Adele as she sipped her morning coffee in a stone-faced daze. From a pay phone in the hallway of an aging hostel, Isabella informed me one evening that she and Alessandra were already tired of each other, which Adele and I took to mean that Isabella was already tired of Alessandra. She'd thought their trip was to be a celebration, she said, a way to let loose, but for Alessandra it was serious, about research. Freed from the confines of assigned reading, Isabella had packed silly, un-complicated novels in a chic leather duffel bag. Alessandra lugged old army maps, dense textbooks, and sheets of archi-tectural drawings in her over-stuffed, utilitarian suitcase, unpacking them each night for further study. She'd trace certain sketches from her textbooks with her finger, with a blank but pleased expression, insisting on keeping the light on, apparently immune to jet lag.

Ever the contrarian, Alessandra reported only a day or so later that they were having a wonderful time. They'd spent a few weeks wandering happily around Florence and Paris, she said, searching for remnants of a world we'd all heard so much about, dark bars, bustling squares, looming cathedrals. They'd laughed, standing in front of Santa Maria Novella, recalling the murals our mother had painted on the walls of our childhood bedrooms, of Renaissance triptychs and Jackie Robinson, images our mother thought were beautiful and would inspire confidence, and that also happened to be the sorts of things she liked to paint. They'd walked from the Tate to the Victoria and Albert Museum, where our mother and Joan had gotten in their first fight, after our mother told Joan that she was going back to Rhode Island to be with our father. My mother says that it was one of the rare times that Joan seemed completely indifferent to the people around her, too angry to care whether she was causing a scene or not. With tears in her eyes Joan had accused my mother of kowtowing to men and to the patriarchy, for talking the talk but not walking the walk.

Alessandra had wanted to spend two weeks in Germany, but Isabella had argued her down to a few days, though she agreed to a tour of Dachau, which she later regretted. Alessandra was hell-bent on recovering Henry's experiences, which in hindsight was probably her way of grieving, though it didn't feel that way to Isabella at the time. She found Alessandra's interest in all things German odd, morbid, with its practical stiffness and flat surfaces. To her Alessandra seemed creepily haunted, almost possessed, by a story Henry had told her during one of their lunches, one that she'd often repeated to us over the years. He'd described seeing an emaciated prisoner about his age emerging from a building at Dachau when his unit had liberated the camp in 1945. The man had stopped, steadied himself, raised his head slightly to make eye contact with Henry, and then he'd smiled. Henry said that it was his most vivid memory of the war. From what Alessandra could recall from Henry's descriptions, she had tried to locate the sites where emaciated bodies had been stacked, where the lines had been of people who'd emerged from buildings, gaunt, practically dead, moving in unison, as if controlled by a machine operated somewhere else. In her hand she clenched the laminated list that she'd found tucked away in one of the drawers in Nana's kitchen, of five of Nana's relatives on her mother's side, people who most likely ended up there. Nana told us years ago that she'd skimmed it twice, but couldn't bear to really look at the names.

This was exactly the kind of single-minded intensity that Isabella found so irritating about Alessandra, and at least part of the age-old conflict between the two of them. Whereas Isabella often struggled to find her voice, Alessandra's steadfast and deep confidence in her own genius seemed ever present. So while Isabella was put off by the idea of tromping through a concentration camp as the denouement to her summer vacation, Alessandra had somehow overruled her, convincing her, assertively, that her worries were trivial, and she did so with no regard for what such an interaction might feel like, because of course Alessandra had never experienced anything like it. This dynamic has played out disastrously, according to Isabella. She recalls a painful history of being too frequently overlooked, despite the two years of acquired knowledge and experience that she has over Alessandra, simply because Alessandra was, and is, so strident, or forthright, or convincing.

While none of us agree with Isabella on this matter entirely, her grievance is not altogether without merit. Alessandra is an asshole, no doubt about it, though she is also magnetic, brilliant, and brave. For example, despite being told repeatedly that her undergraduate thesis concept wouldn't work, she pursued it anyway, eventually winning several prestigious awards, as well as offers of scholarships to three Ivy League schools for further graduate research. Isabella downplays her own academic track, and insists that we all do too. We don't, of course, but there was an awful conversation when our aunt Joan, perhaps rather absentmindedly given Isabella's insecurities, had wondered out loud at Adele's dinner table one evening if it had been unexamined anger that had led to Isabella's thesis topic, and not who knows what, presumably the sort of authentic cerebral seeking that drove Joan and Alessandra. Isabella had fled the table in tears, startling Joan, who hadn't meant to say anything contentious. She'd only meant to say that in her mind at least, there was no such thing as an objective interest. I'd run after Isabella, to the back parlor where she'd buried her face in a silk embroidered cushion, which muffled her voice as she defended her work, though in truth, no one had actually questioned it.

Sometime during her sophomore year, Isabella had read about the Weather Underground, and the young women, women who could have been her, she felt, who'd abandoned everything, devoting themselves, often catastrophically, irrationally, violently, to notions of political change and racial equality. Isabella was struck by the language used to describe them in her required reading, the dismissive misogyny of it, which framed too much within the context of privileged white female obliviousness, which was certainly real, though there was little consideration of the limitations imposed by sexism, the ancient, invisible barriers pitting women against each other, rewriting history as if it were linear and simple, not complex, contradictory, and cloudy. She'd liked those women, she said. They were from seemingly good homes, their needs were met, at least ostensibly, they'd showed no previous signs of deviant behavior, but, she said, smiling with awe, they'd gone ahead and erupted anyway. I did my best not to mention that she'd just proved Joan's point rather impressively, and continued to pat her hand in respectful silence.

Alessandra's thesis concept had crystallized the day the two of them toured Dachau. She recalls losing track of Isabella, and turning around to look for her and becoming powerfully struck by the lines and angles of the buildings that surrounded her. She'd tried to explain this to Isabella later on the train back to their hostel, this notion of architectural schemes and their relation to violence. The existence of that link changes everything, she'd said, enthralled by the detailed arguments she was devising, architectural shapes, the way planes meet, each enclosure and doorway, the symbolism of it, the patterns. They stop being structures, she'd said. They take on other lives entirely. Alessandra felt that Isabella hadn't understood what she was getting at, attributing it to Isabella's frivolousness or sentimentality, and not the nebulous or pretentious nature of her description, or the emotional exhaustion one might experience after exploring a site memorializing genocide. Isabella had apparently begun talking about our father, something she'd done frequently during that trip, more so than she'd ever done before, Alessandra noted. Though he'd often come up for us throughout the years, our memories of him are imprecise, often changing, and sometimes contradictory. We usually focused on the things we could agree on. One of us would recall the bandages on his wrists, because he'd often had tape covering where his IVs had been, or the hats he'd worn indoors after his hair fell out. Isabella told Alessandra that she could no longer picture his face, and that when she tried to, she saw Jackie Robinson instead. She said that she'd spent hours during the years after our father died, late at night, unable to sleep, thinking about him and staring at our mother's murals of Jackie Robinson. Then she'd made a strained face and leaned back and winced before throwing up in a brown paper bag that she'd found on the floor. Another passenger, likely alarmed, said something to them in German that they didn't understand so they'd smiled, shaking their heads.

Isabella told me later that something about the trip brought back strange and painful childhood memories. She recalled wondering often if she were actually invisible. She'd been there with me in the hall the night our father died, she said, but when I told the story afterwards, I spoke as if she hadn't been there. She described my pajamas, the mist that pooled on the floor by the window, that I'd stopped coughing and had begun to breathe regularly, and that we'd swirled and kicked at the white evaporating night air with our feet. Only Adele understood what that had felt like, she told me. When Isabella would try to describe it, our mother wondered if she was misinterpreting things. And Nana would tell her that it wasn't so bad, that there were so many things in life that were worse. But Adele understood that it was bad, and that when Isabella said that she felt all alone, that she actually was all alone. So Adele would hold Isabella's little face in her hands and say to her, well, I see you, Isabella, and then she would describe her. Isabella's purple eyelids, she said, that my mother's family brought with them from Russia, were the color of lilacs. Her dark hair was wild like the waves that crashed against the shore at night. Her toenails were shiny, perfectly square, like tiny dollhouse ice cubes. No one is invisible, Adele would tell her, while rocking her in her arms. Even your father, who is no longer here. Adele still saw him, she said, and then she'd describe him too. But the man that these descriptions invoked for Isabella, despite their vividness, was not our father, but a complete stranger, someone else's father, a man who played for the Dodgers when they were a Brooklyn team, who had no idea that she existed, but who still smiled at her when she was sad at night and couldn't sleep. And Adele always told her that thinking that way wasn't silly at all.

CHAPTER FOUR

My mother remembers the exact instant that my father died. Pivotal moments like that, she told me, like when Martin Luther King was assassinated or when she learned about the horrors of Mai Lai, become forever etched in your mind, even if you don't want them to be. She was in his hospital room when it happened, sitting in a metal chair with thick leather padding, leaning slightly forward, watching his face while he slept. By then he'd been sick for years so she was used to the way he looked when he slept and she was expecting that she would be looking at him, just as she was then, and that one day he would stop breathing. She told me that she forced herself to picture that moment as many times as she could, so that when it actually happened, when he actually truly left, she'd be able to handle it, or at least know what to expect. But it wasn't anything like what she'd pictured, she told me, during one of our long, drawn-out dinners after my sisters left for college. The moment wasn't better or worse or more or less sudden. It was as if it was something else entirely. A few minutes before he died he apologized, and then said something about her purple eyelids, the exact wording she can't recall. But it was the last thing he said to her.

When she learned about my father's diagnosis, my mother was in northern England with his sister Joan, on a weekend break from her painting fellowship in Florence. Joan had an assistantship at Oxford, which she abandoned every chance she got to wander about, conducting her own research, often convincing my mother to accompany her on various excursions. My mother insists that she followed Joan to Europe, that Joan was the brave one. And Joan insists that my mother was brave, too, and that she'd only pursued the Oxford thing on a whim, which wasn't entirely true. Joan has been running or fleeing for most of her life, or that's how we've all come to think of her story, because that's the way she and my mother have always told it. Joan had sought out the assistantship to escape something, her past, her home, her family.

They'd gone away for a few days because Joan was obsessed by some transaction having to do with the Manchester-Liverpool train line. She'd tracked down a middle-management railway official who had original records of some long ago transaction. They'd planned to meet him the following day for lunch. They stayed in a tiny hotel in Manchester and while Joan read, my mother painted miniatures of flowers and still lifes of random things she'd arranged on her nightstand, a blue glass pitcher of water, her toiletries, whatever novel she was reading, using the techniques she'd picked up studying Masaccio, Fra Angelico, and Giotto. Their bedroom at the hotel had two rickety single beds and she and Joan sat on hers, cross-legged and facing each other, while Joan read aloud the letter from Adele that relayed her brother's diagnosis in the same sing-song tone she'd used to describe the roses blooming in the previous paragraph. After Joan finished reading she dropped the letter to the floor but continued to stare at it. My mother remembers that Adele's handwriting looked like one long, looping Hollywood signature.

She'd met my father, Luke, the summer before her senior year in college at a bar she rarely went to. He was in his last year of medical school and he was so tired that he almost fell asleep standing next to her, one hand resting on the bar counter. She told him that she had majored in art history but that she should have majored in biology and that she wanted to be a painter. He told her that he didn't understand why people made claims like that, as if anyone could know the results of having done the thing you think you should have done. The music was loud so she didn't hear him at first and had kept asking him to repeat himself, but by the time she finally heard what he'd said, they'd both independently decided that keeping up their conversation required more energy than either of them was willing to put into it. Not knowing what else to say or how to end the interaction, she told him that he looked tired, which he found funny. She could hear his laugh, which had surprised her, the force of it, discernable even in the haze of the music and the voices that surrounded them. He'd had a wonderful smile, she said, deep and intense, and he had beautiful hair, too, which doesn't matter, but still. Something about his laugh struck her, the power of it, or the confidence. It was a masculine, magnetic laugh. My mother laughed then, too, as she described it, looking almost embarrassed, and then she changed her tone, becoming lighter, almost silly, as she recalled that Nana had described him as looking somewhat like a golden retriever, a rather rude but not atypical way she sometimes characterizes the goyim.

My mother found my father incredibly attractive, perhaps even exotic, worldly and educated the way wealthy people are, a part of a rarified swath who can quote things, recall things, lines from Yeats, for example, or a Churchill joke, as if such things are quotidian. Neither Nana nor Poppy recited poetry and the only politicians they talked about were the Providence ones, and the way they talked about them was far from lyrical. It was more like "that son-uva-bitch did so and so, that son-uva-bitch." Nana recalls feeling as if my mother began to see her differently in those days. She blamed Adele for it, though she wouldn't come out and say so. Next to Adele, Nana felt she appeared crude to my mother, a notion my mother said was preposterous. For her it was simply about exposure to something new. But Nana would tsk-tsk and shake her head. Don't be fooled by this fanciness, she'd say. It isn't real. It's not the stuff that matters. And about my father's illness, Nana would grow stern. You don't have to take all of this on, she'd said. Women think they have to, that they have to save everyone and fix it all, but they don't. My mother remembers being dismissive of Nana, even though what she was preaching, a practical brand of no-bullshit can-do feminism, is the sort of thing my mother was generally quite enthusiastic about. At the time my mother thought Nana was being prejudiced, which she was, but my mother now sees that she'd refused to hear what she was trying to tell her.

My father made a strange face on their first date, the particulars of which my mother can't really explain. It was just odd somehow, and it's the thing that still stands out for her, something about the vacantness of it, which she knew was not an indication of his being vacant, but maybe slightly detached. They ate at an Italian restaurant with red-checkered tablecloths and overpriced garlic bread, and he wore a blue button-down shirt that made his shoulders look wide and straight. She remembers noting that he looked larger and more foreboding than he had at the bar. He had the kind of face that my mother described as stark and angular, with beautiful coloring, unlike anyone from her high school, she made a point of saying, whatever that means. Even without the loud music, she found it hard to keep a conversation going. She'd say something, but because he took so long to respond or didn't seem to acknowledge that she'd said anything at all, she questioned whether he'd heard her, even though they were sitting across from each other. She thought, should I say something more? Was that the end of my sentence? Was I unclear? When she brought her water glass up to her lips her hand was shaking so much that the clinking of the ice cubes was audible, but he hadn't seemed to notice. He'd just continued to look at her, making the strange face my mother came to think of as somehow related to what ultimately came between them. It was a kind of distancing, though she didn't see it that way at the time. Then it had felt like a challenge, a romantic one, to someday break through to a place that he guarded, that would always be inaccessible to her.

My mother offered these accounts to me, these lucid moments, that felt almost like tiny paintings, the jolt she felt after one of Nana's terser critiques, the smell of the air in the summer while listening to a Beatles record, an afternoon spent mending a pair of men's corduroy overalls and then trying to cinch in the waist to make them more flattering for when she wore them over to her friend's house in East Greenwich to garden. These details supplemented the stories she'd told throughout my childhood, adding depth and color to a history of which I had assumed I already knew almost every nook and cranny. They also served to further highlight the enigma that was my father, both the man himself and the memories of her time with him. Sometimes his presence in her recollections was overpowering, as if he were some omnipresent demigod presiding over all of us. Other times it sounded as if he were already dead, though when I thought back on the events she'd described, after some basic arithmetic, it occurred to me that he'd been there too. He must have been, perhaps in his bedroom with Alessandra on his lap, where they'd sat quietly for hours one afternoon while he'd sculpted tiny dolls out of copper wire using basic pliers. One doll had been so intricate that she'd had a ponytail, thick and wild, her copper hair rising in an arc before curling at her lower back. Or maybe he was in the basement near the staircase performing a puppet show for me, about dogs I think, dogs that were frightened of kittens. Or behind the latched door of the downstairs bathroom, vomiting from chemotherapy, the sounds of his retching I had to strain to hear because he'd opened the window and turned on the faucet to hide it from us. It wasn't that my mother hadn't talked openly before, or that she hadn't talked about our father. It might have been that her more complicated memories became less distinct as the years wore on. Whatever it was, I liked that the combination of my age and the fact that my sisters and I weren't all clamoring for attention as we once had, allowed her story the chance to shine just as brightly as Joan's or anyone else's always had, even if it meant that my father's story didn't.

One fall afternoon she'd caught me when I was ditching school. She'd told me that morning that she was heading to Cranston to get canning equipment from a high school friend. I hadn't planned to not go, I just simply didn't. I was drinking my second cup of sweetened warm milk with a splash of hot coffee. I was dressed in tight black flares and a merino wool turtleneck sweater. I think this was the phase where I had a bob, very angular, very Anna Wintour, but without bangs. I'd finished my toast, heavy with a layer of the dense peanut butter we bought from the co-op, and as I watched my mother climb into her Volvo, wrapping her scarf around her neck, it dawned on me that I could stay home. Just for that morning. I could take a bath. I'd use her lavender bath salts. I'd wrap my damp hair in a towel after massaging grape-seed oil into my split ends. I don't remember if I ran the bath, but I recall taking off my shoes and putting on my mother's slippers and looking at myself in her full length mirror, so transfixed that I failed to register that she'd returned, having forgotten something, and stood staring at me staring at my reflection. We didn't fight. There wasn't even an argument. She asked me if I skipped school often and I told her the truth—that I had a few times but no, not often. I asked if she was angry and was struck, dazzled with love and awe and curiosity by her response. I don't know, she said. Is this the sort of thing a mother is supposed to be angry about?

My mother told me that after my father stopped breathing she had stayed where she was, rooted in her leather chair, staring at his face. Doctors and nurses came in and she must have talked to them, she said, but she has no memory of what was said. What she remembers is some point later when she was alone in the room with him again, still staring at him, trying to remember the way she'd planned to tell me and my sisters that our father had died. She said that she'd pictured that over and over, too, just as she'd pictured what his face would look like when it suddenly became still. That's what she'd been doing during all those years that he was sick, during all the scares, the relapses, the frantic drives to the hospital, when she'd worried that she was falling apart. But sitting there then, she suddenly couldn't remember any of the lines she'd memorized. All she could focus on was how tired she felt. She remembers thinking, if I can just get home. If I can just get home I'll sleep for a few hours and then I'll remember how to tell them. The girls will wake up and I'll tell them. And then she thought, actually first I'll make them breakfast, oatmeal with almonds and honey. She recalls, while still looking at my father, picturing the honey with the green label with white lettering that she'd left on the counter, the kind we still buy from the same organic farm in western Massachusetts. She wondered, is there enough for three bowls of oatmeal? Yes, there is. And if there isn't, I'll put the least amount of honey in Isabella's because she won't notice or if she does she won't make a thing of it the way Alessandra or I would, which was rude, I pointed out, but also true. Such an injustice would surely have prompted a fit. She said that she'd started to whisper her thoughts, narrating, not to my father, but to herself, to keep from falling sleep. Then after they eat I'll take them on a walk, she whispered. And then I'll tell them. By then I'll have the right words.

She remembers looking out the window, who knows how much later, and seeing that people were already up. It was three in the morning, or four or five maybe. A man in a gray jacket was walking down the block across the street. She thought, when he gets to the bus stop I'll get up. When he passes the bus stop I'll go home. But he passed the bus stop and she couldn't find the strength to stand, so she waited until a young woman in red shoes came around the corner. When she passes that sign I'll get up, she thought. She kept doing that. Another guy. A couple. A woman in a green blazer. And then no one was around outside. Adele says that she was there in the hospital but my mother insists that she was alone. She remembers turning around after a while and seeing her parents. Nana came towards her and reached out her hand and my mother held it. Poppy told Nana that they had to get my mother home, and my mother didn't say anything. Then Nana gently pulled her to her feet. As they walked out of the room my mother turned around to look at my father again. His jacket was hanging on a rod in the closet by the door. She wanted to know what they planned to do with his jacket. She remembers trying to say something to that effect but that no sounds came out so she left the room with her parents.

I'd never heard Adele's version of this particular day, or Nana's, though I don't know that I ever asked either of them to tell me what they remember about the day my father died. I think this is at least partly because his death loomed so large in the family narrative, especially in respect to how the rest of us thought and talked about my mother's life. It had an almost biblical feel to it. There was the before, and then the momentous first encounter, and then love and marriage and children and tragedy, each phase of her existence situated in relation to my father. She was painting, but he was sick. She was pregnant, but he was doing his residency. This was not, however, how my mother thought about her life. And it wasn't how Joan, or my mother's Providence friends, saw it either. For them it was: Leah replicated a Masaccio, and used the wood of an old barn door to make a frame for it, and Luke was working in an emergency room. Or Leah rolled us a joint in her kitchen, while making ravioli from scratch. She'd filled the sheets of pasta with scoops of butternut squash and herbs, folding them into tiny dough pillows that she plopped in a pot of boiling water and ladled out with a slotted spoon, the joint lit and dangling from her lips, as she laughed, telling some crazy story about seeing

Bob Dylan at a festival. And who knows where Luke was.

My mother can only recall my father's funeral in stark, unrelated patches. She remembers seeing Joan again, after what felt like decades, although it had only been a few years, and that she'd looked as if she were glowing. It was because Joan had just fallen in love, though she hadn't let on about it then. My mother remembers talking to Joan on the phone the day before. She'd called when she'd gotten in, from the phone in the kitchen at Adele and Henry's house. My mother could hear Adele's voice in the background, shrill and anxious, finalizing some plan for the reception or something. My mother didn't know what to say at first. She told me that she wondered if Joan had been angry about how disparate their lives had become, how tragically far away their summer in Europe, so many years before, felt to her then. But her thoughts weren't coherent. She couldn't even really communicate. Her sentences came out awkwardly. She tried to talk as she and Joan always had and then had stopped, unsure why she'd thought she'd needed to pretend. Of all people, Joan, her best friend, would never have asked that of her.

My mother told me this when I told her that I'd like to get on the pill. I was still a virgin. I'd let a boyfriend or two prod about in the area but wasn't sure how to think about sex. I felt immensely powerful, as if I had some sort of secret hidden magic. I was also appalled at the awkwardness of my first sexual experiences, the earnest rubbing, the clumsy handling of bra straps and buttons, the rearrangement of uncoordinated, growing bodies. Walking home from one such encounter it dawned on me what the problem was. I'm a lesbian, I said to my mother, in an exhausted tone, as I removed my jacket, finally home. The kitchen was bathed in golden light, the yellow of the bulb over the sink and the orange of the setting sun glowing through the windows of the sunporch. My mother was sautéing spinach in a pan, her apron on, a wooden spatula in one hand, and her glasses slightly lower on her nose as she glanced from the pan to the obituaries in the paper that was spread on the counter. How else can you learn about all these wonderful lives, she'd say, when we'd point out how morose it was that the obituaries were her favorite part of the paper. She'd barely raised an eyebrow at my declaration. My coming out she took not seriously at all. She moved a few leaves of spinach, throwing a handful of pine nuts into the pan. Give it time, she said, laughing. And then, why don't you tell me what you were up to this afternoon. I described the boyfriend, a crushing disappointment, a nice enough, lanky Irish and Portuguese boy from a big family, who was too shy or terrified or bored or boring to move me all that much. Guilt and his access to marijuana and peach schnapps were what bound us, though I was looking for passion, maybe a pregnancy scare, or a good screaming fight like my friend Serena had with her boyfriend Mark. She'd shriek at him and then hang up the phone and then a few hours later she'd allow him to sneak into her basement so they could have a remarkably brief session of makeup sex on the futon in front of the television. But my boyfriend was too even-tempered for such antics, and had been conditioned by the women in his family, truly lovely women actually, to agree with me no matter what. I don't like being touched by men, I told my mother. It annoys me. I feel like my time could be better spent. But I also so badly want to feel like a woman, a scorned and aching, red-blooded woman. So the pill thing was really just a way to fit in. I wanted to gasp in horror like Serena did when she'd realize that she'd forgotten to take her pill, and then she'd wash down a few with her Diet Coke, light a Marlboro Red and get on with her life, her glossy black hair pulled back tightly into a bun, her foundation perfectly applied, easing into her hairline, just as her mother had taught her. My mother wore blush, but only on very special occasions, like my father's funeral, and the few times we attended synagogue at Yom Kippur. She'd hurriedly apply it to the apples of her cheeks in soft slapping motions, as if she were embarrassed. Focus less on this boyfriend, my mother said, and more on Serena. Build the sisterhood.

Though my mother has never quite come out and said so, it is her relationship with Joan that has been the most profound of her life, and not her union with my father, or the men that came after him, men that according to Adele, didn't really exist, as they weren't true affairs of the heart, but passing, trifling things. Not even worth mentioning really. My mother met Joan early in her relationship with my father. She remembers being startled when he'd brought up meeting his family, given how little they knew of each other. But he'd seemed so certain, she said, so remarkably unconcerned with all the reasons not to, so she'd agreed to it. They'd arrived at Adele and Henry's house well after midnight because my father had attended a late lecture and then something afterwards. She drove his car and they'd kept the windows open so that the wind would keep them awake, but he'd fallen asleep almost immediately after they'd gotten on the highway.

She slept in a guest bedroom down the hall from his childhood bedroom and it wasn't until she woke up the following morning that she grasped how large the house was, with its grand entrance and its porches and its sweeping, manicured grounds. He'd talked to her about his family a bit here and there, but nothing he'd said suggested that he came from the kind of family that lived in that kind of a house. She'd gotten lost on her way to the kitchen. She couldn't remember what wide staircase she'd come up the night before, or which long hallway lined with an oriental runner she'd walked, and she heard no voices, only the faint chirping of birds and the waves crashing lightly in the distance. She thought at first that everyone was still sleeping, but Joan was leaning against the butcher-block counter in the kitchen when my mother finally found it. She remembers thinking that Joan was beautiful, maybe a bit too thin, but with a lively animated face, unlike my father whose expressions she often found so difficult to interpret. Adele was sitting cross-legged at the trestle table drinking coffee, wearing a cashmere bathrobe over a dark red bathing suit, casually running her fingers through her blonde, graying hair. A newspaper was spread out before her on the table and she was smirking at it, almost daring its contents to be interesting enough to hold her attention. That's still how my mother sees Adele, she told me recently. Even now, when she pictures Adele's face, although she knows full well that Adele is dead, she still thinks of her strange expression that was confrontational but somehow still lovely. That morning she'd looked up at my mother and said, Of course you'll have some coffee. My mother had said to her, yes, of course, even though she never talked that way.

Henry spent most of my mother's first visit in his study, a room she thought of as Edwardian, dark and austere. My father had knocked on Henry's study door after breakfast on their first morning there, and Henry had looked up from his reading, surprised. My mother remembers wondering if he'd even been aware that they were coming. She shook Henry's hand, and my father leaned against his father's large mahogany desk and the two men talked formally while she sat awkwardly on the arm of the sofa. Henry mentioned something about a sailing race and my father had responded to him, but my mother thought that neither seemed to know quite what to say to each other.

Dinner that evening was long and ceremonial, each course served on thin, ornately painted china. My mother was surprised by how little the family ate, given the meticulousness of each serving, the rigid lines of cubed carrots, the delicate slices of beef, the tiny mounds of perfectly scooped butter. She was reminded again of the contrast between the two families, hers in Providence and my father's in Newport. Dinners had been chaotic, haphazard affairs for my mother growing up. Nana and Poppy closed the deli at five-thirty, after selling the last of the baked fish and prepared vegetables that the local Jewish housewives had ordered that morning for dinner, to be reheated in their convenient tinfoil containers. Then my grandparents would clean up and do any prep work for the following day and then walk home with their own dinner, usually a variation of what they'd sold to the housewives. My mother would then clear her homework from the kitchen table and lay out forks and knives and napkins, and then Nana would unwind, her pent up sarcasm unfurling, while Poppy imitated a difficult or silly customer, or ranted about Providence politics, and my mother would laugh, the small, warm room filling with boisterous, happy voices. This was talking shop, a quintessential Jewish way of life. My mother grew up believing that all married couples talked this way, debriefing, discussing business, teasing each other, and was shocked when she saw Henry gently kiss Adele's cheek one evening in a timid way, as if she were a new acquaintance.

My mother had to borrow clothing from Joan for that first dinner with my father's family. Whatever she'd brought was too casual or somehow not quite right, and of course my father hadn't thought to warn her that his was a family that "dressed" for dinner, a concept my mother had never encountered before. They'd laughed about it later, she told me, but she was mortified. Luckily her embarrassment was upstaged by Joan's rabid rage that erupted midway through the meal. Joan had left the table abruptly, angrily stacking her dishes while pushing back her chair. My mother could hear her afterwards in the kitchen after she'd stomped from the room, opening a drawer, slamming it, filling a glass with water or rinsing something, and then her footsteps grew faint, first on the back stairs and then in the hall above them. But no one said a word. My mother had looked at my father. He'd reached for his wine glass. They'd been talking about the Nixon administration, a topic Henry clearly wanted to avoid, but Joan had been insistent. Adele had then said something that struck Joan as frivolous or arrogant or uninformed, my mother can't remember which.

After dinner my mother sat with Joan in her bathroom while she smoked. My mother had changed into a nightgown and then tiptoed down the long hall to Joan's bedroom while my father remained downstairs with his parents drinking port. Joan sat glumly on the edge of the claw-foot bathtub with her legs crossed. The window was open next to her and she was tapping the ash of her cigarette into a dish that, to my mother, seemed indistinguishable from the one she'd been served salmon mousse on an hour or so earlier. Joan offered her a cigarette and my mother shook her head, sitting down across from her on a low wooden bench next to a pile of tightly folded pale yellow hand towels. My mother told Joan that she'd agreed with what she'd said during dinner. She recalls reassuring her that she also thought Nixon was a monster and that Joan had nodded. My mother then looked down at Joan's bony ankles, noting the blueness of her veins through her skin. She was thinking, this must be what they mean when people talk about blue bloods, and then Joan asked my mother if anyone had ever told her that her eyelids were purple.

And that's how it all started, the strange sisterly friendship that has been described and praised and dissected by my mother and Joan for as long as I can remember, as if their bond is a sort of sacred fabric that must be constantly rewoven, consistently reinforced with new threads made of stronger fibers. My mother often recalls becoming enamored with Joan, almost like a crush, the way little girls become enthralled by slightly older girls or teenagers, eyeing their curves, their clothing, their hairstyles, projecting onto their bodies childish fantasies about adult womanhood. To my mother, Joan was bold and strange and fascinating, just as my older sisters were to me, their attempts to tease their bangs with organic hair spray seemed sexy, their braces glamorous. Even the most minute of Joan's mannerisms, the way she squinted, or how she smoothed her hair when she was nervous, my mother found intriguing or somehow beautiful. She even began to emulate her, she told me. She gestured the way Joan did, especially when she talked about politics, shaking her fist or throwing her head back. She followed Joan to marches and demonstrations, and to parties she never would have gone to alone.

Before they set off for Europe my mother gave Joan the painting of sliced smoked salmon, and Joan immediately hung it in her bedroom where it still hangs now. Joan told her playfully or ironically, my mother can't remember, that the painting's subject matter indicated that my mother wasn't such a nice girl after all. So she told Joan that she'd only taught herself to paint, and painted such odd things, because she couldn't play on the boys' baseball team as a child. She'd said, laughing but still serious, that it had broken her heart. So play baseball now, Joan told her, and my mother remembers thinking, if it were only that simple. If only she could stomp around the world like Joan could.

A few months later, after they'd each settled in their respective European cities, Joan moved in with a man named John, who she'd met at a bookstore. John was wiry and sarcastic, my mother said, and almost as smart as Joan was. It had seemed like an odd move to my mother, one that would have frightened her, particularly because Joan seemed not to have a plan, no stated desire to marry John, or any hopes about a real future with him. My mother didn't understand at the time that that wasn't the sort of thing Joan thought about. It was new experiences she was after, and she took them in any form that they came to her. On her last night in her apartment, some tiny decrepit rented room, something moved her typewriter off of her desk when she was lying in bed reading, and she swore that it hadn't scared her. She told my mother that she didn't believe in Adele's ghosts, that she refused to, and she used her mother's first name, which my mother remembers her doing more and more after that.

CHAPTER FIVE

My aunt Joan bought her first apartment in Kensington not long after she published her book. It was a third-floor flat, overlooking a small park, with wide plank floors, large windows, and antique radiators that hissed during the winter. My mother was already back in Rhode Island by the time the book came out, late in her pregnancy with Alessandra. She remembers waddling by the bookstore and seeing copies of it on display in the window, Joan's name in a serious-looking font above an image that had seemed inconsistent with the subject matter. When Joan had called to share the news, my mother remembers a distinct odor to the room, as if she could smell Joan's brand of cigarettes and see the smoke as she exhaled, a phenomenon she attributed to hormones and something crystal-related that made no sense to me. Joan says that by then she'd quit smoking, at least for a while, though it wasn't until she saw a hypnotist in Colombia that she quit for good, and that was years later.

During the first few months that Joan lived in the Kensington apartment she'd had a recurring nightmare about distinguished-looking men in tweed jackets with leather elbow patches appearing in the living room. Without saying a word the men began to pack up her books in boxes and then had walked them slowly down the stairs to a dungeon-like room that didn't exist, at least not in her building, although it resembled something she'd seen once in a museum in Portugal. When she met Steven, years later, she told him about the nightmares and he told her that the only thing to do about them, if she wanted them to go away, was to laugh about them.

They'd met at a dinner party a year or so after she'd published her book. He hadn't achieved the kind of objective acclaim that she had but that never bothered him, she always made a point of saying. He'd just laugh and hold her hand and tell her that she was brave, and then make fun of her for blushing about it. He had toiled for years, often without any recognition, over a series of beautiful poignant essays, which she'd never heard of, about the resistance movements to apartheid. Someone at the dinner party had mentioned his work, assuming that she was already familiar with it, and she'd nodded as if she were. Later he told her that she was a terrible liar, and she had pretended not to know what he was talking about.

Before she married him she read his book of essays, almost finishing it on the plane from London to New York on her way back to Rhode Island for my father's funeral. She'd put off reading it at first, and then when she finally did, she was distracted, too focused on trying to anticipate what her father's reaction to it might be. It was as if she needed Steven to pass some arbitrary benchmark, proving that he was a serious scholar, that his thinking was thorough. But halfway through the first essay she realized that she'd been coming at the whole thing incorrectly, and that what she was doing wasn't the kind of thing you do with the work of someone you love. But ultimately it didn't matter, because she felt about it exactly the way she'd hoped she would.

For my father's funeral Joan had stayed at her parents' house in her old bedroom for a week and a half, which was the longest she'd stayed there since leaving for London after college over a decade earlier. She remembers being startled by my mother's painting, hung so many years before. So she called my mother from the phone in the kitchen. Joan remembers my mother saying that she was tired, over and over, as if on repeat, and that she'd looked so awful at the funeral that at first Joan hadn't recognized her. The purple in her eyelids had turned gray and her lips were cracked and dry. Adele had stood next to my mother and had sort of petted her but neither of them was crying. In completely different ways, Joan said, they both looked as if they were confused about where they were and what was happening. At one point my mother had looked at Joan and smiled, not in a happy way, and that was, to her, the saddest part of the funeral. Joan remembers thinking, I've failed her. I failed my best friend. I left her all alone with this.

After the funeral my mother and my sisters and I headed back to Providence, leaving Joan alone with her parents. Joan recalls Henry retreating to his study to read for hours on end, and Adele staring blankly, as she always had, but without even an ounce of the humor that had usually been there too. Joan spent most of her time outside, even though it was a particularly cold autumn, first wandering the cemetery and then just ambling, along the beach, around the outbuildings, in the mulched, muted garden. One afternoon she returned to the house just as it was growing dark. Adele was in the front living room, lighting a fire in the fireplace. She was seated on a low stool with an embroidered horse on it and next to her was a box labeled in her distinctive, exaggerated cursive. There was a set of dates on the label that Joan couldn't quite make out but she remembers that one of them was from the '40s. Adele had leafed through one of the boxes and pulled out a journal, and then she'd put it in the fire and watched as it had started to burn.

Adele hadn't heard Joan come in and Joan didn't announce herself, but remained standing in the dark by the front door, the light from the lamp and the fire not reaching her. After a while Adele had pulled the journal from the fire with the end of a fire poker. It fell to the hearth in front of her and continued to burn and she had stared at it without moving. Then, abruptly, she'd put the rest of the journals from the box in the fire and then walked out of the room, leaving the little stool dangerously close to the open flames.

I hadn't thought of Adele's journals in years, and even when I had, it had only been in a vague way. She'd told me years ago, I think when I was in high school, that she'd burned all of her journals by accident, but years later, she'd told me that she'd done it on purpose, dragging a box of them from the attic and shoving the entire thing in the fireplace a few days after my father's funeral. It wasn't until Keith and I stayed with Joan in Cape Town that it occurred to me that some of them might have survived. We'd slept on a gray linen pullout sofa in the spare bedroom that Joan uses as an office, a space crowded with artifacts collected at various stages of her life. A Barcelona Football Club flag hung on the wall by the door, and the haunted typewriter that had apparently jumped off a table late one night in London in the '70s sat on a desk. On an antique games table that had once been in Henry's office was a set of neatly labeled dictation cassettes that were labeled things like "Jeso 1" and "Kwanele 3," that I assumed had belonged to Steven. And on a bookshelf by the door, there were stacks of leather journals, some wrapped in plastic and others, that appeared to have been burned, were black and charred at the corners. I think I'd said something to Keith about the possibility of them having belonged to Adele, but I can't remember. As we drifted off to sleep one night he'd said that the place felt like a museum.

Joan found this observation hilarious. I told her about it over breakfast on Adele's patio after I'd left New York again, rather abruptly, Keith felt. I hadn't planned to, of course, but then again I hadn't planned to do much of anything. I'd spent a day or two doing laundry and tidying my apartment. Then I'd repainted my nails and walked to Duane Reade to buy more mascara. I'd called Alessandra numerous times, but she hadn't picked up, and because Keith was working on something, attempting to make a very important deadline, I somehow found myself back in the Corolla with Roo next to me, driving through Harlem with the windows down, heading towards the Willis Avenue Bridge, once again on my way to Adele's house.

Your mother knows I took the journals, Joan then said, apologetically or shyly, I couldn't tell. Apparently she'd told my mother about having taken them a few days after my father's funeral. She said that she'd run to the fireplace when she heard Adele reach the back hall, and using the fire poker, had pulled the stack of volumes back out. A good number of them had burned, but she'd saved quite a few. Afterwards she'd sat in the living room late into the evening reading the rest of Steven's book of essays about apartheid. Adele had come back after a while and had looked at Joan and then at the fire. It was clear, Joan said, that Adele had wanted to make sure that the journals had all burned completely but that she didn't want to give herself away by asking about it.

It was through my mother that Joan learned that Adele had died. Joan told me that she had no memory of the actual conversation, only that her first thought afterwards was to wonder how someone like her mother, who had always seemed so bold, and larger-than-life, could die in such a small and silly way, slipping on the path she'd walked a million times before, hitting her head on a rock she knew so well to step around that she could have done it in her sleep. After the conversation with my mother, Joan had sat on the sofa in her living room in Cape Town, staring out the window at the sea, thinking about the way Adele had reacted to her own mother's death. Joan remembers standing with Adele in the cemetery, both of them crying, and that Adele had held her hand, a kind of affection she rarely displayed. Through her tears Adele had told Joan that she'd only just gotten to know her mother, which Joan found puzzling as a child. Adele's mother had died at seventy-six, when Joan was nine, and she felt that she knew her grandmother well.

In fact, she was the subject of Joan's first attempt at historical research, which she worked on secretly for a year or so
after her grandmother died, when she wasn't helping Henry to organize his slides or lecture notes. She'd planned to
give her research to Adele, she told me. She'd had some idea
that if she did it well, that she'd finally win her mother's
approval, somehow redeeming herself, for what she didn't
say. Though she did describe a feeling that was omnipresent
throughout her childhood, this notion that it was expected
of her that she both fill some abstract void for her parents
and also disappear.

This perhaps explains at least part of the oddness of the
interactions I observed among the three of them throughout
my childhood, though for much of it I didn't think anything
was odd, but simply the way it was. In fact, it was hard for
me to imagine Joan not finding Adele irritating, the behaviors so normalized, the rolling eyes and caustic sentences
that Adele reacted to as if they were something else entirely, completely normal, polite even. Though I adored Joan,
I felt sorry for Adele when I observed these encounters. It
seemed that she took the brunt of Joan's anger, which was
rarely directed at Henry, though Joan did let on that she
found him rather insufferable at points, too, his exacting
manner, the way he seemed all too eager to correct people,
his obstinate refusal to participate in conversations that he
found dull, even if he'd started them.

My mother told me that what I was noticing was the result
of pain from the past. Adele and Henry were different people now, she'd said, much more loving as grandparents than
they'd been as parents. And Joan wasn't mean, my mother
maintained, even if she sometimes seemed to be. The story
my mother told to underscore this point was that Adele had
forbidden eight-year-old Joan from crying when she'd broken her arm, because Adele had told her earlier not to hang
from the rafters in one of the outbuildings. Joan had done it
anyway and then had fallen, cracking her ulna and bruising
her face, and then for the drive to the hospital had had to

sit upright and carry on a pleasant conversation because she knew full well that Adele didn't like such long drives.

Joan's grandmother, however, never forbade her from crying. Go ahead and bellow, she had apparently said, because whatever it is, it'll come out one way or another. Her grandmother had also helped Joan find places to hide from her brother when he was being particularly tyrannical, without ever demanding an explanation of their childish conflict. Before she died she gave Joan a four-leaf clover that she had encased in a tiny gold and glass locket. She told Joan that it would protect her. Joan still wears it. But besides that, my great-grandmother left behind very little, a journal, a few letters written to my great-grandfather and a few friends when she was a teenager, and three photo albums without much explanatory information, all of which Joan found in a trunk in the attic one afternoon when she was bored. Henry had offered her little help with the biography because he was busy annotating something a colleague had written about military correspondence, but he'd told her often enough that history was about detective work, and that historians had to look at the world as if it were trying to obscure the truth, so she felt at first that she could complete the project without him. But she didn't know what to make of her grandmother's teenage voice, it turned out, or the anonymous faces in her albums. So she eventually gave up on the project, though she still has the notebook where she'd made a list of everything she could remember about her grandmother a year or so after her death.

Included in this list is that her grandmother had smelled like the lavender soap that she bought in bulk on her quarterly trips to Boston, and that she used to take naps almost every day after lunch. Joan remembers lying with her in the bedroom near the stairs, where I now sleep, after they'd drawn the heavy curtains and removed their shoes. They'd then climb into the walnut four-poster bed, Joan's little feet reaching almost as far as her grandmother's did because she'd been so small, only five feet tall or so, and then Joan would ask her questions about her childhood. My great-grandmother used to laugh because Joan loved hearing about anything that was old. Old books, old furniture, old stories, outdated ideas, learning about what her grandmother used to wear, how she had coped with a sore throat as a child, or how she was treated in school, was more interesting to her than a new doll or whatever it was that children her age were involved in. But the best part of those naps, Joan said, during which neither of them slept all that much, were the stories my great-grandmother told her about Morning, a woman, by then mythic in my great-grandmother's telling, who had worked for her family when she was growing up, doing housework and taking care of her and her siblings. Every weekday, Morning had made breakfast for the family, and my great-great-grandfather would come into the kitchen and say, "Morning" to her, as in "Good morning" so my great-grandmother, who was just a child, assumed that Morning was her name.

Morning believed in ghosts. She told my great-grandmother beautiful ghost stories about women who were trapped, not in purgatory quite, nothing religious, but in states of grief or longing. They'd had full lives that no one around them understood or saw, so they lingered, long after their deaths, in the spaces they'd once occupied. In one of her grandmother's letters that Joan had found later, my great-grandmother linked this sort of thinking to what she had heard in the sermons preached at the Episcopal Church on Sundays. Breaking from the hurried reports of her social calendar and silly anecdotes about her family was a serious attempt to make sense of the world around her, what God meant, what it meant to love and fear Him. She had clearly struggled to reconcile the unyielding Protestant notions of her family and community with the authenticity of Morning's voice and deep beliefs about the afterlife. Joan remembers that though it was never explicitly discussed, it was clear that by the time that Joan was a child, that her grandmother no longer thought much of Christianity. By then my great-grandmother believed, as Morning had taught her, that God was everywhere, and serving God meant being open, and listening for the voices where He or She might be heard. Just as she'd told Adele when she was little, my great-grandmother told Joan that she was haunted, and that being haunted was a gift. She was certain of this because Morning had told her so. When Joan asked what had become of Morning, my great-grandmother's eyes had filled with tears. She'd pointed towards the water, which was partly obscured by a thin layer of fog, and said that her memories were melting, disappearing, that she could no longer even recall Morning's given name.

I don't really know how Joan thinks about Adele's ghost because, like her mother, she has been consistently inconsistent about it whenever I've asked her, sometimes dismissive like Henry, other times sounding like Adele, somber and dramatic. And other times sounding like herself, declarative and nonchalant. She told me once that she hadn't even realized that the notion was something worth noting until she had let an odd remark slip out in front of her roommate in college, something about the cemetery and the stones moving. Embarrassed, she'd tried to take back whatever it was that she'd said, suddenly aware how strange the concept was.

Joan had roomed with a girl named Cynthia, a wealthy socialite from Cincinnati, an anthropology major who drove a motorcycle as a form of rebellion against her parents. In their small, shared closet, Adele's old scarves hung in a clump next to Cynthia's designer sweaters and worn leather jackets. Though they never became close friends, the two girls bonded over clumsily rolled joints about their lack of homesickness. Both felt oppressed by their families, or oppressed in general. Escaping from the tension at home had felt invigorating, Joan told us, and the political tumult on campus had enabled her to find her footing. There were sit-ins and demonstrations, and wonderful parties thrown by the women's lib girls, a cohort Joan was acquainted with but regrets not being fully immersed in. Her brother, Joan said, had seemed somewhat oblivious to all of it, which had enraged her, partly, she admitted, because his nonchalance reminded her of Adele. My mother thought it was because he was just old enough to have come of age before the '60s were really the '60s. By the '70s he was an adult, in a way so many people her own age weren't quite.

Not coincidentally, Joan majored in history, just as Henry had. Her advisor, an emphatic socialist, was critical of the military and the government. His very existence challenged so much of what Henry had stood for, what the professor called the old guard bullshit, but there was also a lot that he pointed out to Joan, she told us, that she found real and relevant, eye-opening and radical. She told us that she had felt very at sea as her beliefs began to coincide more and more with those of her professor and less with her father's. He, too, was a World War II veteran. But unlike her father, he had grown up poor in South Boston, the eighth of twelve children. He told Joan that his father had been racist but that it wasn't until recently that people understood what that meant, let alone talked about it. He'd ended up being honorably discharged from the army, but didn't go into the particulars of his dismissal. He told her all this in his office one afternoon. He said that the way Black people were treated in the military seemed to contradict everything the United States was doing in Europe. He'd said that the scales had fallen from his eyes, an expression Joan often uses. He had his students read and discuss complicated analyses of the trials, which had enthralled Joan. But like so many men like him, his pure politics about justice and the greater good did little to prevent him from treating the women around him poorly. Joan knew of two students that he had been involved with. Both, she said, were bright and attractive, unimaginative and naïve. He'd ultimately come on to her, too, which had both thrilled and terrified her. He had asked her one afternoon to come to his office after class to talk about a proposal for a paper she'd written. She remembers wrapping one of Adele's shawls around her like armor. She'd responded to him fearfully, angrily, surprised by her own strength. She'd had no idea how she might react to something like that, she told us. She concluded that she was naïve, too, but not unimaginative.

Joan wrote her final paper on the liberation of Dachau, which at least on some level, or all levels, was about Henry, though she didn't see it that way then. It had been her attempt at individuating, though it was done without self-awareness, she told us not long after Henry died. She described the argument she conceived as an undergraduate as trite, an overly simplistic exploration of the alleged shooting of SS guards by the US Army after they'd surrendered. Her paper recounted the events leading up to the fall of the camp, the resistance movements of the imprisoned Jews, and the calculations made by the allied powers—all of which Henry had experienced firsthand. It was an academic portrayal of her father's story, the one she'd heard countless times as a child, but she had wanted to poke holes in it. She used the Nuremburg trial sources, raising inflammatory questions to gain favor with the professor, all the while tearing at Henry's myth. She'd written about an event that haunted her father and that he believed defined him, and she had done it to be provocative. But all he said in response after reading it, despite the A she'd earned for it, was that the paper sounded inauthentic and was not truly representative of the way she thought.

So she'd pushed him further, trying to argue the point she'd assumed, rather arrogantly she says now, that everyone else failed to see or was too cowardly to take on. Those SS guards were killed, she'd barked. They were murdered *after* they'd surrendered. That's part of the story too. Finally taking her bait, Henry had raised his voice. But what's the point of all this, he'd wanted to know. What's the point of going back there just to shake things up? She had no clue what she was doing. His tone had startled her, she said. She'd started to sit down in the chair where she'd worked as a child but had stopped and straightened her shoulders, preparing herself for battle, but then Henry's voice became unexpectedly monotone, low and steady. He repeated to her the story he'd told numerous times throughout her childhood, about the man at Dachau who'd smiled at him. That prisoner, gaunt, close to death, had somehow found the strength or the will to smile. Henry had assumed at the time that it was because he'd survived, which to Henry meant that all was not lost. He said that what he had seen in Germany had begun to erode his sense of hope and his belief in the ultimate good of mankind. But that man smiling that way had changed that. It shook him, and reminded him of his purpose there, and what he was fighting for. As Henry spoke tears had formed at the corners of his eyes, and Joan realized that she'd gone too far, had pushed him in ways she hadn't intended to. She began to apologize but his voice overpowered hers. How dare she question what happened that day? How dare she march into his room with such arrogance, waving some childish paper about as if she'd done some sort of service to scholarship? The nerve she had, to suggest that her radical education could trump the facts. The facts remain. Those SS guards were murderers. They didn't deserve to be treated like humans. She would be wise to leave this the hell alone.

It took Joan a long time to understand the depth of her father's reaction to her paper. It wasn't until he died, she said, that she was able to think about that afternoon without feeling defensive. There was too much confusion in the world of academia, she said, too much bullshit to try to sift through. The following summer, after spending week after week alone in the great London archives, she recalls becoming depressed. There was something demoralizing about the dauntingly enormous collections of documents that had once belonged to great men that sat before her; so much of their contents so mundane it struck her as cruel that anyone had bothered to save them at all. One afternoon, completely overwhelmed, she was reminded of the stories her grand-mother had told her about Morning, and was brought to tears thinking of this Black woman who had worked her entire life for the family, living in their house, occupying rooms alongside them. But no one could even remember her actual name. Though Joan really had tried to.

After failing to resurrect the story of her grandmother, she'd attempted to solve the mystery of Morning, but no one seemed to know anything about her, whether she'd had a family of her own, or what she'd thought about, besides the ghosts. Joan remembers being struck by the cruelty of it, an entire life erased. And too little remained of her grand-mother as well, though her grandfather's papers, because he'd been a judge, were stored in file boxes for years and then donated to the archives of some Ivy League law school. It had occurred to Joan then, that she was part of that cycle, too, a young woman, alone, working without pay, organiz-ing some vast, Byzantine trove, painstakingly turning it into something useful, that a male Oxford professor would then get credit for.

It was because she simply couldn't bear the thought of another woman's life being expunged that Joan saved Adele's journals, she said, though she made it clear, repeat-edly, that she hadn't read them, hadn't even flipped through most of them. She wasn't a monster, after all. Yes, she'd put the prettiest volumes, with the colorful spines, the ones that were the least damaged, on a shelf in her office. But she didn't touch them. She hadn't even bothered to order them chronologically as she did with most of her book collection. She'd wanted to wait, she said, until she liked her moth-er, or until she understood her. She didn't want to dissect Adele, pulling and prodding at her story, and the stories that hid her story that she'd so desperately tried to conceal.

But this is not entirely true. The truth is that Joan had been waiting for quite a while to get her hands on Adele's journals. When she was about ten she'd discovered them in a steamer trunk in the attic while looking for traces of Morning and her grandmother. So she had, she admits, read a few entries then, but this was when she was a child, she points out. Adele had written sporadically, and Joan had found her handwriting difficult to read. But she learned that Adele had been in love before she'd met Henry. Though not long after that first reading Adele had put an abrupt stop to her snooping. She never asked, but had returned to the attic one afternoon and found the steamer trunk mysteriously empty.

There were other journals, too, at least five or six volumes besides the ones that Joan had taken with her after my father died, and then carefully packed years later in Cape Town, and shipped to Rhode Island after Adele died. Joan and I found them after dinner one night when we'd wandered about the house, slightly tipsy, and ended up poking around in Adele's dressing room, which still smelled of her, light lavender mixed with musky Chanel perfume. I'd opened one drawer, then another, both filled with the practical accoutrements of privileged self care, white muslin face cloths, expensive hand cream, cuticle oil and sachets of aromatic dried flowers. And then on a shelf, next to her dresser, along with her books, the stack of journals, leather volumes embossed with her initials, the paper they held thin and glossy, lined in faint gold stripes. It appeared that Adele had begun to write regularly, though not daily, sometime after Henry died. I did my best to take Joan's lead, to glance at but not read them. I carried them loyally to Joan who was then perched on the window seat, a handful of letters that had been tied together with a saffron-colored ribbon, now spread beside her on the upholstered seat cushion. Another packet, still bundled, Joan held in her hand. She looked at me guiltily. I couldn't help it she said, biting her lip.

One packet contained letters written by Joan from London, Joan's small, square penmanship filling each page, including the margins. To her mother Joan had detailed the most mundane aspects of her life, revealing a deeply ingrained WASPism she has so aggressively attempted to shed. Her housing in London, she described at length, a rented room in a quaint stone cottage belonging to a professor who was on sabbatical, a portrayal rather unlike the cramped hovel we'd so often heard about over the years. There were other students occupying the rest of the house, she wrote, though she rarely saw them because her assistantship kept her so busy. She'd met John, an economics professor, at the bookstore she often walked past when she had time for lunch, usually eaten quickly at a bustling Indian place with a buffet that included at least six different curries. In a silly girlish tone, which I hadn't thought her capable of, even as a young woman, she wrote that John was her first and likely her strangest love. He made her tea in the afternoon and listened to American folk music while he planned his lectures. He was brilliant, but he couldn't ride a bicycle or pronounce Antietam. Joan did not include that she'd moved in with him in the middle of the summer, or that it was at his table that she'd started one of the earliest drafts of her book. Instead she described trying to replicate a green curry, which she'd failed at, miserably, despite befriending the wife of the restaurant's owner, who gave Joan naan and samosas, and a note card with remarkably detailed instructions, which Joan included with her letter.

Joan shuffled the letters in her hand, smoothing and refolding them. She then moved them to her lap and then back to the cushion, crossing and recrossing her legs. She'd kept the writing project to herself because she'd worried that she'd be unable to complete it, she told me, clarifying the sentiments in her letter as if I'd asked about them. She thought that if she announced that she planned to try to write a book and then failed to deliver on it, she'd lose any leverage, particularly with Henry, that she'd gained after graduating so impressively. Even her father's professor friends, she said, had seemed to find her more intellectually promising than her brother, though of course they included a caveat when talking about and to her. For a woman, they always said. She had such potential for a woman, and such an attractive and little one at that. But by golly, she was smart.

On one of her last nights at the cottage Joan remembers calling home. Henry was out, so she'd sat on a wooden chair in the kitchen, listening to Adele talk about Paris. She could tell that Adele was drunk, or at least tipsy, but Joan had kept her on the phone as long as she could. Adele had rattled on about her strange visions, the geometry of reflected streetlight, a woman who used to walk along the edge of the field near the cemetery, weaving in and out of the mist, disappearing completely and then emerging again. Then that night when Joan was lying in bed reading, her typewriter, which had been sitting on the desk against the wall by the window, that had put her copious notes into concise paragraphs, suddenly slid sideways off the desk and crashed to the floor. It had made a terrible sound, Joan said, but she didn't do a thing. She just lay there completely still, thinking about Morning, the crumbling wall of the cemetery, and her mother in Paris, walking in the hallway at night to keep from having nightmares. Joan did this prattling reminiscing while simultaneously continuing to leaf through the letters and journals I'd found. She distracted me with tales of her past, tales I'd heard numerous times before, while she read, a remarkable feat really, given Adele's handwriting and the age of the documents. This then led us to the boxes in Joan's bedroom.

And that's how we learned what Joan may have suspected all along, though she didn't come out and say so, that Adele had been haunted by much more than a ghost, that my father had been conceived out of wedlock, with another man, the man who she'd loved before Henry, and therefore everything Adele said, and had claimed to live by, the snobby propriety, the decorum, the self-congratulatory rigidity, all began to feel absurd, and sort of hilarious. So in my mind, kind of perfect, actually.

CHAPTER SIX

For quite a while I assumed that it had been the infamous episode at the deli, the one that had proved once and for all, to Nana at least, that Adele was an unequivocal hypocrite, that had been the beginning or at least had something to do with the rift between them that my sisters and I observed throughout our childhood. But I was incorrect. It had actually started long before that, though it wasn't until recently that I fully understood what had actually transpired, partly because for years they all refused to discuss it. Nana did concede at one point, years ago, that if I had observed what she described as a coolness, it might have something to do with the fact that during the episode at the deli, Adele had hurt Leticia's feelings. This only further confused things for me though, because Nana had also hurt Leticia's feelings, albeit only once they both said, and she hadn't done it on purpose, though it had caused their first and only fight. But this Adele thing was different, Leticia told me, after I'd badgered her about it for quite a while. Because Adele had overstepped her bounds, Adele had taken charge where she shouldn't have, which is all to say that the way Nana saw it, her beautiful, only daughter, Leah, my mother, had been manipulated, overpowered, and in some ways stolen from her when she agreed to marry my father and take on the centuries-long simmering angst of an old, too-wealthy-for-their-own-good WASP family. And that was unforgiveable.

Like my mother, Nana often made a point of differentiating herself from Adele, which I always found preposterous because it was so obvious. Nana described herself as simple, which was not at all true; and practical and straightforward and reasonable, which she was, for the most part at least. Leticia said that Nana did this because Adele made her feel insecure, though that wasn't the word she used. I can't remember how she phrased it, but Leticia described looking through the huge boxes of my mother's canvasses with Nana in the back room at the deli, that my mother had shipped from Italy years before, and that Nana couldn't help finding my mother's paintings crude, which made Nana feel stupid, unable to understand art. So Leticia had marched her to the library on Hope Street one afternoon and they'd read up on the Italian Renaissance and learned that the paintings were in fact crude because this was the point where perspective was just beginning to be understood. Nana did understand art, Leticia had reassured her, and Nana was grateful for that, though it did little to quell the uneasiness about Adele and everything she represented.

Nana recalls my mother spending a lot of time with my father when she came home from Florence, doing what she didn't know and never asked, but on most nights she still slept in her old bedroom with the crayon and acrylic paint doodles on the wall that she'd done when she was little. My father proposed right away, only weeks after my mother returned from Italy upon learning that he was sick, and that bothered Nana. Leticia remembers her saying that it wasn't fair to my mother, that it was too much pressure, that she was too young to make the kinds of decisions that had implications like that. One afternoon Nana told her that she overheard my parents arguing in her kitchen. She could hear my father's voice clearly but had to strain to hear my mother. They'd been talking about something a doctor had said, something medical, maybe a new diagnosis, but she wasn't sure. Nana had been on her way out, about to go downstairs, but had turned around and gone back upstairs to her bedroom, her purse and cardigan in her hands, and waited until she heard them leave. This is my own house, she remembers thinking. Why am I hiding from them? But she stayed where she was.

Nana worried that my mother would only understand what it meant to marry someone who wasn't Jewish when she and my father fought, because it's when people are angry that that sort of thing comes out. Do you think he'll punish her, she'd asked Poppy. Do you think he'll hold her Jewishness against her when he's angry, she'd wanted to know. When she told my mother that she worried about that sort of insidious anti-Semitism my mother said that that was archaic thinking, that her generation didn't operate that way, so fixated on who was and who wasn't Jewish. But Nana didn't really believe her, which is not to say that she thought my father didn't love my mother enough because she knew that he did. She could tell that, she always told us, by the way he looked at her, with his strange, blank, amused expression. The night before my parents' wedding Joan had described this kind of look as American maleness, which Nana said she didn't quite understand at the time, and maybe she still doesn't. Nana had mentioned to Joan that my father made such funny faces, and Joan had said sort of angrily that it didn't occur to him that he should be aware of how he's being perceived, that he might have some sort of responsibility in managing the emotional atmosphere that he took part in creating. Joan had been shaking her head while she was talking, her narrow nostrils flaring, while fishing around in her handbag. That's our job, she'd told Nana. That's women's work. We manage that stuff. Then she'd lit a cigarette. They'd been sitting in Nana and Poppy's living room and Nana remembers that she'd almost said to her, don't you dare smoke in here, young lady, but she asked her for a cigarette instead. The funny thing is, Nana now admits, that as far as she knows, my father never said anything like that to my mother; even when they were fighting, he never said anything about her being Jewish. So maybe she was wrong about that part, and that like my mother said, maybe her generation didn't care the way Nana's had about who was Jewish and who wasn't. But she wasn't wrong about the rest of it. She really wasn't.

Nana often talked about the luxuries she had been deprived of, but not in an angry way. It was more that she wanted us to know that although she'd suffered greatly, she'd still had a full and rewarding and enviable life. Of her enduring marriage her line was that she'd married the right man for the wrong reason. That reason being that she'd liked his hair, which was dark brown, almost black, slicked straight back. She simply didn't have the time to think about things differently, she told us, but thank God they liked each other. It sounds silly, she said, married people talking about liking each other, but people forget sometimes just how much that matters. She told us that she'd said the same thing to Adele once, maybe the second or third time they'd interacted. Adele and Henry had come up to Providence and Nana and Poppy had treated them all to dinner at an Italian place in Federal Hill. Adele had worn a fur coat and was testy with the young man at the coat check, Nana remembers, speaking to him harshly, nervous in a rude way that the restaurant's cheap hangers would damage her fancy mink. When Nana told her that she'd married the right man for the wrong reason, Adele had remarked that she found the idea funny, though she wasn't smiling, and that Nana had captured the notion wonderfully. And then she said that she supposed she'd married the right man for the wrong reason too.

Poppy's friends had teased him about how much time he'd spent watching Nana working at the factory as opposed to doing his own work, silly, relatively harmless banter, the way some men talk when women aren't around. To embarrass her, Poppy used to tell people that out of the blue she'd invited him to drink whiskey with her and her cousin one afternoon, which Nana says she never would have done. What she says actually happened was that Poppy had followed her home and then had stood sheepishly on the stoop of her aunt and uncle's house for a while before walking away without even knocking or anything. Months passed before they eventually spoke for the first time and it only happened because Nana asked him to light her cigarette. What was he to do, Poppy would say laughing. She was such a force, such a dynamo. What could he possibly have said to her that would be worth hearing? Not much, he'd tell you. Not much at all. But he could light her cigarette. That he could do. He'd light her cigarette any day of the week, he'd say winking.

Not long after they'd gotten married, Poppy enlisted in the army and Nana got promoted. Though she couldn't sleep at night worrying about him, she got a lot from her work life, rapidly acquiring more status and responsibility at the factory. She loved the constant whirring sounds of the machines, she'd told us often when we were little, sometimes making a little buzzing sound and smiling. She said she'd pace the first floor, smoking and calling out orders, and that the women operating the machines, whose husbands were also away, would shout back their responses. They were committed to the cause, and proud of their remarkable productivity. Before working at the factory, Nana said, a lot of them hadn't a clue how capable they were.

After Poppy came home, Nana got demoted, which she'd cried about, in secret, and then turned her focus to getting pregnant, which was a struggle. Her father told her that it was because she worked too hard or too much, and her doctor told her that she was too thin, too stressed, and that she probably didn't drink enough water. She'd replied that that was true of everyone she knew and didn't change a thing. They hadn't moved to Providence yet but they'd bought what was to become the deli on the East Side. At first they just sold fish wholesale. Nana worked right along with Poppy and the men he'd hired. He knew Lou, Leticia's husband, from Fall River because they used to box together, long before Lou got sent to prison. Nana's hands would get raw and cold from handling the crates of fish so she used to soak them in warm water with cut lemons at night, which

Leticia had taught her, because that was the only way to get the smell off.

Nana didn't get pregnant with my mother until she was thirty. She told us that she'd practically given up at that point. She had shooting pains in her legs for four days straight right before she went into labor and she delivered a few weeks early. My mother was a small baby, but she ate so much in the hospital that Nana only had to stay there until her expected delivery date. The doctor told her that he'd never seen a baby go through so much formula. Nana used to walk back and forth in front of the glass-fronted room where all the babies were lying in rows of basinets. The nurses told her that they put my mother in front because she was so beautiful. And she really was, Nana would say, as if to refute any suggestion of partiality on the subject. She told us that that was the first time in her life that it had occurred to her that something could be perfect. She kept telling Poppy that she just couldn't get over the idea that they'd made her, and he thought it was funny that she thought about it that way. Because my mother looked just like them, especially as she got older. All of their features were there, but for some reason they looked different because of the way they were arranged on her face. She had a good Jewish nose though, Nana's father told her, thank God.

Nana and Poppy didn't go to temple much when my mother was young but when they did, for the entire service my mother would sketch in a little notebook. Poppy usually fell asleep. Sometimes the Rabbi would make eye contact with Nana as if to say, can you do something about that snoring, please? So she'd wake him and he'd stop for a minute, but it would start right back up again. It drove Nana crazy. But it never bothered my mother because she wasn't paying attention. She spent the whole service drawing, covering every square inch of her notebook with little rows of intertwining flowers or leaves.

My mother's first real job was to make the labels for the fish and egg salad and bagels that were sold at the deli. She also wrote out the names of all the items and their prices on a large board that hung on the wall above the refrigerator cases using cheap paint and stencils she'd cut from pieces of cardboard, earning a nickel for each iteration of labels. Nana and Poppy had hoped that the work would help to mitigate her sadness about not being able to play on the baseball team, which was only for the boys back then. She'd cried harder about it than Nana had seen her cry since she was a toddler, tearfully asking why Nana and Poppy hadn't warned her that the world was that way, why they hadn't prepared her for the blunt reality of suddenly being relegated to the sidelines. All along they'd encouraged her love of baseball, so it had never occurred to her that one day she'd have to think about it differently. Nana and Poppy had no idea how to respond to her. They had no way to explain it, really.

Eventually my mother learned to appreciate baseball differently. When she was in high school she'd do her homework in the back room at the deli and when she was finished she'd sit behind the counter painting rows of deli meat while listening to the ball game on the radio, memorizing names and statistics. Because she was so beautiful, Nana said, boys would line up in front of the display case, pretending they were there for a sandwich or a pickle, but they were really there to see her. Sometimes she tried to engage one of them in a conversation about the game, but mostly she talked about other things, the weather, business. By then she'd been making the labels at the deli for years, and still earning nickels, which she did until Nana sold the business after Poppy died, rewriting new prices or items, each label more sophisticated than the last. If Nana and Poppy needed a new one or if they had to make a change to one of them while she was gone, like when she was in college or in Italy, they would cover the old label with a Post-it note to remind her to do it when she got back. Nana has saved all of them. Every single little label my mother ever made Nana keeps in an envelope in her jewelry box with her engagement rings and a ruby brooch that belonged to her mother. It doesn't make her sad to look at them, she tells us. Maybe because doing so recalls what it felt like back then, with Poppy still alive and my mother still young and unburdened. Her favorites, she told me, are the ones from the '70s, with their puffy, hippie fonts and psychedelic colors.

So what Adele did during that infamous episode, was not just an affront to Nana's best friend. It was a mean-spirited invasion of a place that was safe and happy, a rare and unique refuge that had taken years to cultivate. Adele had barged in, her eyes blazing, furious that my sisters and I had been put in danger, in the proximity of a criminal, meaning Leticia's husband, Lou. The door with the little bells that Nana had attached to it years before clanged open, slamming against a small red metal gumball stand that stood next to the bin with the free papers. Adele wore sunglasses, like someone in a mob movie, and her arm was outstretched, with a long, perfectly manicured finger pointing directly at Nana, who was hunched over, refilling a vat of egg salad behind the glass display case. Adele was terrified that we were in danger. Criminals were horrible, unrepentant people, she apparently said, contradicting the nonchalantly espoused liberal values that were so abundant and unchallenged in her own home.

Leticia had been unloading a tray of bagels and Alessandra was doing chores in the front room, refilling napkins and straws, making sure there was enough salt and pepper in the plastic shakers that were kept on the metal tables by the windows. Both of them turned to Nana, who explained to Adele that Lou was a good man, that he had repaid his debt to society, if he'd ever really owed one, but Adele ignored her. Nana then came around the counter and tried to touch Adele's forearm, but Adele had batted her away, frantically, aggressively. At some point Poppy had come in from the back room. Adele had then pointed her finger at Poppy, which Alessandra recalled as looking like a prehistoric weapon, long, bony, and sharp. You let this maniac around the girls, Adele had shrieked. What is it with you people. This *you people* Nana took to mean Jews, though my mother thinks she was referring to her parents specifically, or maybe liberals or radicals, and Poppy didn't care what she meant, he said later. All he cared about was standing up for his friend. So he said very calmly to Adele that Lou had done his time, and that whatever happened was in the past. Adele had tried to say something else but she did it halfheartedly and Poppy cut her off, this time slightly less calmly, saying again that Lou had done his time.

And then that was it. Or that's how the story ended when it was told to me. I unfortunately missed the theatrics because I was busy ogling Leticia and Lou's son Darren, a handsome young teenager who was eight or nine years my senior, but Alessandra relayed the whole scene for us later. She may have seen the entire argument or only snippets of it. The reports that came throughout the following week were almost always different, as was her role in them. But whatever madness occurred, that had temporarily enthralled all of us, eventually subsided, and the matter was only rarely brought up after that, which was odd in some ways, though at the time I didn't think so.

I hadn't even known that Leticia was married until Lou came home, not long after I turned six, though I had certainly heard of Lou. It had just never occurred to me to make that connection as a child. In fact, I don't know how I classified Leticia in my life before then, or whether I'd truly considered what she was to all of us besides a beloved fixture, someone who was sarcastic and hilarious and sweet, who gave all of us nicknames, who had fingernails that looked like blanched almonds, and who, when we were sad, made a thick concoction of warm milk and honey and let us sit on her lap while we drank it. For all of the adults, Nana, Poppy, Leticia, and my mother, Lou coming home was a very happy thing, but they talked about it like it was fragile, as if their carefully constructed sentences might at any moment topple to the ground and crumble into pieces. I found this perplexing. Nobody's perfect, was Poppy's motto, so it was our motto, too, and it enabled us to laugh off almost everything, slaps and insults, shitty grades, petty theft, moments of meanness, trampling the neighbors' peonies on purpose. I asked my mother about it but she couldn't really explain it, and Nana couldn't either. I was also painfully curious about what he'd done, but Nana said that it didn't matter anymore and that it wasn't his fault and that I wasn't to ask Leticia or Lou anything about it, which I did anyway a number of times, despite the explicit instruction not to.

I saw Lou for the first time in the back room of the deli, a hodgepodge of a space that housed the table where Nana "kept the books," as she called it, and the large metal shelves filled with batches of dough in various states of inflation. He was standing next to Poppy, leaning very gently on a wooden shelf filled with jars of mayonnaise, pickling brine, ketchup, and mustard. He was built like Poppy was, with straight shoulders and very skinny legs. Not all people who box look that way but because Poppy and Lou are the only two people I knew who really boxed, I assumed for a while that that was the case. Lou had large, funny-looking, crooked teeth, and I couldn't help but laugh when Poppy introduced us. He had reached out to shake my hand and I'd put my hand in his but I didn't make eye contact with him. I think I looked at the floor. Now when I think about his face I would describe it as handsome, because he really was a handsome man. It might have been that he learned to make other expressions that hid his teeth or that I came to think of them differently. I don't know exactly. But when I saw them for the first time I was startled. I didn't know any other adults with teeth like that.

When Lou left the room Poppy asked me what my problem was and I shrugged at him, also without making eye contact. You don't laugh at people for no reason, he told me. You know that. I think I then explained that I hadn't been laughing for no reason, that, rude as it was, I had been laughing at Lou's teeth. Then Poppy told me that I was being an asshole, and that my reaction had to do with resources. And did I understand what he meant when he said that? I don't remember how I responded to him but I didn't know what he meant. I had to ask my mother about it later and she explained to me that dental work is expensive and that laughing at someone the way I had was hurtful and arrogant and not at all in line with the values with which she'd raised me. I was made to apologize, which I did diligently, and Lou responded to me the way he would for the rest of his life, sort of like Poppy but with a blend of his own mischief, intensity, and evenness. I explained to him that things were pretty bad, that I was an asshole, whether we liked it or not. I wasn't quite sure what to do about it but apologize and try to be less of an asshole in the future. I put my hand on his forearm, something Poppy did when he wanted me to listen and Lou put his hand on mine and nodded at me while I talked. And then he told me that it was okay, kiddo. Nobody's perfect.

Adele's intrusion, and criticism of Lou, may have been behind Nana's rolled eyes, her grimaces, her reflexive belittling remarks about Adele, she told me, behavior she isn't proud of, but at least she'll admit to it. Some people, Nana says, won't even do that. She also points out that her feelings changed about Adele, that she didn't stay angry, though she might have if she were less open-minded. But it took her a while, far longer than it should have, and she isn't proud of that either. Even after my father died and Adele had stood at his funeral looking pitiful to Nana, bent over and misshapen, Nana still didn't do more than hug her. It wasn't until Poppy died that Nana began to see things differently, but by then it didn't matter, because it felt in some ways, as if nothing did. Nana told us that she remembers feeling grateful that she'd never had the time or the inclination to try to picture what life might be like without Poppy, because the truth was that not even in her wildest imagination could she ever have conceived of something as awful as the void he left behind. She'd wanted to die, then, too, she said. She wanted it all to be over, for it all to be nothing. But she still had to function. She had to make decisions. She had to slowly dismantle the life they'd built together piece by piece.

So she sold the deli to the son of someone who knew someone from temple. They tried to run it under new management for a while but the business failed so they sold it to a restaurant developer. It's been a few things since then, a salon, a bakery. Now it's a coffee shop. Then she put their apartment, which was the second and third floors of a two-family house, on the market. Her realtor, who was a neighbor, told her that she needed to paint over the crayon and paint in my mother's old bedroom, which was barely visible by then. The realtor told her that she could pay someone to do it but when he told her the price Nana told him she would do it herself, but she couldn't. She bought white paint and a paintbrush and she laid down a little drop cloth and she opened the paint and stirred it and dipped the brush in it, but she couldn't make herself do anything else. She couldn't bear the thought of destroying one more part of her life with Poppy, of letting go of one more irreplaceable reminder of what had been. So she stood there for a while looking at the wall and then she heard someone coming in. She remembers shaking her head because she always forgot to lock the door behind her. Poppy used to scold her about it. He'd say, Anya, are you crazy, and she'd laugh at him and he'd laugh, too, because she could remember everything, except that she needed to lock the damn door. She may have called out, who's there, but she can't remember. She could hear someone coming up the stairs, and she remembers noting that the movements sounded unfamiliar, not soft like our mother or jumpy like me and my sisters, or sturdy but slowing the way Poppy had sounded. These sounds were plodding, intentional, but also cautious.

The noise stopped at the landing and then ascended the second flight of stairs and then suddenly there was Adele.

She was wearing a shawl or a cloak or something with wide sleeves and Nana could smell her perfume from where she stood in the doorway. Adele had looked at her and then looked at the wall and Nana didn't say anything because she couldn't. She just looked at Adele's face. Then Adele started walking towards her and Nana remembers thinking that Adele looked softer than she used to look. She thinks for a second that she may have tried to figure out why Adele was there, but she was too tired to say anything so the thought disappeared. Adele didn't say anything to her either. She just walked up to Nana and took the paintbrush from her. Adele's hands were thin and cold and her nails were polished, Nana remembers thinking. Then they stood there next to each other for who knows how long, Nana told us, Adele still holding her with one hand and methodically covering my mother's childish doodles with the other.

Nana can't remember what happened next. She recalls waking up in bed sometime later in the evening, her apartment smelling of paint. Adele was gone and the sun had set. She went to the kitchen and drank half a glass of water, wondering if it had been a dream. She called Leticia who seemed to see in the experience something religious, a sort of profound absolution, which Nana didn't quite buy. After she hung up she walked to my mother's old room. The floor was clean, the drop cloth gone. The window was propped open slightly with a tattered hardbound Nancy Drew novel and the wall was spotless, bright white.

Nana went back to her bedroom and put on a nightgown. It was too early to go to sleep, but she didn't know what else to do. She put cold cream on her face and wiped it off, and brushed her teeth, staring at her reflection, seeing for the first time, or maybe just in a different way, the woman she'd become. There were lines in places that had once been smooth, wisps of gray that had once been thick, and a deep red chestnut brown. Lying in bed she concluded that whatever had happened had to do with the world having humbled Adele. Adele's perfect son had died and he had died unsettled, which is the worst way anyone could die. Her daughter had fled the country, had gotten married in Africa without even telling her, and Henry had disappeared into his books. By then Adele roamed about her house by herself, like a ghost, my mother had said, looking for things to remind her of what it had been like when people who still wanted to live lived there. But then Nana began to feel the coarseness of thinking that way. Her chest tightened and her eyes welled with tears. And she realized that she was humbled by then too. Because that's just what happens when you get older.

And that's also why it all changed. Very suddenly, the anger dissipated. Nana's taunting remarks were noticeably absent, and miraculously, a genuine friendship developed, which would have been hard for all of us to grasp if it hadn't appeared so natural, and in some ways, simply right. In fact, it happened so seamlessly I might have missed it had I not asked Leticia, a few weeks later, what she'd been up to lately. Twice a week I'd walk to Leticia's apartment to help water her plants, which were abundant, hanging from the ceiling of her porch, framing the stairs of the front stoop, and lining the edges of her living and dining rooms, so that the feel of the place was that of a warm tropical paradise, regardless of the season. I'd accidentally killed every plant I'd tried to raise in my own bedroom, and Leticia had offered to teach me how to nurture indoor greenery. She also always had a snack waiting, and would let me eat it while I followed her around, because she trusted me to handle my crumbs like a grown woman. As she gently pulled a dead leaf from a potted geranium, she explained to me that it had begun with just a dinner. A few months after Poppy died, which was not long after Lou died, Adele had called Nana and told her that everything would be all right. She didn't mention the painting of the wall. In fact, they never discussed that day again. She simply said that Nana and Leticia should come down for dinner. Adele was very sensitive to Nana and Leticia's feelings about the unspeakable horrors of traffic so she'd arranged a driver. Lauran, "the one with Sapphic desires " Adele made a point of saying, a landscaper, a woman who could haul boulders with the ease of a man, who transformed the grounds surrounding the house each spring into patches of English country perfection, would come collect them in her pickup truck. Lauran arrived in Providence bearing a picnic basket loaded with cucumber sandwiches, candied nuts, small pouches of potato crisps, and little thermoses filled with iced tea and seltzer water infused with blackberries and lime. Nana accepted the first invitation to be polite. Leticia accepted out of curiosity. For so long she'd heard about the house with the three different living rooms, the sound of the waves crashing against the shore, the small pathways, lined with lilac bushes, along the edge of the gardens near the family cemetery, where we played elaborate games of tag and spy and Madame Warlord Super Tyrant that we'd explained in detail to anyone who'd listen when we got home. Because Adele didn't cook or serve, besides her two signature French dishes, the meals were prepared by Lauran's girlfriend, Charlotte, who went by the name Charlie, which Adele thought was very strange indeed, but she was a classically trained chef, a real artist, so some sort of quirk was to be expected.

Lauran and Charlie were exceptional hostesses, nearly charming the pants off of Nana and Leticia, who'd spent their entire lives caring for everyone else. They were absolutely tickled to be swooped up in the arms of a robust, kindly woman and carefully deposited in a large, sturdy-seeming vehicle loaded with delicate snacks, only to be carefully removed an hour or so later and placed on a cushioned surface and fed Cornish game hen and cold radish salad, after a course of fine cheese. After that first dinner, Leticia told me, laughing, that she wanted to take those ladies home with her. She really did.

CHAPTER SEVEN

eticia, I was shocked to learn, is not Jewish, although she is a masterful baker of Jewish things and was responsible for making challah and rye bread and rugelach at the deli for almost the entire time that my grandparents owned it. Starting in the late 1950s she had taken a bus from her neighborhood, a bustling collection of tree-lined blocks that was eventually split in half by a highway, to the cluttered Jewish part of Pawtucket where my grandparents lived. Then she and Nana would walk to the deli together, plotting and planning, because even though it was Poppy who owned the place and Poppy who signed the checks, it was Nana and Leticia who managed and organized every operation, from the delivery of fish, to the placement of straws and napkins, to the proportion of chopped carrot to noodle in every single serving of matzo ball soup.

When the highway split Leticia's neighborhood in half, she had to walk twice as far to get to the bus stop for a ride that took almost twice as long, and she could no longer walk to her sister's house because it's physically impossible and unsafe to cross a highway. Both Leticia's and her sister's buildings were torn down, as were many others, to be replaced by government housing, structures that were box-like, unimaginative, stripped of the meaning and charm of the original buildings. Leticia's new apartment, erected not far from her old building, was drafty and beige, and had low stucco ceilings that were impossible to keep clean. Her small living room window faced the new highway and she told me she got so angry that she shook every time she passed it. Eventually she moved, which she hadn't wanted to do because it took her too far from her friends and family to maintain old routines and customs and relationships, but she minded the Portuguese neighborhood less than what had become of her old one. It was the intrusion of the highway into Leticia's life and the way she was able to talk about it with my grandmother that truly cemented their friendship, Leticia told me. Nana grasped the significance of what she was telling her, without ever prying, because it was something Jewish people had experienced too.

Leticia was not pleased when Poppy had suggested that I might be an asshole. Asshole was too strong a word, she said, shaking her head and mouthing the word asshole so as not to really say it. I relayed the whole saga to Henry and Adele the following weekend on the patio before dinner—Lou's teeth, my rudeness, the notion that I might be an asshole, my apology. Adele was wrapped in a stole, to ward off the ocean breeze, and she had her sunglasses on, large tortoiseshell ovals that covered her eyebrows unless she raised them. Henry was dressed like a deckhand even though he hadn't been on the boat in months. Like Leticia, Henry was not the kind of person who would outright call me an asshole, not because he wasn't concerned about that being a possibility, but because that was the sort of thing one just didn't say. Though brilliant, and full of exactingly cultivated opinions, as I said before, he wasn't much of a talker, unless he was pressed or it was a topic of his choosing. He often told us that he left the talking to Adele, and then he'd imitate her, complaining about the weather or something in a sing-songy way, while keeping his chin stiff and slightly protruded.

In a moment of gregariousness though, Henry had once described his and Adele's marriage to me as an uneasy peace, though I can't recall if I'd asked him about it first. Sometimes they laughingly compared themselves, after a round or nine of predinner gin and tonics, to Hitler and Stalin, describing the truce that they'd been living with as being comparable to Hitler promising Stalin that he'd leave Russia alone. They never said who was Hitler or who was Stalin but the more I learned about Hitler and Stalin the more perplexed I was by such a characterization of their marriage, especially because the thing that all of us, Nana and Poppy and Leticia and Lou, too, revered so much about Henry, and the reason he was the way he was, had to do with Hitler, the liberation of Dachau, the experiences he'd never recovered from.

Adele and Henry had conflicting stories about where and when they first met, but they do agree that they met through Henry's younger sister Joan, a lively young woman who died in a car accident when she was twenty-two, and who my aunt Joan is named after. Joan the elder, who Adele called Pea or Sweet Pea because she was quite small, was Adele's best friend. The two knew each other socially, through school and dance lessons, and debutante events. Henry told us that he first saw Adele at a party, that she was seated with her legs crossed, on a wrought iron chair on the veranda, smoking a cigarette and half-smiling. He said that she was the most beautiful woman he'd ever seen, but when she stood up and he realized that she was a few inches taller than he was, she suddenly seemed to him a little less attractive. Adele resented this telling of their story both because she insists that it's factually incorrect and because it focuses on her height, which she was self-conscious about and is also the reason she walked in a slouched slant for her entire life and was never a terrific dancer. Pea, who was built like a hummingbird, was a lovely dancer, but she also had the added bonus of being able to practice with her older brother, whereas Adele, an only child, had no one to practice with at home. But because Pea was such a good friend, she demanded that Henry also practice with Adele, and it was on one of those dance-practicing afternoons that Adele claims she and Henry met for the first time.

There have been suggestions that Pea suffered from some sort of mental illness, but Joan says it is much more likely that it was depression, or repressed rage, or alcoholism. Pea was alone when she took the car out, having ducked out of a social gathering after arguing with a man she may have been involved with, and no one can agree whether she'd been drinking or not. Her body wasn't found until the following morning, a few yards from her wrecked car, at a sharp bend in the coastline road. Adele remembers that Pea had had night terrors and bouts of awful melancholy but she bristled at the thought that Pea dying the way she did was anything but an accident or that anyone could possibly misconstrue it as something she brought onto herself. Henry was away in Germany when it happened and didn't receive the news for weeks. An informal memorial was held when he came home after the war ended, and it was the following night that he had his first flashback, a seemingly unprompted episode, precipitating a pattern that plagued him for the rest of his life. Once when I asked him about the flashbacks he responded by telling me that he was the one who was supposed to have died if it had been either of them, and I realized that even forty years later, he still associated the death of his sister with the trauma of his experience in Germany.

Adele cried so hard at Pea's funeral that she fainted, and someone carried her to a spare room and laid her on a sofa. She woke up to see Henry staring at her. She said she barely recognized him because the war had changed his face so much. She said that he was always serious, and he'd always looked serious. But when he came home, he looked as if he'd been destroyed, even though he hadn't been. She told me that she wanted to save him and that he wanted to save her so they got married only a month or so later in the small chapel of the Episcopalian church with only their parents as guests. When I asked Adele what Henry was saving her from she said that they were young, and that they wanted to save each other from the world, that everything had felt so fraught back then. But the truth, Joan and I learned, so many years later, is that she had wanted to save him from what he'd experienced in Germany, which she never did, and he had wanted to save her because she was three months pregnant and unmarried and they both knew that if he didn't, according to the rules of their very small, very elite world, she would be ruined.

But Henry didn't save Adele, because he wouldn't or couldn't, and I now believe that she suffered, in her own way, for a long time because of it. Yet, for years, this had been invisible to all of us, but particularly to Nana and Leticia. Long before they were wooed to the dark side with breakfast trays of soft boiled eggs and freshly made jam, they'd adamantly maintained that someone like Adele had not suffered at all. Not really. Or at least not in the way that they had. Her entire history, they'd said, existed in an alternate reality. She had been cocooned by vast wealth and absurd privilege. She had never worked, not the way they had, and she never had to answer to anyone. Nana, on the other hand, grew up on the lower east side, before it was the Lower East Side, in a yellow brick tenement building filled with some Russian but mostly German Jewish immigrants. Her mother died when she was little so as a young girl she took on the responsibilities of the household, which meant managing her father and brother, who she adored, but who were also in many ways quite helpless. She got her first job when she was just nine years old, doing basic stitching in the shop of a Russian seamstress. Every member of her family who stayed behind in Germany died, some at Dachau and some at Bergen-Belsen, which effectively extinguished her mother's line.

And Leticia suffered because she grew up poor even though, just like Nana, she, too, worked for her entire life. And because she is Black, she had to understand and attempt to temper potent hatred that was flung at her from all directions long before she was old enough to understand what racism was. By the time I knew her, she'd been doing it for so long that it was second nature to her and I didn't pick up on it, even though it felt to her, she told me, like something that was slowly, inevitably, eating her alive. Then she lost her

family history when the highway cut across her neighborhood because to her, family history is inextricably connected to place. And she felt further disconnected when Lou was
sent to prison, an anguish that manifested as physical pain,
making her joints ache and her temples throb and her chest
feel compressed when she took deep breaths at night when
she tried to keep from crying herself to sleep. So she got sick
and lost weight, but she still saved money to take long bus
trips to see Lou, which she did when she wasn't working,
which was rare. And when Lou finally came home Leticia
continued to suffer because in many ways he was a different person and he knew he was a different person and he
struggled to connect with who he'd been before. At night he
put his clothes under their mattress instead of in his closet,
because that was how he'd kept his clothes from wrinkling
while he was away. And at first if Leticia moved furniture
around, which she'd always done periodically, the unfamil-
iarity of the arrangement startled him, and so did certain
noises and people walking behind him and sometimes open
spaces. And then Darren was sent to prison, too, because he
did something awful, which Leticia blamed herself for even
though it wasn't her fault and in many ways it wasn't his
fault either, but that sort of thing spreads like cancer. That's
what Poppy was talking about when he told me not to laugh
about resources.

What was interesting though, was that Nana and Leticia
seemed to feel differently about my father, another tall privileged WASP. As happens too often, Joan has frequently
pointed out, even some of the best, most just and fair-minded
of the female sex, are harder on women than they are on men.
So my father's snobbery, his highbrow education and taste,
were often overlooked or explained away. For example, his
expensive leather luggage, monogrammed, of course, was
actually not really so ostentatious. His habit of correcting
the mispronunciation of French words, no longer a biggie.
He was a doctor, after all, and quite busy. And he was a

provider, which is quite admirable, and though neither Nana nor Leticia would ever acknowledge the double standard, in their minds a man who provides is more valuable than a woman who provides, which is remarkable given all the providing they've done. So when my father died, the depths of the tragedy for them registered on levels other than emotional and psychological. This was also a financial assault on a family, a violent blow to the very core of a basic, necessary ancestral structure.

My mother hated their pity, because though they denied it, Nana and Leticia were certain that without a husband, her life would be very hard, very troublesome, full of suffering. Just think of the poor girls, they often said, which my mother resented because she felt that such sentiments, though true and understandable to a certain extent, also invalidated both her role in our lives and her strength and good sense as a mother. And, it felt to her as if she thought only of her poor girls, but somehow that wasn't enough. Leticia often sent her son Darren to our house to help us, with what I wasn't always sure. Often he'd simply show up and stand shyly at the front door, moving from one foot to another while he explained to my mother that Leticia was worried and wondered if we needed help with anything. In all fairness to Leticia, there usually was something, some silly task that was easier to accomplish with a tall teenager than one-to-three distractible children, replacing a difficult-to-reach light bulb, moving a piece of furniture, checking one of the various contraptions in the basement, the water heater, the furnace, the fuse box.

I was profoundly grateful for these visits because Darren was the first person to awaken in me the urge to know a man biblically and for that, though our love was never consummated, I'm forever grateful. He was quiet, like his father, and he had a beautiful face. At around age sixteen, he had a faint dusting of dark hair above his upper lip, and the irresistible gait of an overconfident and underweight baby giraffe. My sexual awakening was consumed almost entirely by devising ways to extend his visits to my house, so I often regaled Nana and Leticia with tales of my feeble mother, characterizing her daily efforts the same way one might describe the travails of a tiny baby bird. We are starving, I would wail. Or, mom might truly be losing her mind, I'd say solemnly. We lived only two blocks from the deli and one block from Nana and Poppy's apartment, as Jews tend to shtetl when they can, but because Jews also interrupt each other, finding a way to articulate my mother's pitiable predicaments in a way that was heard and that made clear that the only real solution was Darren's presence, was a profound challenge. In fact, almost all my attempts failed to come to fruition, which is why when I finally had an opportunity to pounce, I did, pinning him against the radiator in the hall next to the den where my mother did most of her painting, and hugging him with my eyes closed while he attempted to untangle my tiny clenched limbs from his so that he could escape. Lesson learned. Some men need to be approached with kid gloves.

This attempt at coupling occurred on the afternoon my mother had asked Darren to help load her canvasses into a rented truck because she had been invited to exhibit them at a local feminist art collective. My mother had pried me off of Darren, who displayed no detectable sexual excitement at all, and then she scolded me for my aggression and made me sit on the stairs, where I watched and cooed at Darren while he skillfully hoisted up each piece without looking at it, and carried it deftly from the room. My mother then became distracted by our neighbor, Monica I think her name was, who was hysterical; I could see her from the window, gesticulating wildly at Darren. Fearing competition from a woman with actual breasts, I pounced again when he returned for another load, but tripped, entangling myself in a sheet of bubble wrap, and had to abandon the assault to tend to my wounds.

The paintings had initially been used for a textbook on the history of venereal disease and for the months my moth-

er was working on it, huge stretched canvasses depicting vaginas and penises in various states of disrepair and health
stood leaning against almost all the walls in our house. My
sisters and I were fascinated by them, and were heartbroken at the thought of them going. They'd inspired numerous
games, art installations, conversations about the existence
of God, and for me, reflective, character-building moments
alone, where I'd perched on the edge of the bathroom sink
with one leg braced against the medicine cabinet and examined my own, very teeny vagina. All the paintings were sold
at the gallery and the house felt cold without them, and even
though my mother admitted that in some ways she missed
them, too, she much preferred the money, which just goes
to show that for the Jewish people, everything goes back to
resources.

Resources were important to Leticia as well, though not
because she wanted them to be. Unlike Adele, she'd previously pointed out, she didn't have a choice. And she didn't
have a choice about too many things, which is why she and
Nana fought so bitterly that time years later, sometime
during my high school years, which resulted in our first so-
journ to the dank miserable prison outside of Providence
where Darren was locked up. It was an experience that I had
no context for, no way to truly understand, at least not deeply, so it never properly settled, but has remained hanging in
my mind as a crystallized, anomalous incident, an ominous
blip in the sequence of moments that made up the narrative of my life as I saw it. What I remember is the strain in
Nana and Leticia's faces on the long bus ride there, a kind
of hardness that comes from sadness or desperation that
most times, on them at least, was obscured by laughter or
sarcasm or practicality. And I remember realizing that despite having forcefully attempted to make him my husband
a few times, and having shared summertime lunches with
him in the back room of the deli, and in some ways, having
moved in the same rhythms throughout parts of my child-

hood, I didn't really know Darren at all. If it hadn't been for the flash of rage or recognition that flickered quickly behind Leticia's eyes, he would have been indistinguishable to me from all the other Black and brown men in that room who walked dejectedly but with intention, playing a role, along with the visiting women, that had not been picked, but had been given to them. But even if I had recognized him, that wouldn't have changed the oddness of the moments that followed, when Nana, Leticia, and I were shuttled from checkpoint to checkpoint, met with suspecting stares as if we were guilty of unspeakable crimes, and then seated at a table in a large but eerily cramped room, overpowered by fluorescent light and the smell of damp, contaminated air, only to talk about the Celtics as if everything was the way it should be.

The fight between Nana and Leticia began with a joke. A silly one, a few throwaway lines, repeated so many times over the years that they'd lost their meaning. They weren't best friends, they'd always said. Even though they were practically inseparable. Even though they finished each other's sentences and used the same expressions while making the same face. Even though they are a tiny but mighty army, a fiercely united front of two very small, very direct, very capable women, bound together inextricably by the fact that they both suffer, and have suffered, and will continue to suffer, and will do everything they Goddamn can so that the rest of us don't have to suffer the way they have. But they were not best friends, they said. I always found this line preposterous as a child. Because it was quite clear, from where I stood, that they absolutely were best friends.

They eat a late lunch together almost every day, which they've been doing now for over fifty years, first at the deli, then at one of their apartments after the deli closed. They also eat dinner together once a week at a small Portuguese restaurant a few blocks from Leticia's apartment that has a weekly cod special that tastes fine. Years ago, when a different family owned the restaurant, the cod special was delicious, but times have changed. Yet because Nana and Leticia feel both a sense of neighborly loyalty to the former owners and a responsibility to guide the new ones to prosperity, they still eat there every Thursday evening and they never complain about it. Until quite recently, they walked there, each armed with a small square pocketbook filled with mints, a little cash, tissues, and ancient cell phones that they frequently turn off when ending calls, on purpose, because doing so preserves batteries. Credit cards, forms of identification, and health insurance information are left at home, hidden. Despite their deeply guarded independence, my mother has begun to drive them to the restaurant for their weekly dinner out because she worries that the amount of time allotted by the stoplight at the corner makes it impossible for them to walk at a comfortable pace and she can't bear the thought of them feeling rushed. Not after all they've been through.

When they have lunch at Nana's apartment they sit in the kitchen at the small table by the window and nibble on whitefish salad on crackers that Nana makes using the same recipe that she used at the deli. They drink coffee without any cream or sugar and they never run out of things to talk about. Favorite topics include traffic, the internet, the Edelmans next door who can't seem to get a break, the rapid changes occurring on Hope and Wickenden Streets, and sometimes Adele.

Nana and Leticia are not particularly fond of discussing their fight. They claim to have forgotten the particulars of it, though they agree that it occurred around Thanksgiving. Leticia had been on her way to Fall River, to see her family, her sister-in-law, and some distant cousins. She'd been baking for two full days. My mother had dropped Nana off at her house and Nana remembers that the counters of Leticia's kitchen were covered with pies and tarts and iced cookies shaped like pumpkins and cornucopias. They had plans to have lunch and Leticia noted that Nana was late, which she was, but only by five minutes. So Nana apologized but

Leticia didn't respond. So Nana asked her if she was tired and Leticia snapped at Nana. Of course she was tired. She was always tired. When had Nana ever known her to have not been tired?

The truth was that Leticia was sad about Darren, sad about Lou, sad that her family got ripped apart and taken away from her, sad because sometimes the accumulation of deep injustices, piled on century after century after century, becomes too much. But Nana didn't know that then. Or she didn't know it in the way that Leticia needed her to know it. So she didn't think about what she was saying. It didn't occur to her that when she began talking about my mother and me and my sisters, saying that she was sad, because she missed Poppy and worried about my mother and wondered how everything would turn out, as she put it, seemed profoundly, and cruelly, unfair to Leticia. Leticia told her later that sometimes, even within the safe and loving boundaries of their unique and solid friendship, she felt alone and unseen.

Nana remembers that Leticia's face had started to change while she was talking, but Nana misread her expression. She hadn't realized that Leticia was angry. And when she finally did, she stopped talking, and watched as Leticia's eyes narrowed into slits though she still said nothing. So Nana had asked her if something was wrong and when Leticia responded her tone was abnormally steady. She said that she was angry that Nana joked that they weren't best friends, though this was something she'd joked about too, often. Just like they'd joked about Nana being ten years older. Leticia used to tease her about it, that Nana nagged Leticia like her mother had. They used to say that there were so many reasons that their friendship didn't make sense. Leticia had been raised by women, and Nana by men. Leticia wasn't Jewish. Leticia rarely swore, and Nana did, frequently, even though because of Leticia she tried not to. They told each other everything. They relied on each other. Nana never doubted that she could count on Leticia, so she assumed that Leticia never doubted that she could count on her. So Nana said something like, why are you so angry? What have I done? I've never done anything to hurt you. And then Leticia told her that that was the problem, that Nana had never done anything. She said that Nana hadn't been there for her. She asked if Nana had kept track of how long Darren had been away. It had been years at that point. And Nana hadn't gone with Leticia to visit him. Not one single time. Nana needed Leticia in her world, but Nana wouldn't come to Leticia's.

Nana told me that she left the room after that; that she stood in the living room for a few minutes, but Leticia says she stayed rooted where she was. No, no, Nana insisted to me, her face stark and sad, like a coward, ashamed and embarrassed, she'd absolutely walked out of the room. Because Leticia was right, she said. Nana had recognized then that she'd let Leticia down, and she couldn't bear it. When Nana apologized Leticia had at first told her that she was just like Adele, that deep down, she, too, thought she was better than Leticia was. But then she took that part back, saying she hadn't meant it. She'd just lost her temper.

My mother was away the weekend after the fight so Nana was watching us. Alessandra and Isabella had plans or were off doing something else, so Nana took me along on their visit to Darren. My mother was enraged when she got back, accusing Nana of using me to prove that she was a good friend. Now I had nightmares and couldn't sleep. Nana tried to explain to her that it had nothing to do with me, and that she wasn't trying to prove anything. But she also admits now that maybe she was.

Neither Nana nor Leticia drove at that point so we took the bus. I was fidgety for the whole trip, Leticia remembers, picking at the leather seats and drawing on the window with my finger. Leticia was fidgety, too, biting her nails and chewing at her cuticles. She said she'd been trying to contact the prison's medical services because Darren's asthma was getting worse. Darren hadn't been given an adequate inhaler, she told us while looking out the window. It was because of the highway. That awful highway. That's how he got his asthma in the first place.

The fight didn't last long. Leticia apologized as if it had been her fault the day after Thanksgiving. She held Nana's hand like she'd done at Adele's house, when she'd gotten frightened because she thought she saw a ghost. Nana told her that she had nothing to apologize for, that Nana was the sorry one. Then they didn't talk about it again for a while. But Nana started going with her more often when Leticia went to see Darren. Nana would pack her a snack for the bus ride, or she'd bring her a book. But Leticia was usually too distracted to eat or read. Then they just sort of drifted back to the way it had always been. Dinner at the Portuguese place. Lunch every few days. Long talks about books and their families. Then one day Leticia slipped in Nana's kitchen. She didn't actually fall but she came close, catching herself on the table, and then sitting down quickly. Leticia says that Nana came and sat across from her and they just stared at each other for a while. Then Nana had started hyperventilating so Leticia had laughed, wanting to know why Nana was breathing so hard when she wasn't the one who'd almost fallen. Then Leticia put her hand on Nana's hand because Nana was trembling, and Nana told her that she'd always made a point of saying that Leticia wasn't her best friend because Leticia was her sister. They were not best friends, she'd said. They are sisters, and Leticia had to be more careful. So Leticia told her that she would be more careful and had continued to pat her hand until Nana stopped shaking. Then Nana got up because the kettle was whistling. That was the fight.

At the time, I'd had no clue that Nana and Leticia had had an argument, and assumed that it was my unstoppable bad-assness that had made me a desirable travelling companion, and not that my mother had left me with my grandmother for the weekend while she was wined and dined in Vermont

by a man who turned out not to interest her very much. I'd
been excited by the prospect of seeing Darren, though since
he'd been away, he'd lost some of his luster, and had been
replaced by similarly unsuspecting members of my cohort
in school or around the neighborhood. I didn't understand
what my presence was supposed to mean to Leticia, and did
mean to Nana, or that the whole awful thing, Darren being
contained in a man-made structure, was part of something
much bigger and more intractable than I could have imagined at the time. Though sometime later, when Alessandra
returned from college, I think during her sophomore year,
laden with dense textbooks, rolled-up sheets of paper containing photocopied architectural drawings, and the kind of
insufferably earnest, highbrow intensity typically only seen
in the young male upon completion of his first work of non-
fiction, she did attempt to lay it out for me. She sat on the
floor at the foot of her bed, a blueprint of a concentration
camp in front of her, explaining what a section was, a floor
plan, an elevation, clarifying tiny symbols and etchings and
line weights. She expounded on theories of architecture, the
minute decisions that were made about spaces, what they
should do, how they should feel, who should be in them.
Those successive decisions that then lead to more detailed
successions of decisions, she told me, were evident in each
drawing if you understood how to read them. She'd stared
intensely at the renderings of Bergen-Belsen and Auschwitz
and Dachau that were splayed out around her. What I needed to understand, she said without looking up, was that the
point of all of it, every corridor and room, every slant of a
roofline, the edge of each enclosure, was to warehouse people. And that meant destroying them.

She was by this time already in the throes of her mighty
undergraduate thesis, something I got around to eventually
as well, though unlike both of my sisters and Joan, I do not
extol the virtues of academic scholarship. I find it all a bit
dull, and much too confining, which explains my choice of
college, really more of a camp for dirty adult children, nestled

high in the hills of rural New England. I'd initially planned to write about the Victorian lady greats but had changed course to Virginia Woolf when I began a short-lived, tumultuous affair with a tall chain-smoker who wore leather bracelets and admired the Bloomsbury set. Our passion died quickly, but my love of all things Bloomsbury did not, and a few months after I'd actually completed the thesis, Adele and I got in our first real fight. In between sips of coffee one morning, she asked me in a rather pained way why I hadn't so much as mentioned to her that I'd been writing it. She pointed out that I'd asked my then-boyfriend repeatedly for guidance—by this time I'd moved on to a Theater Arts major, or maybe it was Applied Arts, I can't really recall—even though, unlike her, he didn't even like Virginia Woolf. He found her too experimental, too unformed, too hard to categorize, too something else he refused to bother further explaining. Adele's question took me by surprise and I don't remember how I initially responded to her. The appalling truth is that it hadn't even occurred to me to ask her to read it.

The next thing I knew she'd left table. Her half-drunk coffee remained, as did her crumpled napkin, which hung precariously on the arm of the wooden chair where she'd been sitting. I then heard her at the other end of the house, or I heard something, a knocking, some cacophonous racket, which turned out to be Adele banging a fire poker into the knot of wood on the wall that opened the sliding door to the library. It was the damn humidity, of course, she said, that was preventing the spring from releasing. I offered to help, and she responded by waving the fire poker in my direction, almost as if she planned to whack me with it. I nodded at her. I've upset you, I said. Let me explain. She rolled her eyes at me. She was not the least bit upset, she told me. Not at all. And then she flounced from the room after flinging the fire poker into its wrought iron stand, making a horrid clanging sound that reverberated throughout the room like a dismal church bell. I was made to chase her as she marched through the house with some of the most glamorous and self-assured passive aggression I've ever seen. Please stop, I said, as she ran her finger along a line of the wainscoting in the hall, inspecting for dust. But of course she couldn't be bothered, as she was much too busy. Let me make this right, I pleaded, as she re-fluffed an already beautifully fluffed throw pillow. Adele, please listen to me, I begged, as she straightened a painting of some majestic old relative. This went on for quite some time and I don't know that it would have stopped if I hadn't tripped on one of the narrower treads of the back stairs. My goodness, don't be so careless, dear girl, she said, and then she sat down beside where I lay in a dejected clump.

I then straightened myself out and asked her if she'd like to hear about my thesis, and then I proceeded to tell her about it because she ignored my question. It was just a silly exploration of Virginia Woolf's nuanced feminism, I said. Adele stared straight ahead of her. I reached for her hand but she moved it to adjust her woolen cardigan that she wore on the mornings that she pretended to garden. Adele, listen, I said. She turned to face the wall. I tried again. What I did, I told her, was uncover a profound truth, a fundamental tenet of the female experience too long obscured by the patriarchal gaslight we all exist in. Still nothing. My argument, I went on, is that the strength of each narrative, in so many of Woolf's novels, is dependent on the way the female characters discuss it. Which means that men are lionized and celebrated not because of who they are or what they've done, but by the way women talk about them. The war heroes they prattle on about don't die heroic deaths. They tumble off horses or die of typhoid. They are nothing like the conquerors they are made out to be. Adele moved her head slightly, not quite nodding. She's saying that we are the war heroes, I said. We are the kings. We are the ones who hold this whole thing up. Well, of course I know that already, Adele told me, not patting but sort of tapping my knee with her pointer finger. Then she got up and returned to her breakfast and we never discussed the incident again.

Of all the stupid things I've done in my life, this stands out as one of the most idiotic and preventable failures. Because I knew that it was Adele who had introduced my mother to Virginia Woolf, leaving a stack of her favorite novels on the nightstand in the bedroom where my mother often slept when she'd begun to visit more regularly. It was Adele's copy of *The Waves*, filled with her notes, in her distinctive, floral cursive, that had inspired the names my mother ultimately did not give us. The night after our fight, I crept down to Adele's library, quietly tapping at the hidden spring-release door, and entered the large rectangular room where she stored her Brontës, her Eliots, her Austens. I sat on the floor, moonlight flooding the room, in awe of the space, the beautifully organized Western canon, the tiny glimpse of a part of Adele that despite, on some level, having known was there, never bothered to truly consider.

CHAPTER EIGHT

J oan informed my sisters and me by email that she would take ownership of Adele's house after all, instead of selling it as she'd often threatened throughout the years. I assume her chosen mode of communication was a result of her not yet being quite comfortable with the prospect of it, though I didn't ask. She would not, she wrote, be selling the house in Cape Town. Nor would she commit to any particular schedule or system, but would continue to live her life as she had before. I was about seven feet from her when I received this briefing, sipping my morning coffee, but I stifled my excitement. I was overjoyed by the news but didn't want to go on and on about it, as my eternally peripatetic aunt, like a house cat, tends to scamper off when met with wild shows of emotion.

Wisely, in her estate planning, Adele had assumed that it would take some time for Joan to come to her senses on this matter and had set a plan in place. So until then, our grand New England manse was to remain under the management of the platoon of aspiring folk heroes and squatters and artists and poets who we found clustered in the eaves and such, scribbling in journals hours after dutifully completing various household tasks, raking, seeding, making pie crust, polishing silver. Their exhaustive work is funded by an obscure trust established in the late '80s, one of many golden eras of establishmentarian WASP stewardship, the sort of thing Joan rails against and benefits from in equal measure.

When we finally discussed the matter later that afternoon, Joan declared that she would absolutely not be taking on the role that her parents had, which she didn't expand on. She still had writing to do, places to visit. She would use the place as her headquarters, she told me, the way one might describe using an unfurnished studio in Pawtucket to park one's belongings while other more serious matters are attended to. Though this was exactly the kind of out-of-touch elitism that Joan had found so appalling about Adele, she talked about her decision as if she were doing us all a favor, which she was, to be perfectly honest—I would simply shrivel up and die if that house were no longer in my life—and that she was the most reasonable, practical woman on the planet. Oh, I'll just stay here, I suppose, she'd said generously, and do my work, whilst traipsing about the globe during the unforgiving New England coastal winters.

I was in no place to scrutinize another woman for being an out-of-touch elitist, however, as I had spent the better part of the previous two days in silk pajamas on a sofa. I had yet to commit to a date on which I would return to New York and I was in no mood to be lectured about it, though Keith lectured me anyway, pointing out that I was running from both him and my problems. Outraged, I'd doubled down on my sabbatical by arranging to rent out my studio for a week to a couple that my high school friend Serena had befriended in Israel, even offering them the seeded kosher crackers I kept in the cupboard, despite the fact that neither the couple nor Serena is Jewish, though she met the pair on a birthright trip, the details of which remain a mystery to me.

A week passed. Maybe two. I spent my days with Joan, cooking and reading mostly, and making plans about what to do with Adele's belongings, which generally consisted of us naming our favorite articles of her clothing and then wandering off somewhere to nap. I renegotiated my rental agreement, extending it for another week or so, this time with a friend from college. I contemplated bangs. I grew out my leg hair. I sat in Henry's office, at his desk, and using Adele's monogrammed stationary, composed letters to a woman named Jay who I'd gotten to know while working on the prison garden project. My sisters joined Joan and me at the house on some weekends, as has been our habit over the years, particularly in the summer, though these visits were decidedly different than they had been in the past, namely because my sisters began to exhibit behaviors that suggested they were at risk of unraveling, or had already unraveled, both scenarios I'd previously thought impossible. When they'd marched off to college, years before, all eyeliner, baby barrettes, and attitude, I'd honestly felt sorry for the people and environments they'd surely soon vanquish. That anyone or anything might defeat either of them was simply out of the question. But ever thus is life in the patriarchy, I suppose.

Alessandra was settling into her new place uptown and was no longer eating meat, though she was reluctant to be labeled a vegetarian. She just had to make some major changes, she told me. I'd collected her in front of her local bodega, half a block from her building, in the 1984 Toyota Corolla Adele and Henry had used for long-distance errands like a trip to the post office or the big box grocery store, where they'd purchased bulk items like tonic water, dish soap, and Goldfish crackers. Alessandra's hair was wet and her sunglasses covered her eyes. We listened to the Bangles, which was my idea, mainly because I needed a real and unbreakable distraction to keep from spilling the beans about Adele's illicit past. Joan, per usual, had remained unequivocally unexcited. She seemed not at all eager to tell my mother, which made me wonder how much of Adele's story she'd already known, or had at least gleaned on some level. I felt that a conference with my sisters had to be the first step. Then we'd of course have to tell my mother that her well-bred first love may have been sired by a plebian pauper after all, which he was not, by the way, but he was sprung from the loins of the nouveau riche, which, at least according to Adele, was actually much worse. Then we'd tell Nana and Leticia, because though they would claim not to, they would absolutely love this sort of thing. I was stupidly unaware at the time that focusing my energy on the drama of Adele's secrets that way was at least partly a diversion, saving me from the misery of truly grieving for her.

Isabella met us at the house. Her daughters were with Jason on the Cape or in Maine, some other fancy ocean getaway. She fretted about them constantly while telling us that she was the kind of mother who was perfectly comfortable letting things go, not at all a helicopter parent, but a very relaxed one, maybe too relaxed really. Joan, conveniently, hightailed it to the Catskills to see an old friend or an old flame, she claimed, but really to avoid discussing her role in pilfering her mother's journals. I waited thoughtfully until my sisters and I had sat down for dinner. I'd prepared a salad with greens from the garden that I garnished with the candied nuts Adele's house elves had left in labeled jars in the pantry. Isabella made linguini with tomatoes, basil, and hunks of mozzarella, while Alessandra meticulously sliced a lemon, perhaps for her water, though she left it on the counter arranged in an arc. I uncorked and poured our wine, a crisp Sancere, and I sipped mine before placing the journals and letters in the middle of the table and announcing that our beloved grandmother had actually been a bit of a hot mess after all, just like the rest of us.

Their reactions surprised me, and said much more about their own lives than Adele's. Isabella was concerned about being judgmental. She threw the term "self-righteous" about a good deal, saying that relationships are complicated, really complicated, and that people do crazy things, stupid things, hurtful things. People stray in marriages, she said, as if such a notion were a revelation, foreshadowing her tantrum that was yet to come. Alessandra, on the other hand, was hurt. Why hadn't Adele confided in her, she wanted to know, expressing a cloying, vulnerable, neediness that was wildly unlike her. But I told her my secret, she said. Why didn't she tell me hers? We chatted for a bit, our conversation much like a poorly played game of ping-pong, no real rhythm or point, but this was because Isabella had

had a bit too much to drink and Alessandra had had to gear herself up to talk, which she finally did, about an hour after we'd all stopped eating and the candles had begun to melt in a way Adele would have tsk-tsk-ed about.

He took up an entire doorway. That was the secret Alessandra had told Adele. Or that's how she told it to us, by presenting patchy information in shapes, using the strange geometric associative configurations through which she understands the world. She'd misread the signals, she explained. That Seth had taken up space that way, his wide shoulders mirroring the frame of the door, to her, had been indicative of strength of character. She saw him as a protector, this conclusion the result of some strange biological algorithm she'd created, about masculinity, connectivity. On some level I understood what she was getting at—men are hunters or some such sexy compelling nonsense—but I also felt as if I were in the presence of a stranger, some weak and broken woman who's story came flowing uncontrollably from her mouth like a ribbon being tugged at, by what I don't really know.

I recalled a conversation I'd had with Adele in my early twenties about my sisters, as our adult lives had begun to develop, and Alessandra had grown even more remote. I'd described the blueprints Alessandra had brought home from college, her certainty and strength back then, so palpable, unquestionable. I told Adele that I'd felt that she'd abandoned me. I'd assumed, when I initially moved to New York after college, that Alessandra and I would live together, a promise she'd made to me long before, when we were little girls watching Madonna videos on MTV. But when I got there, she had a studio that she loved, and seemed to have forgotten all about me and Madonna. For years her work, and then later, Seth, seemed to take up most of her time. Looking back on the memory, and what I'd relayed of it to Adele, felt depressing then, somehow dark. Had that been the last instance of her unquestioned strength? And if it was, how could I have missed it? I felt the crushing embarrassment I'd experienced after realizing that our neighbor's yelling the afternoon Darren had helped to pack up my mother's paintings had been because she assumed that he'd been robbing our house. A tall Black man, she said—though he was not at all a man yet—was going in and out of our house, taking things and loading them in an unfamiliar car. No matter that my mother was there directing him, that I was there trailing after him like a badly behaved puppy, that the unfamiliar car was a U-Haul, conspicuously emblazoned with its logo and phone number so that the whole world could see that this was a vehicle used solely for the purpose of transporting things. I'd thought nothing of it at the time. This was a woman who always yelled. She got hysterical when I'd decorated the fence, beautifully I might add, with my own puff paint that I'd saved for and purchased myself, for God's sake. Of course she was yelling.

Seth had crept into our world quietly, eerily quietly. Alessandra had been single and dating around for years, never really interested in anyone all that seriously, and then suddenly there was a presence, a man she described as brilliant, complex, damaged. She liked that he'd had to fight so hard for his success, that he identified as an underdog. She began to question all of us, our privilege, our ways of doing things, which I found annoying as shit. Must you take everything so fucking seriously, I'd said to her when she lectured me after I'd purchased a fantastic pair of Balenciaga slides that even on sale were still wildly, atrociously expensive. I'd rarely interacted with Seth, and I increasingly rarely interacted with her, though I did see her. There was the occasional walk or dinner, random phone calls, but an undeniable gulf had formed. And as the years went on, without thinking much of it, I began to gravitate towards Isabella and the new depth and strength she'd either acquired after becoming a mother or that I'd only then recognized she had always had. None of this was conscious, on any of our parts, at least to my knowledge. When I'd vented to Adele on the telephone my irritation and sadness at the thought of Alessandra having outgrown me, Adele had dismissed it, as I knew she would, explaining that relationships, over time, take many forms, and it's best not to fight such changes and reconfigurations. She'd said something like, memories are of course murky. Let life happen, darling. So I'd done my best to take her advice. And I'd found Isabella refreshing in a way I hadn't really when I was younger. Where before she'd seemed too obedient, a stand-in for our mother, I now found her complicated, flawed, kind, and surprisingly understanding of the oddities of my life at the time.

Isabella's face grew grave as Alessandra spoke, and I saw how much she'd begun to resemble our mother, which, I think because of Adele's death, signified the passing of time to me more than anything else. The faint lines at the corners of her mouth and at the sides of her eyes moved just like my mother's did when she smiled or raised her eyebrows. I couldn't tell if I was comforted or saddened by seeing Isabella this way, or if the wine and Alessandra's talk of shapes and signals was getting to my head, so that Isabella's face became a collection of moving planes, a puzzle, an equation to be deconstructed. Alessandra's voice had taken on a sort of background quality, so I heard first the waves outside, and the buzzing of fireflies, and then, far away somehow, her strange story, as if it were being carried by the wind, having originated oceans away.

There were moments of rudeness, like when Alessandra went out of her way to make it clear to us that Seth had found her. She hadn't sought him out. Because she wasn't like we were, like Isabella who, with her gaggle of girl-friends, had flailed at boys in high school, losing herself in a momentum she couldn't control. Or like me, she said, who chased and pounced and felt trapped and then screamed, only to do it all over again. I was surprised that Isabella seemed unbothered by this, though she may have been too distracted to register what Alessandra was saying. I was myself rather pleased by the description, though I only said something like, I don't know what you're talking about, just to keep her going, because she'd paused. She knew she was being vague, of course, she told us, but she didn't know how to explain something that she couldn't understand herself.

Then she faltered, her voice cracking. It was like being in that maze again, she said, the one that Henry had made for her when she was a child. But no one came for her this time. No one came to show her how to get out. At night, she said, when she was dazed, aching, half asleep, she'd tried to make sense of it all, but then had determined at some point that she wasn't really after a conclusion. It was far easier, for a while at least, to exist in a kind of numb darkness. Because she knew, she told us, that if she let her thoughts travel further, they'd erupt, wrenching her awake and then she'd have to face that there wasn't any sense to make of it, and that that was the point. She began to have horrific, violent dreams where she'd stab Seth, following him into the bathroom at night when he was half asleep. Or she'd choke him, his eyes bulging as she squeezed his throat, her grip unusually strong, the way one is in dreams.

In one of those half-asleep deliberations, she recalled our mother yelling at her from the bottom of the stairs in high school because she'd let her prom date drive her home drunk. The memory came back to her vividly, she said, the smell of cheap whiskey, the underwire of her push-up bra digging into the skin of her chest. She hadn't wanted to go with him. She'd thought seriously about asking around for another ride. But she'd balked. In that moment, avoiding humiliating him had outweighed her fear of driving with him. Our mother had gotten tears in her eyes when Alessandra told her what had happened. Embarrassed by our mother's reaction, she'd clomped from her room, slowed by the platform sandals she'd borrowed from Isabella. Our mother had asked that she stop, that she turn around, but she'd continued towards the staircase. She'd actually wanted to tell someone about it when she got home, she said, how she'd braced for the entire ride, checking and then rechecking that her seat belt was buckled, as her date swerved around the East Side of Providence, but she'd become frozen, too ashamed. So she lay in bed for a long time, eventually falling asleep to the sounds of our mother running her bath.

When our father was alive, our mother had taken baths almost every night. It had been her way of unwinding. I have no memory of these baths, though to Alessandra, they remain one of her clearest recollections from childhood. Our mother had installed an old claw-foot bathtub that she'd found at an estate sale not long after our parents bought their house. She'd cleaned and painted it herself, and had found an antique cross-handle faucet for it just like the ones at Adele's house. She used to sit cross-legged in the steaming water, Alessandra said, picking dried paint from underneath her fingernails with the end of a metal nail file. When Alessandra couldn't sleep as a child, she'd walk to the bathroom and stand with the side of her face pressed against the closed door and wait for our mother to notice her feet under the door. Sometimes our father sat in the bathroom too. Our mother would rest one leg on the edge of the tub and our father held on to one of her toes and he'd sort of wiggle her foot while they talked, which neither of them reacted to. Alessandra remembers wondering if either of them was conscious that he was doing anything.

One night they barely said a word to each other, Alessandra told us. She set her wine glass down in front of her, and was tracing its outline on her place mat, her brow furrowed. She remembers that our mother was angry with our father, or that he was angry with her, because she'd overheard them arguing. And during dinner she recalls that our mother's purple eyelids had been tinged dark red and that her nostrils were slightly flared, which only happened when she was upset. After a while our father had brought Alessandra back to bed. Whispering, she'd asked him if he was going to apologize to our mother and he told her that he was. She'd wanted him to explain to her what had happened. He'd seemed uncomfortable, she said, annoyed by her probing curiosity. So she was silent for a while, not sure if she should push him further, or why she even wanted to. He didn't say anything for a while and then he'd smiled. He told her that it was like our mother always said. It's science. The biggest thing, the thing that matters more than anything else, is that he loved her.

How is a child supposed to know what that means, Alessandra asked us. Neither of us, by this time, knew what she was getting at. Encouraged, Alessandra went on, nodding. This is why, she said, she had spent so much time in the bathroom after our father died, when our mother no longer took her nightly baths. Leticia had told her that it was because it was too hard for our mother to sit still. Baths were no longer comforting because they'd been the place where she'd let her mind wander, an explanation Alessandra now understands differently. But as a child, when fatherlessness felt like it was suddenly everywhere, in every corner of her mind and in every breath that she took, she'd longed for those moments of watching him, being awake when she knew both of our parents wanted her to be asleep. So after brushing her teeth before bed, she'd play with our mother's lavender bath oil or clean her metal nail file with a washcloth, content to be occupying the space where she'd observed it all. One night, Alessandra recalled, I joined her, lying on the bath mat, kicking at her ankles while she futzed with the toiletries. To avoid me Alessandra had moved towards the window and watched as our neighbor Monica slowly emerged from her station wagon. She'd pushed the car door shut with her hips, making a barely audible clunking sound. Then she'd walked to the back of the car and pulled a few grocery bags from the trunk, which shut just as smoothly as her door had. The she'd dropped the grocery bags, and their contents crashed to the mottled pavement of the alley, but Alessandra couldn't hear a thing because the window was closed.

Early in Alessandra's relationship with Seth, they'd attended a benefit that was affiliated with the brokerage firm where he worked. When they'd met, about a month or so earlier, at a small house party in Chelsea, he'd touched her shoulder while she was talking, which had startled her, but he hadn't seemed to notice. It felt to Alessandra like some signal, like our parents at night in the bathroom, the edges of their bodies connecting without either of them acknowledging it. Seth had been wearing a navy-blue overcoat, a real adult garment, his body filling the material completely, looming in a way only men can. After they'd been together for a while, Alessandra had shown our mother a picture of him. In the photograph Alessandra wears gray jeans and Seth is smiling. They sit close to each other, the tops of their legs touching, his hand on her knee. His wasn't a kind smile, our mother had said about the photograph. She'd been right, of course, though Alessandra couldn't see that then. She'd thought instead that the work of being near him, the conflict, had meant that it was right. She'd believed that she was doing the right thing, that she was like our mother, striving, eyes red and weary, dutifully committed to fixing the thing that resisted her.

At the benefit Seth had touched her constantly, her wrists, her arms, her waist. She felt shy at first. She wasn't used to socializing with people in the financial world. Her circle consisted of college friends and the busy academic types she worked with, intense and intelligent, but less focused on social polish. She'd gotten into a playful political argument with someone on Seth's team. This man was quick, very funny, and a Republican, she told him, because he didn't have to consider not being one. Laughingly, he'd accused her of being a bleeding heart liberal. Alessandra hadn't realized that Seth was angry until he began to guide her towards the coat check. He'd walked forcefully, his hand clasped on her arm. In the cab on the way home he accused her of flirting and of showing off. Most people can't argue that way, he'd said. She didn't know how to react, she said. She thought that he was being ridiculous, but his anger was chilling. She'd tried first to assuage it but ended up losing her temper too. She started yelling back. In her apartment he hurled his overcoat onto her bed, covering half of it, the sound a heavy, lumpy thud. He slammed her against the wall near the door. They could hear her neighbors in the hallway, happily yelling, home from dinner or the bar. She thought for a second about calling out to them, saying that she'd made a mistake, that she'd misread the signals, whatever that overcoat meant, the perfect symmetry of those shapes, the certainty she'd felt about the work of tending to him. She needed help now getting out of this. But instead she said nothing. She made eye contact with him, silencing him, protecting him, saving him from acknowledging in the real world what he did to her when he was angry.

As Alessandra talked I recalled the bruising I'd seen on her neck and upper arm not long ago. I remembered the haziness of the colors, a crude yellow that faded into the olive of her skin, a purple, a blotched hardened irregular pattern. But I hadn't asked her about it. I'd absolutely noticed. I'd sensed something. But I'd done nothing. I thought of her stark white shelves, the books that she'd crammed them with, the intensity with which she'd declared that her life was all right, that the breakup meant nothing, that the shapes of the windows refracted light in a way that her previous apartment's windows hadn't.

So that was it, I thought, that was the thing that had come between us. My eyes filled with tears, out of rage or confusion or terror I don't know what. I looked at her face, oddly serene, all things considered. A flood of questions rushed about and parts of them came out in fragments. Was that how it started, how this all began, that awful night at the party downtown? Was that what prompted the move, the change. Why are you only telling us this now, and how bad was it, are you still you, and am I still me, and will you ever be okay. Yes, yes, she would be okay, she said, her voice composed and firm. And yes, the night she was talking about was when it started, though it wasn't really. Because the first night that it happened wasn't the first night that it happened. Because of course it never really is.

She'd started going to a group in Washington Heights, she said, and that, along with the blood one night, had been the turning point. She saw an advertisement for the group on a bulletin board at work, one of the ones by the basement door where the ads stayed on for months without being updated or reorganized. Most of the flier had faded to pale pink. When she'd reached for it, to pull off a phone number, she'd moved it slightly, revealing a section that was untouched by the sun that was much brighter, almost magenta. She'd called the number that afternoon. She'd whispered. The woman on the other end spoke to her very clearly, enunciating each word. Alessandra pegged her as a teacher, though she learned at her first meeting that the woman and her sister ran a family bakery. The flier had read, is somebody hurting you, in bold print.

She told the women in Washington Heights that she'd considered an abortion when she learned that she was pregnant. They'd sat in a living room that was large, at least by Manhattan standards, in the apartment of a woman named Leslie, a space with beautiful old windows that faced the Hudson. Leslie was a crisis counselor. She ran various groups, mainly for women, some affiliated with a nondenominational church a few blocks away. Alessandra described sitting in a square, stiff chair in the lobby of a doctor's office about a month or so before, a room without windows somewhere in midtown. A very thin, young girl who had been seated across from her had looked her up and down nervously. Alessandra had smiled at her and she'd looked away. After Alessandra's name was called she'd started shaking. She'd been holding a bottle of water that she'd bought on the way there. It felt then as if something inside of it were moving or pulsing, so she'd set it on the floor near her purse. The doctor had the kind of face that probably used to be nice, Alessandra explained, but had started to look mean, not because he was mean but because he was tired. Right away she'd said to him that she wasn't sure she could go through with it. Because it had suddenly occurred to her that she didn't want to, but there was nothing moralistic, or even logical about it. He'd put his hand on his forehead, and with his thumb and the tips of his fingers he'd pressed his temples. With his other hand he'd taken off his glasses and then he'd moved his hand from his temples to his eyes and had started to rub them. He'd said all right, wearily. She'd apologized and told him that maybe she hadn't thought it all through. He then looked at his clipboard on the table next to him, having forgotten her name, and then addressed her, telling her that she really had to think it through.

In the group they'd talked about safe spaces, whether there were strategies to cope with their current situations, how they might take steps to extricate themselves from them. Walking towards the subway when it was over, Alessandra told a woman named Rafaela that as a child she used to like to sit on her bed and watch people from her window. She especially liked watching as people shut their car doors when her window was firmly shut, so that the sound of the car door slamming was inaudible or at least muffled. From where she sat the motion was fluid, an easy click, a carefully crafted arithmetic configuration in which everything fell into place. She liked picturing the mechanics of it all, the greased gears and hinges. Alessandra had started laughing while talking. Rafaela had laughed too. During the meeting Rafaela told the group, stone-faced, that her boyfriend had slapped her twice in the middle of a family dinner. Alessandra told Rafaela that she still watches for car doors, that when she's terrified, sometimes it's the only thing that helps. Rafaela told her that she liked to walk to the end of the hallway and take off her shoes and stretch her toes, pulling them back towards the tops of her feet as far as they can go.

In describing this to Adele, Alessandra told us that she had talked about Poppy, how he'd told us that the way you fight says something about who you are. When Poppy fought with Nana he'd sit down, after pulling the legs of his pants up, which he did because it wasn't fair that he was so much bigger than she was. She's gotta be able to really yell at him if she needs to, he'd told us. Poppy had hated the story that my sisters and I loved so much, about him knocking out three guys at once. He wouldn't even tell it to us. He'd said that his knuckles had bled and that he'd been scared. That's why he did what he did. He told us that most things aren't worth fighting about and that it's the toughest guys who know when to walk away. But he also said that if you do decide to stay and fight, if the thing is really worth fighting for, to never balk, and that's what Nana and Leticia and Lou said too. Adele had said to her, yes, yes, I agree completely, I suppose.

Alessandra recalled my asking Lou what he'd done to get thrown into prison, how I'd sung out, what did you do, Mr. Lou? Did you strangle someone? Did you cut somebody's throat? And how Poppy had scolded me and then told me to try to imagine what it would feel like to be known for the rest of my life for the worst thing I'd ever done, which was ultimately the wrong tactic, as I'd found the notion quite appealing. So Poppy had held my face in his hands and laughed. Then he'd said what the hell are we gonna do with you, kiddo.

Oh Lou, I remember Lou, Adele had said to Alessandra, without acknowledging the fear and rage she'd once felt about him. Alessandra told her that Poppy believed that Lou had been made out to be a monster, but that it was the people who make others out to be monsters who are the real monsters. Adele had only nodded at this so Alessandra began to recite the Niemoller poem, the way Poppy had when he'd talked about Lou. He'd say, first they came for the socialists and I did not speak out. He rarely quoted more than a few lines but we knew what he meant. It was the same thing Nana talked about, what it does to peoples' souls when they get gathered up and removed. In the basement at the

JCC the entire poem was typed out and taped to the door of the room where the Hebrew lessons were taught. Nana told us once that she wished they'd take it down. She said that what the poem said was true, but that it was also misleading, because people did speak up. They did resist. But that the forces that oppressed them were ultimately too powerful. She'd tell us that we had to remember when talking about the suffering, the displaced, that it wasn't their fault what happened to them.

When Poppy got sick, he called us from the hospital and told us ridiculous jokes in Yiddish. Jokes he'd already told us, too many times to count. I hadn't realized at the time that it was his way of saying good-bye. He hadn't wanted us to visit him because we were already fatherless, already too familiar with death. He thought that it would be too traumatic for us to see another man dying. He wanted us to think of him forever as a fighter, a never-balker. He didn't want our memories clouded with images of loss. I'd found this devastating, when it finally occurred to me what was going on, but Alessandra was relieved. She didn't want to see Poppy looking the way our father had those last nights in the bathroom, with his protruding veins stretched over his emaciated limbs, and his eyes like wet stones pressed into the concaved hollows of his eye sockets. She wanted men to look like men, and strength to be unquestionable. This is where her wires got crossed, she told us. This was where she began to misread the signals.

After a particularly horrible fight one evening, Alessandra told Seth that someday she might snap too. And then they'd just looked at each other blankly because neither of them believed that she actually would. Hours earlier he'd hit her hard enough that her head had slammed into the cabinet behind her and when she'd slumped forward afterwards she could taste blood in her mouth. Later, he'd held ice on her face, slowly shaking his head. Seth's father had been violent too. Seth remembered watching his mother cowering near the back door, her nose swollen and her lips bleeding. During his senior year in high school he'd punched his father so hard while trying to defend his mother that his father's whole body was briefly suspended in the air, and when it hit the ground it had bounced, his father's limbs crashing in ways bodies shouldn't move. Seth said that it had broken his heart. He said that he didn't want to be the thing that made someone's body contort that way. He told Alessandra these things afterwards, when she had bruises forming on her neck and upper arms, a scab on her lip where he'd split it. With tears in his eyes, he'd ask how it had all happened. He wanted to know how he'd become his father. He told her that he wasn't a monster. He said it over and over again. He was not a monster. He was not a monster. He loved her and he was not a monster. And because she was lost in the maze of him, and because no one came to get her, she told us, to lead her somewhere that was safe, where she might catch her breath and gain perspective, in those moments, that explanation somehow made sense, and she believed him.

CHAPTER NINE

I don't know that there's a way to properly react to hearing that one's older sister, and not just any older sister, but the more formidable one, the scary one, the one who'd always seemed unstoppable, had been victimized in this particular way, and not just once, but repeatedly, for months, years, who really knows because her story kept changing. For the next few days I experienced a wave of emotions, and when I could, I hugged her, too desperately, until she rebuffed me. Stop, stop, she'd said laughing, pushing me away. I'd shut my eyes, trying to reconcile my preconceived notions about the kind of women who wind up with abusers with the woman I'd grown up with, a brilliant thinker, not a pitiful or pathetic bone in her body. It's because it's not just one thing, she'd said, though I hadn't asked her about it directly. It's like what Nana always says about that poem, that you can be a fighter, you can be strong and clear-eyed. And you can still get clobbered.

And what had Adele thought of all this, I wanted to know. Alessandra wouldn't say. Like Adele, when she'd decided that the conversation had run its course, she simply made it disappear. She cocked her head to the side playfully, making Adele's silly tsk-tsk noise, and reached for the journals. She then sipped her wine and cleared her throat and began to read aloud from a volume from 1947, a year that was inconsistent with the events being described, though by then nothing seemed to be adding up. It was well past midnight and the candles had now burned out completely. The night sounds of our lush coastal ecosystem were faint and soothing. A fog had descended, and soft wet mist had begun to seep into the room where we sat.

Dashing was the word Adele had used to describe him, not kind or attractive or bright. The sense of his constant movement seemed to be what she was trying to convey, though from the packet of pictures enclosed in a disintegrating envelope that fell from the pages at the back of the journal, this man had also been handsome, but he was handsome in the way that too many men like him are, Isabella pointed out, incapable of managing their own psyches so they invade yours. I didn't see all that in his face, the way she did, as I was distracted by the youth and ebullient spirit of the man I was certain was the old Robert Redford who'd trudged up the long driveway and then stood sadly off to the side at Adele's funeral. Alessandra told us that she believed that this was the same man who'd come to our father's funeral, too, though Isabella wasn't so sure. His name was Howie, Alessandra told us. Henry had told her about him once, when she'd tried to talk about our father, though it had not led to a real conversation.

Howie and Adele had grown up together, Alessandra read out loud, on the same wide street in Newport, in a cluster of imposing estates. Only a stone's throw away, Adele had written, higher on the hill above the water, was the massive stone mansion that belonged to Henry's family, an infrequently used summer showplace, really just a place for his family to park funds, a minute portion of their considerable assets. They spent most of their time in Manhattan, in a large apartment in Gramercy Park, a pale brick building with an elevator encased in a gilded frame that ran behind a grand front staircase. Neither Howie nor Henry was an ideal suitor for Adele, according to her parents. Henry was not a regular in Newport, so he knew little of society goings-on, and he refused to bother trying to, and Howie's family was the kind of rich that Adele's family found distasteful, ostentatious. They were boisterous, new money boors, not stewards of ancient wealth. That they made their way to the center of the most elite circles signaled, to Adele's ilk at least, the beginning of the end. Howie had three brothers. A friend at a party described all four sons, Adele recalled, as rough-and-tumble sorts, rebellious, charismatic, and never dull. They liked to drink, to fight, to carouse. They had fast cars, access to money, a sense of the world as limitless, because to them, at least for a while before the war, it had been.

As a young woman, Adele had picked up the habit of smoking. She'd told us that it had seemed glamorous to her, dark and secretive, that it kept her thin. She smoked after her parents went to bed, on the second floor balcony, dangled precariously over the railing, to prevent the smoke from wafting back into the house where her parents might smell it. Late one evening, Adele wrote, Howie had apparently spotted her. He told her at a neighborhood party a few days later that he'd seen a small white form against the dark stone of her house while driving by. He'd thought that it was a ghost, and not a young woman in a white nightgown.

Adele had always described falling in love with little sentiment. It was something that happens to you, she'd told us, an invasive force. It was not to be trusted or taken all that seriously. Men come and go, she'd said, and most of them are more alike than they are different. We somehow knew that she meant none of this. She had had a way of communicating that often further obscured whatever the topic was. Yet despite her opacity, we felt compelled to believe her, to root ourselves firmly on her side, to blindly accept her version of the world, even when we knew full well that what she was telling us was likely untrue or a direct contradiction of something else she'd said. So it should have been unsurprising that her written voice sounded nothing like her, dripping with earnestness and melodrama. But nevertheless we were shocked to read so many run-on sentences, ridiculous proclamations, silly hopeful musings.

Though Howie was never Adele's "beau," at least not in the way that she'd experienced before, she grew to rely on his company. Before going to bed she'd tie one end of a long piece of string around her big toe and hang the other end out her bedroom window so that Howie could tug on it to wake her, when he snuck over late at night. Then she'd climb from her window to a large tree, then to a wall near the patio, and they'd sit outside, talking and smoking until well after midnight, or they'd take long drives along the coast. When she told him that she was pregnant he promised to marry her, but he left town the following day. For page after page Adele wrote of her longing, her confusion, her deep lamenting sadness at having been tricked, betrayed, taken for a fool, and not the respectable woman she wanted to be and insisted that she still was. And then her tone became stark, and her sentences grew clipped, almost manic, as she attempted to make sense of and to assert some control over her circumstances. Their relationship had never existed in daylight, she admitted, and their world was total chaos, young men regularly leaving suddenly for the front. It had surprised no one when he disappeared, she noted, and it shouldn't have surprised her either, this sentence she capitalized, chastising herself.

At first she had tried to conceal the pregnancy with draping clothing, but confessed, in a moment of terror, to her mother, begging her not to tell her father. Her mother had agreed to this at first, and then told him later, another betrayal, Adele wrote. Enraged, her father had forced her to walk up and down the stairs backwards, for hours, every day for weeks, to abort the child, which, unsurprisingly, didn't work. She just grew slightly rounder. Henry intervened only weeks before she was to be sent away, back to a Scottish relative, to protect the reputation of the family. Of course he was hardly in a state to take care of anyone. He'd come home to the death of his younger sister, convinced that his mind was beginning to deteriorate because of the onset of flashbacks. The preposterousness of making a young woman walk the stairs that way was what galvanized him, Adele wrote. It was not his love for her or his pity or his goodness. It was inane action in the face of a relative crisis, or really stupidity of any form, that Henry found intolerable. And this was a good quality in a man, she wrote. This was a principled man, a man who was soft-spoken, less overt. He didn't dazzle her, of course, but he was unlikely to hurt her. He promised to save her. He told her that she could keep the child and that they'd raise it as their own, though she wasn't to talk about the particulars of this pact, certainly not to him, and she was forbidden from contact of any sort with Howie. Though not ideal, this was a man and a situation Adele could handle, she wrote. And then for a few months, the writing stopped.

Adele told me, when I was a teenager, that being romantic was much easier for men, because most men didn't have to bother with being practical. At the time it had been unclear to me exactly what she was talking about, though I realized, listening to Alessandra's recitation of Adele's account of early adulthood, that it was Howie that she was talking about, and that what she had been trying to tell me was that her life changed irreparably for something that he could write off as a trivial mistake. She'd told me that part of the reason she'd loved Henry so much was that he was only practical. When he died, only months after that conversation, she had had paroxysms of weeping, where she tried to purge the house of anything that reminded her of him, which was impossible, so she'd then demand that everything be put back. On one of these occasions, I'd helped her, refilling a leather trunk with the items she'd emptied in the hall. I recalled finding a pocketknife with unfamiliar initials etched into it, and that Adele had taken it from me hastily. My sisters have no memory of this, though I'm sure I mentioned it to them at the time.

Alessandra suddenly wanted to go to bed. She'd become moody, perhaps annoyed by the suggestion that she'd forgotten something, a pet peeve of hers. Isabella flashed me a look, which I took to mean that I should let Alessandra retire to her bedroom and not argue with her, so I reached for my water glass. Alessandra shrugged, said good night, and then left the table. Isabella and I remained sitting for a while before moving to the back porch to look at the stars, which was something we'd done one evening as children with our father, a brief moment that has since ballooned in our memories. We were out there for hours, we recalled after he'd died. He'd pointed out the Big Dipper, Orion's belt. We'd been certain that he was some sort of genius, effortlessly deciphering the vast constellations of our disorganized universe while we could only make out an irregular pattern of sparkling white dots against a deep navy-blue sky. So we exchanged our customary exclamations, two grown women, clinging fiercely to a dreamed idea we'd developed as little girls: Daddy knows everything and he will never go away.

Isabella asked if I remembered when he'd recognized such and such an astrological cluster. Yes, yes, I do, I told her, and this too. After we'd recounted the experience fully, more fully than it had happened, we wandered back inside and upstairs. Isabella offered to sleep in my room with me, like she'd done when we were children, when I was too scared to sleep alone, usually after being rebuffed by Alessandra who rarely tolerated my kicks and snoring. We lay in the dark talking for at least another hour, and as it so often happens with sisters, we became our little girl selves again, the darkness providing a sort of cloak that allowed us to admit even the most ridiculous of our deeply held beliefs. Part of my shock about learning of Adele's strange secret, I told Isabella, was that I'd always assumed that Adele talked to me more intimately than she did to my sisters, that our conversations were deeper. Isabella admitted that she'd thought the very same thing. Alessandra likely did, too, we concluded. So we began combing our memories for clues. Maybe Adele had said something. Maybe we actually were special somehow.

Isabella recalled an odd exchange she'd had with Adele a few weeks before she died. They'd been talking about

Isabella's divorce, though Adele never said the word out loud. She had been at times very encouraging, but could also be the opposite. When Isabella brought up concrete matters, issues of money, custody, and planning around holidays, Adele had become evasive, saying that men always come back, which is something she'd said before. She then went on about the pain of losing someone. She spoke as if Jason were leaving Isabella, as if Isabella were bereft, destroyed, even though Isabella had told Adele repeatedly that the split had been her decision and that she was all right, though not unscathed. You must consider what people will think, what people will say, Adele had said, as if Isabella hadn't. She talked about the hard work of trying to hold a family together, which Isabella found insulting, though now, she wonders if Adele had been talking about herself, her own set of decisions. At some point Adele had begun to look dazed, Isabella remembers, unhappy. No one has a perfect life, Isabella had said to her, and Adele had looked at Isabella blankly. You understand that that sort of thinking was unavailable to me at your age, she finally responded, and she wasn't sure that she bought it now. There had been a long pause. What is there to buy, Isabella had asked her, and Adele had rolled her eyes, smiling, indicating that the moment had passed, that part of the conversation settled. Now tell me what you plan to do, she'd said.

Isabella had tried to explain to Adele that she wanted to disengage from all of it, not simply to split. She wanted her life to feel like her own again, for the patterns of her marriage, their ideas and rituals, to fade. So she'd bought a different brand of organic cleaning astringent for the bathroom, and white dish towels, which she'd always wanted but that Jason had argued were pointless. Why use white, he'd said, when you know full well that they'll get ruined. But I don't ruin things, she'd wanted to say, you do. By buying them she felt that she was conveying, this is who I am now. This is what I can do without you. Adele had seemed confused. Jason had been right, she said. Why not try beige instead.

Isabella was quiet for a while and then began to twirl her hair, which she'd done in her sleep as a child, but now her eyes were open. Obviously she hadn't really been talking about towels, she explained, and Adele knew that. She let go of the twirled lock and then picked up another, and was silent for a while. Changing course, she admitted that she'd sensed something about Alessandra. She'd known that she was off. But she'd misread the signals, too, she said, employing Alessandra's odd terminology, which made her sound less sympathetic than I think she actually was. I realized that Isabella was ashamed of herself. She told me that she and Jason had met Alessandra for dinner in New York not long ago, and that Alessandra had displayed the disconnect-edness that Isabella had tried to describe to Adele, though at the time, she hadn't recognized it for what it was. They'd been in town for the night to see an old college friend of Jason's. The friend ended up canceling or somehow got held up, so they'd called Alessandra, assuming, Isabella told me, that she'd be busy. Isabella was surprised that Alessandra had agreed to join them for dinner, that she was so cheerful on the phone, offering to meet them downtown. Then she'd arrived with Seth, one of the only times Isabella recalls interacting with him. Alessandra's hair had looked straggly, Isabella noted. Five or more necklaces hung from her neck and her lip gloss was pale pink, a color she'd never worn before. Seth was stern, handsome in an odd, mechanical way. Alessandra seemed unaware of him, Isabella said. Not that she ignored him. She didn't. But it was as if she were drugged, or somehow subdued, not entirely present. At one point she'd gotten up to use the bathroom and had to slip behind Seth's chair and she'd lurched back, going way out of her way not to touch him.

Jason later remarked that Alessandra had finally found someone as callous as she was, a comment that at any other time in her life, Isabella admitted, she would have welcomed, but then it had felt mean to her, inaccurate and off base. But Isabella had been exasperated by, her, too, she said now,

her eyes filling with tears, because of Alessandra's aloofness, her bored, hollow eyes. Isabella had wanted to shake
her. Give me something, she'd wanted to say. Make visible
your participation in all of this, that old, angry childhood
rage once again rising. But instead she asked about Seth's
work and he'd responded in a nonchalant way, the complex-
ities of whatever it was he did he dispensed in small dull
doses. So Isabella had stopped paying attention.

Jason and Isabella fought on the walk back to their hotel,
but not about the comment he'd made about Alessandra. It
was something else for both of them. He'd accused her of being rude to Seth, which hadn't occurred to her, Seth being so
odd and standoffish. And Isabella had been too angry about
Jason having repeatedly interrupted her to think about what
her tone might have been towards Seth anyway. Jason apologized while rolling his eyes but pointed out that she had
hemmed and hawed, an expression she hates, as it makes it
sound as if she were slow, simpleminded. Washing her face
that night in the hotel bathroom, Isabella noticed that the
darkness under her eyes seemed particularly stark. She told
herself that it was the lighting, though she knew it wasn't.
So she thought of our mother, the way she'd looked at our
father's funeral, pale and angry, her face defiant, her stomach concave even though she stood straight. Isabella recalled
crying, huddled in a pew of the Episcopal Church, clutching
Adele's bony hand. She remembered her terror at the thought
of people being pulled from their lives. One day there and the
next day yanked somewhere else. It could happen to me, she
thought. It could happen to my sisters. It could happen to my
mother. She'd looked at our mother, who had smiled at her,
her face suddenly flooding with color. Her eyes were rimmed
red, but bright. Isabella had waved at her, though she was
only feet away. Our mother had waved back to her, but there
was something about that darkness under her eyes.

The following morning I slept in, waking to find myself
alone, abandoned even by Roo who'd been enticed by the

smell of eggs and toast, and fragrant coffee. I stumbled
downstairs in my robe. Roo was lying on her side in a patch
of sunlight. A small plate rested next to her head on the
floor, clean but for a few streaks of egg that she'd missed
because she is now lazy and spoiled, confident that more
eggs are likely coming. She needn't agonize over every last
drop the way she once had. The vestiges of shelter life only
a faint memory, she now turns her nose up at kibbles, even
the overpriced organic ones. Why spoil one's appetite, her
expression reads, when one of the women who coddles me
will soon bring me a plate of roast chicken, smoked salmon,
or another perfectly poached egg?

Alessandra sat at the table with her coffee and fried eggs.
She was still in her pajamas, a Paw Sox sweatshirt that had
to be at least a decade old, and white jersey drawstring
pants, both articles she'd found in the drawer of a dresser
in one of the guest bedrooms, though not hers. She didn't
greet me when I came in but immediately got to her point.
The man who impregnated Adele had been at our father's
funeral. And that made sense, she said. After all, it was his
son who had died. She pointed towards the brass-framed
photograph she'd laid on the table, one that had hung for
years near the back stairs, clearly a photograph of Howie,
and not some distant relative in a US Army uniform, as we'd
always thought. Or had assumed without thinking about it.
There were too many framed photographs to really keep
track of anyway, none standing out as remarkable. To us
they had simply been part of the scenery.

Alessandra held the framed picture next to one of the
photographs from the envelope in the journal. It was unmis-
takable the resemblance, which then of course led us to a
discussion of this man's resemblance to our father, and to
us. We'd always attributed our Scottish coloring to Adele,
and from what we could remember, our father had looked
a lot like Adele. Or had he not? Was this just something
she'd told us that we'd accepted as fact immediately the way
we did with so much of what she'd told us over the years?

Isabella shut her eyes. Jackie Robinson, she said. All I can see is Jackie Robinson. We ran to the front hallway where most of the photographs of our father were, and from them we got nothing and everything. Was that his real expression or was that just the way he looks in a photograph, like an imposter, uncannily similar to him but definitely not our father. Had his eyes always been so deep, we wondered? Was this taken when he was sick or when he was healthy? Was that Adele's smile? Yes, it had to be. But back to this strange man in his army uniform; had Henry known his photograph was there all these years, we wondered? Had our father?

I didn't know what to make of the idea of this strange lothario, my biological grandfather, having been at my father's funeral, and I wasn't sure that my sisters did either. We were only children, our memories unreliable. But of course Alessandra had it all figured out. She recalled overhearing Joan telling our mother that the sight of him had appeared to take the wind out of Adele's sails. Hours later Alessandra had asked what the expression meant, hoping for more information about the man, death, Adele, all of it. But Joan had either forgotten that she'd said anything or coyly played dumb. She explained that the expression meant that a person would appear to wither back, folding into herself, like cloth. Isabella remembered this exchange, too, though she recalled that it had happened a day later. All I could remember from those days were my attempts at deciphering all the interactions around me. I'd tried to take cues from my sisters, but they were at sea, too, though they pretended that they weren't. None of us could make sense of the reality of the moment, each change too strange and severe to articulate. That our father was now dead, that we would soon drive home to Providence without him, that our mother would resume her life and we ours, that at dinner we would not ask when he'd be home from the hospital, and if we were playing downstairs that our mother would no longer tell us to be quiet so that he could rest.

Isabella wondered often about how the absence of Jason would seem to her daughters, if it would feel to them like it had for us when we lost our father, like a sudden inexplicable disruption, odd and uncomfortable, but in some ways less devastating than we'd feared. The imagined or anticipated trauma that preceded his death, had for us morphed into nightmarish apocalyptic visions. But the reality, Leticia calmly told me, while gently attempting to run her hand through my tangled hair, is that life really does go on. Time passes. We are stronger than we think.

After another cup or two of coffee, Isabella and I left our breakfast dishes on the table and headed to the beach for a walk. Alessandra remained at the house, curled on the sofa rereading a collection of letters between the Mitford sisters or something, having closed up again, punishing us, like she had when we were children, for having witnessed even the tiniest glimpse of her vulnerability. I felt a pang of guilt that my spirits jumped slightly at the thought of her staying behind. I wasn't quite comfortable admitting to myself that what Alessandra had told us the previous night was so confounding that a part of me wanted to put all of it, including her, out of my mind completely. It was too much to take. Adele had only just died. We had only just begun to disentangle the mystery of her. And now this.

Though she didn't say so, it seemed that Isabella felt the same way. She, too, was eager to get out of the house, hurriedly slipping into her running shoes and zipping up her sweatshirt. As we walked towards the water, we talked about her divorce, a somber topic in some ways but also a welcome distraction from everything else. Consuelo and Vanessa seemed to be taking it all in stride, she told me, while deftly avoiding the more jagged rocks that separated the waist-high sea grass at the bottom of the hill from the coarse sand of the beach. They'd inherited Jason's nonchalance, his cool, easy demeanor. It had once been a joke between to them actually, the way nothing seemed to faze their children. When she and Jason had broken the news,

Consuelo had laughed and made a sarcastic joke, emulating them. It nearly brought Jason to tears. He told Isabella that he felt as if the world was caving in on him, that he was walking through rushing water. But she was relieved, she said, smoothing her wind-whipped hair. Their reaction indicated to her that she'd raised strong girls who remained sturdy when the world shook.

Weeks later she'd helped him pack. Another metaphor, she recalled thinking. He didn't know where any of his things were or what belonged to him, because keeping track of those sorts of things, for so much of their marriage, had fallen to her. He became emotional in ways she hadn't seen in years, not since they'd started dating. He'd sat on the bed, muttering, while she pulled suit jackets from the closet. She'd hoped that cooperating this way would bode well for future co-parenting situations, and in some ways it did. But Jason also had a way of roping her into conversations she didn't want to have, that no longer mattered anyway.

One afternoon after dropping the girls off at a soccer game, he said that he wanted to talk, almost always an ominous sign. They'd stood in the parking lot of the local field, leaning on cars that didn't belong to them. He was convinced that Isabella had met someone else, and that that was really why she'd left him. It wasn't the case, at least not in the way that he'd meant it. He pointed out that their sex life had changed, which it had, but it had happened a while ago, and that alone had meant little to either of them, Isabella told me. It had changed numerous times in the ten or so years they'd been together, even before they had children. But change alone, even spells of seeming disinterest on either or both of their parts, wasn't what he was getting at and she knew that. It was the absence of real feeling. It was that the spark that truly had stayed vibrant and real had finally, protractedly, died out. She remembers realizing this at a dinner party, and then its realness, its undeniability, became visible to her everywhere. It was as if she'd learned a new word, and then coincidentally seemed to hear it all over the place, at the grocery store, in a commercial on the radio, as she walked past a conversation among strangers on the street.

The dinner party was an event for his firm, held in the back of a once trendy restaurant. She'd worn a gray sheath dress and had straightened her hair. On the way out the door Jason had said that she looked too thin, but not in an overly concerned way, so she hadn't responded to him. At the restaurant she'd talked to the wives of his coworkers, women who were kind and smart enough but who she actually had no real interest in. Instead, she'd been watching Jason as he held court, talking easily, clearly enthralling the two men at his professional level and a younger admiring cohort that had gathered around him. Isabella found herself disgusted, totally uncharmed by him. How could they be falling for that, she thought. Couldn't they see the arrogance? That he was talking over everyone, even if what he was saying was clever and relevant? She had an urge to expose him, to tell the innocent lemmings groveling before him, what a pain in the ass he was to live with, how oblivious he was to the needs of others, how different his thoughtful words were from his actions.

She'd tried to stifle it, whatever that feeling was. She told herself that she was tired, which she was. But then it happened again weeks later while she was folding laundry. She became suddenly physically uncomfortable, frenzied. It occurred to her that she was furious, livid. She felt an urge to wreak havoc on something, on everything around her. What it was about the laundry, she doesn't know. Perhaps it was that that burden, like every other household burden fell on her. Or it might have been that she couldn't focus because she was too preoccupied with all of their details, whether they'd paid the cleaner, the dog walker, whether she'd packed Consuelo's soccer gear, what to make for dinner, whether she'd run the dishwasher, that she was again hopelessly behind on her work, that she still had to deal with the refrigerator because Jason had spilled a container full of

pasta and oily sauce in the vegetable drawer and had hastily, barely cleaned it up, knowing full well that she'd come
along after him to tend to it thoroughly. She was clenching
her fists while folding his undershirts, she recalled, slamming his boxers into a pile of sturdy squares on top of the
washing machine, violently shaking his pants before folding
them. She began to feel faint, so she'd walked towards her
daughters' room. From the hall where the washing machine
and dryer stood, she could hear them playing, but they grew
quiet as her footsteps approached. When she entered they
looked at her blankly as if to hide that they'd been playing, which filled her with an angry, desperate sadness. She
walked towards the window because their room faced the
backyard. She started to close the window. A car alarm was
going off. She pretended that that was why she'd left the
laundry. She'd sat down on Vanessa's bed. Mama, sometimes do you just hate everything, Vanessa had asked her,
and Isabella had laughed in a forced way, out of confusion
or awkwardness or rage. Then she felt a kind of tightness in
her throat, and tears forming, so she'd started towards the
door, back to the laundry.

It occurred to her then what she looked like to them,
what she and Jason looked like, that her daughters were
witnessing the great American female charade, without the
intellectual resources to comprehend it. She leaned against
the dryer, trying to catch her breath. The competing de-
mands, the impossible standards, all bait she'd gladly taken,
had reduced her to her crudest elements. She didn't want
to do it anymore. The unwinnable game of trying to stay
interesting, amusing, to maintain her looks, her weight, to
remain sexually exciting, all while clenching at the last of
the self-esteem she'd brought to the marriage. She wanted
to get off the ride, to give up the Sisyphean experiment of
trying to hold herself together when the needs of children,
a husband, a work life, a home, required that she break into
parts. That was it for me, she said as we reached the far end
of Adele's property line, marked in proper WASP fashion

by a decaying wooden fence, so mottled and worn by the wind and water that it was barely distinguishable from the sea grass.

What Jason had been after when he'd asked if she'd met someone else was something tangible, distinct, something besides the slippery, often defensive, circuitous explanations she offered, the indirectness that gave him so little leverage in an argument. He was right in sensing some vast gray area, something she wasn't articulating, she acknowledges, but he was wrong in his certainty that its existence was an indication of deceit on her part, or of the weakness of her stance. And Dean was only a harbinger anyway, she practically whispered, her embarrassment and her insistence on not being embarrassed both palpable. She bent down to pick up a stick, attempting to look serious. I almost broke into a jig. How absolutely perfect, I said. You saucy, saucy tart. Did you have an affair, I asked, my wonder and adoration growing by the minute. No, no, she said, but then went on talking about a man, a visiting professor, a young sociologist from California who specialized in restorative justice. Dean had shared an office with Rene, her closest friend in her program. He made a point of asking her about her students, her research, something Jason rarely bothered to do anymore. He dug up an old article she'd written years ago and used it in a lecture. He told her that it had inspired an intense seminar discussion, and thanked her, profusely. He wasn't her type, she told me. He was too casual or flighty, so for a long time, she gave him little notice. I nodded and listened as she then went on and on about all the notice she'd given him.

Dean was convinced that there were very few problems that couldn't be solved by thoughtful dialogue. When he was questioned, when someone pointed out that his hypothesis assumes that people are inherently reasonable and actually want to find solutions, he was able to argue that for the circumstances he worked towards, there was no historical precedent, so no way to discount what he was saying. But he was never rude, never dismissive. He was a runner, like Isabella, and he noticed one afternoon, after a lecture, that she had the gait of a runner, something she'd never before considered. The notion itself didn't matter, but his saying so induced in her something long dormant, some fibers of connectivity to another person, something deep and visceral. The moment brought her to tears. Driving home that day she found herself sobbing. Jason knew immediately that something was wrong. He'd tried to hold her, to be playful, but she was unable to submit to whatever he was attempting. It was too late. So she went rigid. She felt desperate, she said, and hopeless. She no longer had it in her to remain open, which she was certain had been the thing that all along had kept them solid.

One afternoon, as their friendship developed, she'd described to Dean witnessing Adele yelling at Nana because of Lou. She'd stopped by his office, again, looking for Rene, she claimed. He'd asked her to sit down, though Rene's desk chair and the extra folding chair that was usually there had been lent out, taken elsewhere for some reason. He began to stand up to offer her his chair. She shook her head and sat on Rene's desk. She'd been holding her purse still, and a bag of books. He'd looked at them and she'd set them on the floor. He was struggling, he told her, writing something about class, forgiveness, race, imprisonment, deterrence. Isabella then began to ramble, she recalls, recounting having overheard Alessandra describing the scene at the deli a few days later to Joan on the telephone, as if she'd actually been there, when she'd really been in the back room, and had missed everything, Isabella insisted, which was news to me, though I didn't let on about it. Isabella recalled her frustration at observing Alessandra talking so casually, making the experience that Isabella had so meticulously reported hours after it had happened, her own.

Joan had then responded to Alessandra's description of Poppy calming Adele, which was not what had stood out most for Isabella. That's sexism, Joan had said, that your poor grandmother tried to say the same thing to Adele and nobody heard her—that's sexism. Don't make the mistake of thinking it's anything else. But what had seemed so remarkable to Isabella was that someone like Leticia could be frightened of someone like Adele, and that's what she'd tried to tell us so many years ago. Leticia was the kind of woman who could stare down anyone, whose quick retorts could silence an entire room. So why had she shrunk back the way she did? Why hadn't she put Adele in her place, the way only she could? Isabella couldn't make sense of it at the time, all the mechanisms at work, the issues of class, gender, race, and power. But she understood it now, she wanted Dean to know. And she wanted me to know that she'd recognized something then that Alessandra had missed with her lying, her dramatic retelling, her diluting of the essence of the scene, her inability to interpret the chaos.

Isabella tried to explain to Dean something about the inherent complexity hidden within the multitude of layers of those sorts of interactions, a concept she applied to her research and that he'd found compelling in the article she'd written. She realized that Dean was staring at her mouth while she talked to him. He was smiling, admiringly, but had stopped when she'd paused, suddenly self-conscious. He began to ask her questions. She became embarrassed. She told him that she hadn't a clue why that incident was on her mind. He wasn't as smart as Jason, she remembers thinking afterwards, or as competitive, as willing to destroy his opponent in an argument, or even a discussion. But she'd left the room feeling smart, full again with her own complete history, that she'd somehow forgotten was there.

Isabella had attempted to make sense of Leticia's reaction so many years ago, she told me. She'd brought it up weeks after the incident, when Leticia was walking her home one afternoon. She remembers being struck by how deliberately Leticia walked, despite being weighed down by bags, a bus pass clenched in one hand, and Isabella's hand in the other. But Leticia had dodged her question, or maybe hadn't understood what she'd been getting at. Instead she'd winked at Isabella, calling her "little muter," and then had abruptly changed the subject.

Leticia still calls her that, though less frequently, and also mame, which like muter, means mother in Yiddish, which Leticia picked up while in the company of my grandparents at work. Isabella looked at me and smiled in a funny way, turning over the conversation in her mind. Did I know what Leticia calls her now, she wanted to know. I had no idea. Leticia calls her Sad Eyed Lady of the Lowlands, because our father used to rock us to sleep singing the Bob Dylan song, Isabella told me. Did I remember him singing that to us, she wanted to know. Because for the life of her, she couldn't. I couldn't either, though I did recall that Leticia had, for as long as I can remember, called our mother things like Van Gogh, or Monet, any painter really, which our mother thinks is silly, especially now, because what she currently does for a living, developing repeating floral patterns for large scale printing, she insists is not real painting. I told Isabella that I remembered telling Nana and Leticia after our mother's business began to take off, that it had never occurred to me to think about who might be responsible for the kinds of designs my mother painted. Leticia had nodded and said that it had also never occurred to any of us to think about who might be responsible for the images in textbooks either, and then Nana had said, and to think your mother could have been a doctor. She could have learned German and gone to medical school and been any kind of doctor she wanted.

CHAPTER TEN

My mother, like all true artists, has a complicated relationship with money. And when talking about it, like all good Jews, she constantly contradicts herself. Like Poppy always said, show me three Jews and I'll show you ten opinions. As a young woman, entranced by the carefree ethos of the 1960s, my mother had preached and sometimes practiced a kind of aversion to material things, and claims to have been capable of separating notions of art from those of commerce. Painting, she felt, was spiritual. To think of it in terms of earning a living was the worst thing she could do for her creativity. She was also—and she remains—absolutely ripshit that her mother never gave her any credit for having honed a skill in college and then immediately landing a well-paying job because of it upon her return to Providence a few months after graduating. She had always planned ahead, she told me. She always knew that she could be an artist without starving to death. Like Poppy always said, show me a woman who's never changed her mind and I'll show you a woman who doesn't have one.

Though her paintings of diseased organs and elaborate tendon systems and such were both works of art in their purest sense and commissions for which she was paid, just to be one step ahead of I don't know what, she copyrighted all of her images. On the advice of one of her childhood baseball friends—a man who grew up to be a somewhat successful copyright lawyer in Cranston, and had a silver BMW, a stucco three-bedroom ranch, and a cottage in Little Compton—she set up a database using relatively new technology. Then when the textbook industry moved to digital images, she had a vast trove, and, as Adele said, she made a killing, the word intended to convey both the crudeness of money matters and the amount my mother earned, which my mother says was not really all that much if one were to compare it to Adele's wealth, but it wasn't nothing either.

She didn't want to completely sell out though. She didn't want to lose what she described as the tactile authenticity of real art. So when a pothead friend of hers asked her to participate in a small trade show downtown that had something to do with promoting local businesses, she set to work, happily recreating the images she'd loved as a child, interlocking floral patterns, sea shells, vines and leaves, the kinds of things she'd doodled in her journals at temple, and still doodles on the notepad she keeps by her landline, which she uses for her daily calls to Nana and Leticia, what with the danger of radiation that leaps from mobile phones and all. She was given a stall with a few racks for the show where she displayed her images on postcards and notepads. She ended up selling everything and taking orders for more. Then one of the people she made orders for put her in touch with a company that offered to buy the rights to some of the images, to be printed on paper and paper-related products, cups, plates, pencils, bound books, bookmarks, wrapping paper, tote bags. Very quickly, she abandoned her convictions about the integrity of the Italian greats, consulted another lawyer, signed a five-year contract, and then bought new furniture for the living room and her bedroom. A few months later, her floral patterns covered plastic to-go cups, mouse pads, lampshades, and tablecloths, so she redid our kitchen and replaced her used Volkswagen with a brand new Volvo with leather seats and a CD player.

This had actually been a long process, her going from hand painting large canvasses to digital images to flowers to everything else, but it felt sudden to my sisters, I think because they experienced almost every change after our father's death as traumatic, a dredging up of old pain. I, on the other hand enjoyed all of it—the plush sofa when I was in kindergarten on which I arranged my paper dolls before I set them on fire in the patio grill, the new easy chairs the following year. Then our mother's king-size bed, a few years later, where I'd take my afternoon naps. When I was in high school she bought the six-burner range with the gleaming hood, the centerpiece of the all-white kitchen with a full wall of glass-fronted cabinets and an island with two wooden stools. Isabella still eyes each of these items with suspicion, as does Alessandra. They talk of the good old days, the days of the brown corduroy sofa and the handwoven blanket, so tattered at the edges it had resembled a massive ball of yarn by the time our mother finally retired it.

After our walk, I agreed to accompany Isabella on her drive back to Providence, partly because it allowed me to put off further my return to New York, to Keith, to all the things I knew I had to face eventually. Jason had asked Isabella earlier if she'd minded if he kept the girls for an additional night, which had enraged her. Repeatedly, she dissected the wording of his request, looking for passive aggression, rudeness, anything, and then convinced herself that she was overreacting and relented. Because Jason still had Consuelo and Vanessa, we first drove to our mother's house. Alessandra had packed up early that morning and taken the train back to New York, leaving behind a strange gloom. So Isabella and I had cleaned some, talked a good amount, and then lay on the patio sunbathing until Joan arrived from the Catskills. Joan had arrived with a cold. Very hoarsely, and perhaps exaggeratedly, she said that she was going to bed, that she was sparing us from her illness, and of course also sparing herself from having a conversation she seemed not to want to have anyway.

Our mother had just come home from some arts festival when we arrived, something about local artists, local materials. She'd sold a decent number of prints, but not everything, so Isabella and I helped her unload the remaining items from the trunk of the Volvo, all packed and neatly labeled in white boxes, and put them on the shelves in the basement, a spot Isabella noted was newly cleared of our childhood Barbie detritus, though this was not the case. It had actually happened years ago. Isabella was that way about the kitchen, too, talking as if the room were newly renovated, even though there were chips in the painted cabinets, worn hardware, permanent damage done to the farm sink. Just as she always did, Isabella inspected the avocado plants that were hardly plants, but she was ever hopeful, always eager to get excited about some sort of potential sprouting, though there was rarely any.

We considered going out to dinner but Isabella thought that the news we were about to share with our mother could not be told in public and that cooking at home made more sense. But of course we couldn't get down to real cooking what with the anticipation and all so we made a sort of hodgepodge spread out of the contents of the refrigerator, hummus, leftover lentils, cold chicken. Our mother seemed to have two reactions to our news, as she leaned casually over the sink, rinsing tomatoes and cucumbers from her garden. She appeared to be both absolutely shocked, and also not at all surprised, a sort of, oh right. Of course. There was always something a little amiss, and obviously so too. She was also certain that Joan hadn't known, though she agreed that she might have known something.

As we moved to the table and began to dissect it all, our mother recalled a strange encounter she had had with Adele not long after our father died. Apparently Adele had wanted us all to move in with her. Our mother remembered that Adele had been strangely earnest in this request, almost pathetic. The suggestion was preposterous, that my mother would leave her own house and lose the proximity to her parents. But Adele had been strange in those days, our mother told us. She was forgetful and she cried constantly. There was something theatrical about it, something that had seemed artificial, but our mother realized later that what she'd assumed was forced, wasn't that at all. It was just that Adele hadn't known how to express herself.

Adele had asked our mother one evening about her painting. She'd come up to Providence alone, which she rarely did. At first she'd talked about our father. They'd been sitting in the living room after we'd gone to bed. The light was fading, my mother told us, and despite the overwrought conversation, the room had felt peaceful, really beautiful, all the colors muted. Adele had said something about my mother moving on. She assumed that our mother never would, never could, that dating after our father would be impossible because of course she would be too grief-stricken. Adele spoke softly, our mother remembered, unemotionally, her wording somehow off, but it sounded as if she were issuing an order. You will never move on. You must never move on. Years later, my mother said, when that man suddenly appeared, however surreptitiously, she'd had to bite her tongue. A part of her had wanted to yell at Adele, she said. She'd wanted to remind Adele of the evening that she'd come over, uninvited, unannounced, and in some ways demanded that our mother preserve a memory for her that wasn't true, that had never really existed, that wasn't her business.

This was the first Isabella and I had heard of our mother knowing anything about a new strange man in Adele's life, and yes, she said, it was the man who'd come to the funeral. What in the actual fuck, I wanted to know. It turns out that our mother's hippie-dippy ways, her crunchified refusal to pass reasonable and necessary judgment had clouded her ability to reason, because this was the sort of gossip she should have reported to us immediately. What do you know, we practically shrieked at her, and what did you see. Well, actually, not all that much, unfortunately. And this was of course entering very complicated territory. Because it was no longer about Adele's life or Adele's, well, deceit I suppose, but something much more complicated. A woman's *right* to her own life, our mother said. A woman's *right* to own her own story. Then contradicting herself she recalled a rather tawdry incident where it had been quite clear that a man other than Henry, likely this Robert Redford tart, had been at the house. A few years ago, while staying there one weekend, our mother had come across a man's watch in Adele's bedroom. Adele had wanted advice about a new color for the trim in her bathroom, so our mother had wandered in with her Benjamin Moore paint deck and there was the watch, which Adele said must have belonged to Henry. My mother pointed out that Henry would never have worn such an ostentatious piece, that the watch he'd worn for over sixty years wasn't much more than a child's toy. Adele had ignored her. My mother had repeated herself, but Adele claimed to have no idea how it had gotten there. So then what, we'd wanted to know. What drama ensued after that? But there had been none, our mother said, none that she could remember.

She also can't remember exactly how she'd responded to Adele about us all moving after our father died. She may have said nothing, she told us. All she can recall is that Adele had behaved bizarrely. She'd paced the room, examining the paintings that were leaning against the wall near the door in our living room. My mother had offered to turn a light on and Adele hadn't answered her. She just crouched to look at the paintings more closely. Our mother remembers being struck by how nimble Adele was, almost like a cat. Then, though nothing had happened, Adele's mood darkened. She grew serious. She'd wanted our mother to explain each painting. But her questions were phrased awkwardly. Our mother couldn't tell what Adele was getting at. She'd started to describe a technical aspect of color mixing, but Adele interrupted her. She seemed to think our mother had a better understanding of medicine than she did, given the subject of the paintings. She got up suddenly and then sat back down on the sofa. She held her face in her hands. Then she stopped making sense.

Adele told our mother that when she was pregnant with our father, she had walked up and down the stairs backwards. Up and down, up and down, she'd repeated, and had made a strange movement with her hands. Adele's father had made her to do it, she explained, because he had been angry about the pregnancy. Our mother hadn't known what to make of this, she told us. She'd never heard a thing about Adele's father's reaction to her pregnancy. The stories that were told sounded idyllic. It had all been perfect. Our father had been the light of everyone's life. Adele had seemed to sense our mother's confusion, or shock, our mother remembers. Adele had smiled in a strained way. It was only that, silly as it may sound, she worried that walking the stairs that way might have had something to do with our father getting cancer, Adele then said, in a light tone, as if what she was saying were banal. But before our mother could respond, Adele had said, oh never mind. It was a crazy thought. Then she told our mother old stories of the spirit that lived in the house, as if my mother hadn't heard them all before. The spirit had protected Adele, but not our father, Adele had said. Then Adele had stiffened suddenly, and wanted to change the subject. She then grabbed my mother's hands in hers, pulling her slightly forward. She told my mother that they were both broken, together, and that the sadness they were experiencing would probably never fade.

Our mother had asked if Adele wanted to stay the night. Adele rarely made drives like that alone, and our mother didn't want her on the road tired or upset. Adele said that Henry would want her at home but was effusive in her thanks. My mother can't quite remember what it was Adele had said, because her phrasing had been odd throughout the evening, but as she put on her coat she alluded to men demanding things of her. It was said in a funny way and our mother wasn't sure if it really was a joke or if Adele had been trying to open up to her. They'd never discussed anything of the sort before, nothing about men or relationships, at least not seriously. That was the thing with her though, my mother said. So often it was nearly impossible to understand what Adele was getting at. My mother remembers laughing, because she was so uncomfortable and also probably over-tired. Adele had laughed, too, and then belted her coat around her waist, and our mother said something about how thin she was. She had been saying it in a concerned way but Adele had thanked her, as if it had been a compliment.

Adele then called the following morning, my mother told us, and spoke as if the previous night's visit hadn't happened. She wanted my mother to know that she'd heard, through some remarkable tangle of gossip, that our neighbor had been abandoned by her husband. She talked in a loaded, provocative way of Monica's pitiable situation. She hated to say so but Monica had very likely brought it upon herself. Adele attributed this to the arrogance and rage with which the women of my mother's hippie generation had gone about their lives, what with their wild talk of liberation and their wanton behavior, which was quite selfish really, because now these angry man-less women were raising children in the most precarious of ways. My mother had wanted to scream at her, she told us, revealing a complicated, somewhat tortured component of her relationship to Adele, territory we'd previously assumed belonged solely to Joan. Though this was absurd, of course, Alessandra pointed out later on the phone. There had been something strange about Adele's relationships to all of us. What was odd is that none of us acknowledged it, perhaps because we didn't know it was there. Or didn't want it to be.

What had actually happened with Monica, the asshole who had screamed at Darren, was that her husband, after browbeating and undermining and yelling at her for years, had simply left. My mother can't remember his name. Only that he had been pretty awful. One time in particular, she recalled, this had stood out with sharp prominence. It was because Monica had mispronounced a word. They were all on the sidewalk at the end of the driveway between the two houses. My father was still alive, standing next to my mother, and Monica's husband had made a point of correcting Monica, laughing, drawing out the moment that my mother and father had planned to play past. My mother can't remember the word, though she knows that it wasn't a particularly complex one, and that it was odd that Monica had mispronounced it. But as Monica's eyes filled with tears and her face had darkened, it had become clear that the mispronunciation had had nothing to do with her intellect and everything to do with a specific kind of exhaustion and hopelessness. She'd begun to break down, my mother realized, because she was constantly criticized, scrutinized, invalidated, among so many other things. Monica had mentioned to my mother once that she'd started to trip a lot, sometimes catching herself but often falling, dropping a child every once in a while too. She was so self-conscious, she'd said, that basic tasks began to present to her enormous challenges. Her husband was constantly watching her, so things like parallel parking, slicing an onion, drying dishes with a dish towel, had become grounds for potential shaming. She was so uncomfortable being studied this way that she'd often fumble, inviting the reproach, therefore deserving it. And each of these things, she'd insisted, she could do perfectly fine when she was alone.

Our father died four months before Monica's husband moved out, so it's unclear what he would have thought about the sudden departure, though Monica chose to see my mother in a light similar to her own. They were both abandoned women. They were in this shit together. But our father had been sick for years, my mother said, so she at least had had some warning. Monica's husband, on the other hand, just never came home one day. My mother recalls Monica's appearance changing, that she'd no longer resembled the woman she'd appeared to be years before when my parents moved into the house next door, awkwardly potting plants, struggling to bend over because she was so pregnant, but smiling, glowing, still youthful. Her hair had grown stringy and her makeup sank into the creases in her face, which she was still too young to have.

My mother felt as if she were falling apart then, too, she told us, but she was no Monica. That's what she would tell herself. At least she was not Monica, an awful thing to think or feel, she admits, but it's the truth. She described one evening watching Monica carrying two grocery bags from the garage to her back door and one of them ripping. My mother had been taking the garbage out. She'd stopped to help Monica, or she'd tried to, but Monica said that she was fine and her tone had been so bitter that my mother had backed away from her. Monica had been glaring, not at my mother, just in general, and then she'd bent over to pick up what had fallen from the ripped bag, but as she did, her purse slipped off of her shoulder and hit the other bag, forcing more to spill from it. The ground around her was a mess, her misshapen groceries spread out around her, dented apples, mangled packages of cheese, ripped pieces of brown paper. She'd dropped her purse to the ground and began to cry. So my mother put her garbage bags down and began picking up the items that had spilled and then Monica had said something like, what did we do to deserve this? My mother remembers looking up at her when she said that. My mother was embarrassed, because she couldn't say what she was thinking, which was that she couldn't possibly be as bad off as Monica was. But in Monica's mind she must have been.

Alessandra had watched the whole thing from the bathroom window, my mother told us, which we already knew. Alessandra had known that something about the scene she'd observed wasn't quite right. But there was nothing to do about it, my mother said. Being honest was out of the question. My mother couldn't tell her six-year-old that the world was unfair sometimes, particularly for women, that some women, even racist, asshole women, might find themselves sobbing in the alley when their groceries spilled, because of a litany of injustices, their accumulation striking just as all the reserves necessary to shield oneself from the pain of them runs out. Alessandra was just a child. That would have been too much. But telling her that everything was all right when it absolutely wasn't hadn't felt right either. That would be committing a kind of cardinal sin, my mother felt, subjecting her daughter to what she'd experienced as a child upon learning that little girls couldn't play baseball the way little boys could. That women couldn't really either. That that was the kind of world she lived in. But everything was all right. Really, it was.

Alessandra had told our mother that night that she'd found it strange to see an adult crying. She thought of Monica as a mean woman, someone who yelled for no reason, but she'd felt sorry for her then too. Our mother had run her fingers through Alessandra's hair, humming a lullaby or something, and Alessandra had stared at the wall, unblinking, softly describing elements of the mural that faced her bed that my mother had painted years ago. Our mother stayed there humming until Alessandra's breath got deep and even, and then she'd crept to the bathroom and stood in front of the mirror. She had wanted to see in her reflection that Monica had been wrong, that they were not in any way alike, two broken, abandoned women. But, she told us, her voice growing somber and hollow sounding, that in some ways Monica had been right. Staring back at her in the dim light of her bathroom, a place rife with painful memories, was a woman who looked old. Her time come and gone. That was the first time throughout all of that, my mother says, where she honestly just felt sorry for herself. She wasn't thinking about what our father had gone through or even what my sisters and I were experiencing. She was thinking only of her shitty luck, of the bullshit aching agony of watching someone who she'd tried to build a life around slowly die.

Poppy thought my mother's conclusion about this experience was ridiculous. She didn't look a thing like Monica, he told her the next day at the deli, that dumpy potato-looking shiksa with an attitude problem. And she didn't look old either. Did my mother want to know who actually looked old? Her mother, he told her. Her mother looked old. My mother told Poppy that he was being rude and not funny, though she'd also laughed, and Nana had made a face, sort of smirking, and said nothing. Don't get hysterical, you two, Poppy had said to them. He looked old too. Because he was old. He'd lived a lot and he had the face to show it. And Nana did, too, God bless her. God bless every one of the experiences that made her look the way she did. Because all of them had made her who she was. And she was damn near perfect, if you asked him. But my mother didn't look that way yet. She wasn't old. Sure, she'd gotten a little banged up with all this. But she still had a lot of life to live. Her time had not yet come and gone. Here, have a sandwich, he'd said to her. You're not thinking clearly. You must be hungry.

Alessandra had also observed what my mother now considers the worst night of her marriage to my father, though the fight that had caused it, she refused to go into the particulars of. All she'd say is that they'd both wanted to move past it, though they couldn't, because they were too angry to let go. So their conversation never picked up steam. Their jokes failed, each of them letting the other's attempt hang in the air, looming and empty. They weren't more than three feet from each other, my mother said, but it felt as if they were miles apart. He was staring at the floor and she was talking without looking at him. The reason the content of the fight didn't matter, my mother said, was that by then the undercurrent of all of their fights was the same. Which is to say that something else had taken over, some sinister force, and they'd both stopped trying. He couldn't help being enraged at her for failing to keep him alive, and she hated him for having asked her to try. And then suddenly Alessandra was there, my mother said, peeking in through the crack between the bathroom door and the door frame, witnessing all that ugliness.

My mother talked to Joan on the phone often around then, she says, though she avoided the most painful or serious topics, even if they were what were on her mind. She and Joan went through phases where they talked all the time, phases that would eventually taper off, and then months would pass without communication, for no real reason, and then they'd reconnect and promise to never go that long without talking again, although of course they would. It might have been that our mother didn't know how to talk about our father's death, she told us. She was incredibly self-conscious about it, even around Joan, which was a first. Because the agony of it, though different, was Joan's too. Finally our mother came out and said just that, which Joan said was relieving. Because Joan felt that way too. But Joan was also consumed by guilt, because her life was picking up, full and happy. She was in love, she realized, for the first time. She knew this because it felt nothing like anything she'd experienced before. She told our mother that she'd find herself suddenly aching, just looking at Steven, a man who never felt real to my mother, she says, despite all of Joan's descriptions of him. Joan said that he'd be seated across the room from her, reading or writing or something, just as she was, but that the sight of him, and her profound recognition of all that he brought to her, felt physically painful. She was planning to move to Cape Town, which felt sudden to my mother, even though it wasn't, my mother acknowledges, at least given the pace of Joan's life. Moving from country to country seemed not to faze her. Joan wondered if our mother would move too. Our mother told her that she'd considered it, which she hadn't really, not more than in the tiny moment that Adele had suggested it and she'd immediately dismissed it.

Joan had seemed distracted when my mother talked about Monica and about what Alessandra had observed. Wasn't Monica kind of a bitch? A bigoted one? Who cares that she cried after spilling her groceries. But what my mother was trying to tell her, was that Adele had been wrong, and that their anger—and she meant the anger of the women of my mother and Joan's generation—was still misdirected and misunderstood. They thought that they'd made breakthroughs, she'd said, and maybe they had. But not enough of them. Or not the right ones. All of this was interesting, this opening up of a part of my mother's psyche I thought I already knew. But the conversation had taken a turn. No longer were we talking about Adele, but about women in general. The ways we can be assholes. The ways we are made to be assholes. The loneliness of being an asshole when you have been made to be one. My mother felt very alone then, she told us, alone with the series of decisions she'd made. Men didn't have to defend themselves the way she'd had to. Men aren't asked to constantly justify the very act of living. It is assumed that men are doing the best they can, whereas she felt that she'd had to constantly point out that she was too.

In order to prevent us from the unnecessary suffering her mother had warned her about, my mother had tried to limit the number of sudden changes my sisters and I would face after our father died. My mother had told Nana that she would try to keep things smooth, just as they'd always been. But Nana told her that that was impossible and that suffering was simply part of life. It couldn't be staved off so my mother shouldn't exhaust herself trying, which was a rather dramatic departure from Nana's previous stance, but this was never discussed. Particularly because Nana and Poppy were incredibly helpful during those first few months, my mother told us, and afterwards too. And Leticia, my mother says, came over all the time. She'd call before she left for work or have Darren come by, often with a casserole or something, bread, cookies, a few jars of pickled vegetables. My mother recalled my obsession with Darren, that I was fascinated by him, by everything he did. If he used a particular word, I'd use it, too, sometimes out of context. Because he loved the Celtics, I'd informed my mother, before bed one night, that I did too. One evening I'd used a peculiar expression. My mother can't remember what it was. But something about the conversation, the way

I'd phrased things, made her realize that the changes she'd hoped to stave off had happened anyway, but not in the way that she'd imagined.

Isabella had become clingier, following my mother around, usually without saying much, even waiting for her outside the bathroom. When my mother would drop us off with our grandparents Isabella would watch the clock, and ask Nana repeatedly how long our mother would be away. Alessandra and I formed a bond that sometimes concerned our mother, because Alessandra could be so controlling. Or not controlling quite, but headstrong, something, and I seemed beholden to her. My mother thought about taking the three of us to therapy. She thought of going herself. But Nana kept reassuring her that everything was fine, that she should trust herself, that no stranger with a fancy degree could tell her a damn thing about her own children that she didn't already know. Instead we were to keep on keeping on, to be grateful for our health, to eat well and to move around and to kvetch when we needed to, but for the most part to just recognize that everything really was all right.

After Isabella had returned to her own house I dragged my suitcase to my childhood bedroom, telling my mother that I only planned to stay for a night or two, which was both true and untrue. I changed into my nightgown and sat in front of the bookshelf that stood between the two windows that faced the backyard, flipping through worn copies of *Nancy Drew* and *The Baby-Sitters Club*. That night I lay awake thinking of my childhood, the most mundane moments of it that had occurred in that house, the salami sandwiches I'd eaten on the back porch, the scabs I'd picked, the way the driveway had looked when covered with ice. I'd stayed up too late arguing on the phone with Keith. Something about the evening with my mother and sister had made me miss him, or made me think that I missed him. I really wanted to miss him. I wanted to want to participate in my real adult life, not my current one, the one I was cultivating as a means to avoid a real adult life, all the while claiming that a real adult life was what I truly wanted. While my mother talked I'd thought about the best parts of Keith, his normalness, his disinterest in the sorts of things that fascinated me and my sisters, my mother and Joan, how we could spend hours analyzing and theorizing about a topic it wouldn't occur to him to think twice about. It was a particular kind of confidence that he had, an ability to be present. He wasn't tempted to try to figure out the things that were out of reach, only what he could control. In that way he'd created a life for himself, one that worked and that made sense. He had no desire to expand beyond that, something that I found comforting and admirable in some moments and enraging in others.

What had become of Monica, I'd said to him, while staring out the window, assuming that he, too, would be curious. When had she and her family moved, I wondered. The house was now a different color. An addition had been constructed off the back porch where she'd once parked strollers and children's bikes. The yard was now exactingly cared for by the Sri Lankan couple who currently lived there with their young children. They drove a Prius and had built a shed that hid their garbage and recycling bins. Some years ago, the alley had been repaved and was now one-way. No longer were there the constant traffic jams, two cars bumper-to-bumper, their drivers attempting to figure out who should back out and who should stay the course, while asking after each other's families and making fun of that asshole we love and love to hate, Buddy Cianci, who had to be responsible for this mess in the first place, right?

Keith wasn't at all concerned about Monica or about the conversation with my mother and sister, and he didn't seem to understand why I was so fixated on Adele and the aspects of her personal life that she'd clearly wanted to hide. He seemed unable to access notions of curiosity, even in the abstract. What was I even doing, he'd wanted to know, and when was I coming back to New York. He then rattled off a series of arguably helpful orders packaged as suggestions, adopting a sarcastic, authoritative tone, like a leading man in a trite romantic comedy. In real life, those men—like Keith, I was learning—tend to be the sort of men who claim to want a confident, feisty woman, but who actually want to be the thing that tames a confident, feisty woman, and believe that that's what the feistiness is really about anyway. I turned so that I was lying on my back and sighed in a kind of resigned, exhausted way, because I didn't know what else to do upon realizing that I was living out a tired old trope that I hated.

The next day I walked to Nana's house to help clean her kitchen drawers, a seasonal task I've now been assisting with for six years because her arthritis makes it difficult to hoist and bend and scrub. Because I can do all three of those things just fine, whilst talking and eating matzoh with butter and cinnamon, no less, it is now our custom. When I walked into the apartment all the ingredients were laid out on the counter, the tiny jar containing Nana's perfected proportions of cinnamon to sugar, the butter dish with the large slab of unsalted butter that she still buys wholesale and stores in the freezer, and a box of matzoh.

Nana was unusually sprightly that morning because my asshole sister had called her the previous night. While I'd been occupied carefully crafting arguments both to myself and out loud to Keith, Isabella had regaled her with the tidbits we'd uncovered in Adele's journals. Isabella made most of her calls at that hour, I learned, usually after putting her daughters to bed. She often called Leticia, too, because one of the things she'd liked about marriage, and that she now missed, was the unwinding at the end of the day, the did I tell you about the interview on NPR that I heard while on the way to pick up Consuelo, or, should we have the gutters looked at. She told me not long ago though, that this unwinding, that had once felt so comforting to her, had begun to feel lonely after a while, as she'd realized that Jason wasn't really paying attention to her, but was reading the *New Yorker* or something, looking up every now and then and nodding.

Nana's response to the Adele revelation was magical, adding validity to my side of the argument with Keith. Nana was a good and reasonable woman, but she also really wanted to talk about the nitty-gritty. She was appropriately fascinated, a little appalled, maybe a bit smug. I filled a bowl with warm water and dish soap and retrieved a sponge from under the sink, one that was too worn to be used on dishes, but perfect for cleaning the insides of cupboards and drawers. Nana sat down at the kitchen table with her coffee and prepared a square of matzoh for me. We covered a lot of ground, everything from our thoughts on repressed WASP childhoods to the sexual politics of the early '80s to the white gloves Adele wore when she read the newspaper because God forbid she get ink on her hands. It wasn't until I'd reached the last set of drawers, with only the cabinet above the sink to go, that Nana mentioned in an offhand way that Adele had given her weed brownies after Poppy died, but only to help with her arthritis of course.

Nana explained that she'd developed what she referred to as "a taste" for marijuana in the '60s, and had asked my mother to bring her some. It was all the rage back then, she told me, and she'd wanted to know what the fuss was about. And why shouldn't she? She'd never gone to college. She'd never gotten to paint in Italy or kvetch in a circle with women who didn't shave their armpits. And maybe she would have liked to. So why couldn't she smoke a joint every now and then. Quite a reasonable line of thinking, I agreed.

The first time she smoked, she and my mother hotboxed the upstairs bathroom and then they'd walked to the deli to get sandwiches. And what fun it was, Nana said, the smell, the coughing, the burning lungs, the haze of smoke in that tiny room. Leticia wouldn't touch the stuff, and Poppy wouldn't either. You'll rot your brain with that drek, he'd told her. That stuff is poison. My mother and Nana had walked there arm-in-arm, which they'd never done before. They'd never been affectionate that way, Nana told me, because remember, this had been a tense time for them, what with my mother's shiny new fiancé and her ridiculous painting of the relics of the goyim. Nana had tried to determine whether her high had worn off as she stumbled about the neighborhood, clinging to my mother. Then she'd forgotten how to wave, or couldn't figure out if waving was a thing that people actually did. Had she just made it up? Was this flailing of her arm at the Silvermans a normal thing to do? Did they know that she was high as a kite and fantasizing about corned beef on rye?

Nana has never been a real smoker, she told me. She'd simply wanted to try it, and she liked it fine. So she'd maybe smoked a handful of times after that. But when Poppy got sick and she was all alone with the tasks at the deli, it really did help. Not just physically, but emotionally too. And Adele somehow knew that, Nana admitted. So maybe she had been a snob and an asshole and a shiksa princess at times, but she'd also been there for Nana at the strangest of moments, moments that made no sense for her to have understood, let alone participate in. For example, it had been Adele who had nodded without judgment when Nana had said in exasperation that she'd wanted to leave Poppy when he got sick. Why was Adele there at the deli that day, she can't recall. But she'd had some fancy hat on with fur on it. And she'd taken it off and put it on the table while Nana vented. It had been only a few sentences, really, sentiments that she couldn't admit to herself even. But a few days later Adele came back with a few neatly rolled joints in a silver and tortoiseshell cigarette case. It had looked to her as if Nana's back hurt, she'd said. Here, have these.

It was that when Poppy got sick, he got mean, Nana said. That's what she'd accidentally let slip out to Adele. It had broken her heart. Her Irving, who'd never been mean, was suddenly mean. Nana found it unbearable. It was as if he became somebody else, somebody she didn't know at all.

She thinks it was that he was scared. Because for most of his life he was rarely sick. Even with the flu or a stomach bug. Things like that just didn't get to him. He was used to his body working. Or used to not having to think about it. But when he got sick he started snapping at Nana, sometimes even yelling. He'd ask her to do something for him, like get him a glass of water or straighten a blanket but he couldn't explain exactly what he wanted her to do so she couldn't do it the way he wanted her to. The problem was that he couldn't face that he could no longer do those types of things himself, Nana said. So he took it out on her. That's what happens when people get terrified.

After he'd yelled at her for what felt like the hundredth time she thought, I'm done. I'm leaving. She even walked out of the hospital room. She got all the way to the cafeteria and sat down at a table and drank a Coke. But then she thought, where the hell am I going to go? She was in her seventies. She didn't even know how to drive. On the elevator back up to Poppy's room she thought about how he sat down when they'd argued. She'd actually hated it. It felt condescending to her. He'd tell her that he'd always fight fair. Even when he was angry. And then he'd pull his pant legs up and sit down. She'd tell him, you want a cookie? You think I can't yell at you when you're standing up? The first time she said that to him he'd laughed at her. Really laughed. Nana doesn't remember what they'd been fighting about but his laughing just made her angrier. He'd tried to hug her, in the midst of their fight, and at first she wouldn't let him. But then she'd laughed, too, and had reluctantly hugged him back. In the hospital elevator, on the way back up to his room, Nana started crying. She wasn't alone. There was a young family with her and they'd behaved as if nothing was happening, as if she were just a sad old lady, which she was, a realization that made her cry harder. Poppy was fast asleep when she got back to his room so she sat on his bed and held his hand and just kept crying. Then that night she lit one of those little joints in that fancy case. It was freezing outside but she didn't care. She had her coat on over her bathrobe and she inhaled and held the smoke in her lungs and then coughed like crazy, just like she'd done with my mother. And then she went back inside and fried herself an egg and watched *Jeopardy* and laughed until she fell asleep.

Lou died only a few months before Poppy did, but Leticia's experience was different. Poppy had developed lung cancer so his body had deteriorated, but Lou had Alzheimer's so his mind deteriorated. Leticia sat with him in the hospital for hours and he was as polite as can be, but he didn't recognize her. Sometimes they held hands and sang the songs they'd liked when they were younger and every once in a while, for a second, his eyes would light up, as if he remembered something, but when he tried to explain it to her his words failed him. Leticia thought she wouldn't be able to go on without him. She told Nana that she was certain that she'd die in her sleep within days of his death. He forgot everything, she said. He forgot who she was. He even forgot that he loved her.

All of this was particularly painful because the possibility of Lou forgetting Leticia was something that hadn't occurred to either of them. Leticia forgetting Lou though, was something else entirely. Please don't forget me, he'd asked of her before he got locked up, so for years Leticia had done everything she could to reassure him that she wouldn't. She'd written him letters every day, each letter addressed with a different silly nickname, because Lou loved nicknames. His father had told him as a child that the worst names are the ones that never become nicknames. You never want to be the kid without a nickname, Lou had often said to us, justifying all the absurd things we were called. But because there are only so many nicknames you can make with the name Lou, Leticia had ended up calling him the names of notable athletes, politicians, anything really, just like she'd done with my mother with the painters and my sisters and me with the Yiddish and the Bob Dylan songs. It was to be funny, of course. But it was also her way of telling Lou that she would never forget him.

Lou had liked routines. He said that it was because of having been in prison for so long. He didn't like surprises. He wanted to know what was going to happen each day and at what time. Nana is the same way. She always has been. But Leticia didn't understand it. She told Nana that she found the regimented part of her life with Lou difficult. He never wants to just go out to eat some night, she told Nana. She had to tell him about it first. Leticia eventually got very regimented herself. It started because she wanted to accommodate Lou's needs but she ended up liking it. Then she'd tap her wrist and make a tsk-tsk noise if Nana was late. As Lou got sicker he no longer needed his routine. He didn't seem to understand the concept of one either. So Leticia would try to cover for him. She'd say that it was time to leave or that it was time for lunch, when before he would have been the first one to say so.

Nana got rides to the hospital to visit Poppy from one of the neighborhood kids she'd hired when Lou could no longer work either. Renzo was his name. Renzo started to drive Leticia around too. And because both of their husbands were often in the same hospital, for a while they coordinated their visits. In the car on the way home from one of them Leticia told Nana that she had to learn to drive. Nana told her that she didn't want to, that Poppy wouldn't want her driving anyway. This isn't about Irving, Leticia said to her, and she had a point. So Nana walked to the DMV a few days later and enrolled in a driver's education course. Leticia went to some of the classes with her. She thought they were boring, but Nana loved them. She liked memorizing the rules and practicing in the parking lot. She started looking forward to the days she had class. Those little breaks made Poppy's temper and sickness more bearable. When he was cranky she would shut her eyes and picture driving across the Seekonk River with the windows open. But after she got her license she only drove once. It was four days after Poppy's funeral and she didn't even make it to the Henderson Bridge. She got a few blocks from her apartment but the glare from the sun was so bright that she couldn't see a thing. So she'd turned around and gone home and called Leticia, telling her that it had all been a waste. It wasn't a waste, Leticia told her. She had needed to show herself that she could do it. And she could do it. If she really wanted to, she could do it. In the meantime Renzo could drive them wherever they needed to go.

After they were both widowed, Nana and Leticia thought about trying to run the deli themselves but my mother talked them out of it. Leticia had thought that it would give them something to do, something to fill their days. By then she was living in an in-law apartment at her niece's house. And Nana was living in her new place, too, which my mother had painted, the first floor of a two-family a few blocks closer to us. My mother had also removed the stucco in the kitchen, replacing it with bright white tiles, and had put in hand rails for elderly people in the bathroom, which Nana didn't really like but she knew my mother was trying to be helpful so she didn't say anything. Nana started reading a lot more then and Leticia did too. They both love biographies. Their favorite for quite a while was one about Louis Armstrong. One night Leticia called Nana close to midnight, or maybe after. Louis Armstrong was addicted to laxatives, she'd apparently said, completely absorbed in the book and unaware of the time, something that had never before happened to either of them. They did their grocery shopping together once a week and they still had lunch together almost every day. At first they went to the diner where many of their old regulars from the deli went. The regulars used to come up to their table and talk about the good old days. Poppy had loved those guys, Nana recalled. He loved that people thought of the deli as theirs, too, that they'd come every day and sit in the same place and eat the same thing. He used to offer people samples, but not small samples. He'd scoop large portions of smoked bluefish into to-go containers or cut three or four slices of pastrami and wrap them in wax paper and hand them out. He'd get excited when they got new items or a particularly good batch of something. In that way Poppy hadn't really had a mind for business, Nana says. He had good instincts about people and that's not nothing, but it was Nana who kept the books, Nana who managed the finances. Sometimes Poppy pushed her. Not often, but he'd do his sort of strutting thing and talk to her as if all her precautions and planning were meaningless. She'd tell him not to scoop out that much fish, or to only give half a slice of meat for samples, or not to give out any samples at all. They'd made money but not that much. During lunch at the diner one day Nana told Leticia that she'd gotten angry sorting through old business papers after she'd sold the deli. They could have done better, she said. They could have made more money. But Leticia told her that she only felt that way because she was sad. This was grief. But God was playing a trick on her. He wouldn't let her just be sad.

It was around this time that Adele began to call Nana and to talk as if they were closer than they were. She'd sounded so silly on the telephone that first time, Nana said, that she thought that Adele was singing. But that was just the way Adele talked apparently, Nana learned. Adele told her that she wanted to be helpful to her and Leticia, which they didn't know what to make of it at first. But Henry was still alive at this point so they assumed that Adele felt sorry for them because they'd been widowed, which they had to admit was very nice. And they'd always thought very highly of Henry, Nana said. For years they'd actually felt bad for him, trapped by Adele and her problems. It was after dinner one evening at Adele's house that Nana sampled her first weed brownie. It was just the three women. Henry was either out or in his study. Leticia, of course, opted for decaf only. But Nana got stoned again, and then had to ask the kind young man who'd been outside chopping wood, the one who'd made the weed brownies, to help her up the stairs to a bed-room. Then, because she was so high, she'd curled up in bed and talked to this young man for quite a while. He told her that he made weed butter in Adele's kitchen and used it in a variety of baked goods. He should talk to Leticia, Nana told him. Leticia was the best baker she knew. But that's all she remembers.

CHAPTER ELEVEN

This was all a bit much. Or I was a bit much. I couldn't
tell. That my grandmother smoked weed, that I was,
according to Keith, unwilling to let go of the things
that held me back because I was obstinate, that it felt as
if the whole world was spinning precariously. I was struggling to make sense of all of it, and struggling, Keith said,
to maintain the childish buffer I'd developed. In a rare
analytic moment, he pointed out that my obsessing over
Adele's past, however understandable, was also enabling
me to avoid truly considering my present circumstances,
not just Adele's absence from them, but their directionless
absurdity. Not unlike the way that dogs often respond more
deferentially to male authority—I think because of a particular baritone arrogant certainty women often lack—I took
Keith's bait and thought for a bit about returning to New
York, to bravely face it all, but hours later found myself instead back at Adele's house, sitting in the driveway in the
old Corolla just after the sun had set. I called Keith back,
knowing full well that he wouldn't pick up because he'd
sensibly and predictably be at CrossFit, having paid for a
yearlong membership to throw around giant truck tires in a
basement with intentionally harsh lighting. So I left a heart-
felt voicemail because adults leave voicemails as opposed
to corresponding solely by text, and headed inside to sulk
and eat eggs.

Joan was back too. She was in the kitchen, drinking
wine, the remains of her dinner on a plate that had been

pushed to the side, overcooked asparagus, a picked-at baked potato. She ate this way at home, she told me—and I was struck that she called the place home—because it reminded her of her childhood, the years when Adele had been happy, years I'd never heard her describe before. It was when Joan was about thirteen, she said, or maybe sometime later. Adele had told her that she didn't want to be so formal anymore, that she was exhausted being so set in her ways. This coincided with a trip Henry took to Paris. He went alone, Joan says, for what she has no clue. But there were weeks, maybe a month, or it could have been only a few days, that Adele had done the cooking. The two of them had sat on the porch one evening barefoot. They'd eaten boiled potatoes with butter and no salt. They'd talked about ghosts, about the certainty of the waves, all the while also saying that there was nothing certain about them.

I began to cry. Something about the haziness of Joan's memory, my exasperation with Keith, my hunger, my inability to recall an image of Adele. What had she looked like, sitting there, decades ago, on the porch, eating boiled potatoes. What was she wearing, and how was her hair styled. Did she laugh, or ask Joan to sit up straight. Was she already slipping away. I fried two eggs and sat down next to Joan, her hands, I saw for the first time, so similar to Adele's, long fingers, and veiny, bony knuckles. Don't worry so much about this boyfriend, she said, or the particulars of life that can't be controlled. I nodded at her, whatever that meant. So we began sifting through the journals again. Joan had brought down a stack from her bedroom, having noted, in my absence, a strange gap, a disruption in the regularity of Adele's entries, but even more shocking, for her but not me, were Adele's entries about Joan, Adele watching her conquer the world, with love and awe and wonder. That Adele had ever felt this way was news to Joan. She'd always believed that Adele hadn't known what to do with her, she said, which was understandable. Adele hadn't.

Joan also admitted that she felt horribly guilty reading

the journals. They recalled an experience she'd had years ago, when she was living in Barcelona in her late thirties with a strapping, black-eyed anthropologist named Arturo, and Alessandra had called to tell her about the scene Adele had made at the deli. She'd said that Adele had yelled like a madwoman. It was that word that had struck her, Joan said, because it wasn't one she'd heard Alessandra use before. Joan had been sitting in the hall of the apartment she'd been renting, which she'd turned into a writing nook, stacking her books by the entryway, and using an antique console table that she'd bought at an outdoor market as a desk. She'd gotten up and had started straightening the books in a frenzied way, she said, not accomplishing anything.

She spoke to my mother a few days later and she remembers how she was sitting for some reason, awkwardly perched on the ottoman at the foot of her bed, and that my mother had had a sore throat so she hadn't sounded like herself. At the beginning of each of my mother's hoarse sentences, Joan had cringed preemptively, she told me, her whole body tensing, because she'd expected that my mother would say something about the way that Adele had behaved too. But my mother wanted to hear about Joan's life, about Arturo, Barcelona. She told Joan that she'd been shocked by how hard Joan had taken the criticism of her book. She'd assumed that that sort of thing wouldn't get to Joan. My mother's comment upset Joan. Not that it was off base. It wasn't. But it made her feel lonely. She remembers wondering self-consciously if it looked to my mother as if she were flailing, swirling in chaos, while my mother rooted herself in marriage and motherhood.

Later Joan had tried to sort out her reactions to these conversations with Arturo and he'd been oddly combative, or simplistic, or both. Only you control how you feel, he'd said. That little girl and your best friend and your mother, they can't do this to you. Joan felt defensive. Do what to me, she'd asked him. All she'd said was that the experience had been confusing. The issue was that it was what she'd always wanted, she told me. She was the one who, all along, had insisted so vehemently that everyone acknowledge all of the things about Adele that were suddenly so visible that day at the deli. She was the one who had wanted to tear Adele down, to expose her, to pay her back for all the years of indifference and disdain. And the truth is that a part of her had liked that Adele's upper-class bullshit pretensions had been revealed. But she'd found herself simultaneously feeling sorry for her too. As she listened to Alessandra talking that day, mesmerized by the peculiar, unexpected behavior of the adults she knew so well, she felt a protective, poignant love for Adele, faults and all.

This then led to collective wallowing, me in the fog of a stupid argument, and Joan in a past she couldn't help herself from revising as she relayed it, despite her training as a historian. She swirled her wine in her glass and began to wax poetic about Barcelona, the city that had saved her, she said, that she'd been certain, at numerous points, that she'd never leave. I raised my eyebrows. Because if I know anything it's that Joan can't—and has never been able to—keep herself from fleeing one ancient city for another. She ignored this though, and instead talked about Arturo. She'd met him through her publisher, she told me, though she'd already heard of him, as they'd been in the same circles, years before in New York, a colorful crowd of radical '70s intellectuals. They'd run into each other at a party in London, one that Joan had been nervous about attending, because at that point socializing had overwhelmed her. The backlash after the publication of her book she'd found unbearable, she told me. All the critiques, the strange ways she was torn apart, or her words were, all of it in permanent, indelible print, in the publications everyone she knew read. She couldn't escape talking about it, no matter where she went or how hard she tried to change the subject. She was accused of both intentionally destroying the legacy of a great man and of abandoning women, of failing as a feminist scholar, because she'd focused so little on female roles, though she hadn't ignored them, she points out. In one particularly stinging review she was accused of attempting to exclude women from the historical record. And this callous rebuke, she said, had been written by a woman, a fellow historian, one who had very likely experienced similar backlash throughout her own career. So Joan had responded to the journal, attempting to explain herself. This was a retelling of only one particular aspect of financing, she said, one that had been administered by one man. This was not a rejection of women or feminism. She'd simply been writing about something else. But her response had only generated more criticism. She'd gotten to a point where she hated leaving her flat. She sequestered herself, she recalls, with books, rations. It was grandiose, Adele pointed out to her on the telephone, which was absurd coming from Adele, Joan thought, even though she was absolutely correct.

Henry had warned her about this sort of thing, Joan recalled, but at the time she hadn't really paid attention to him, or she hadn't understood what he'd been getting at. And of course Henry had loathed all reviewers anyway, considering them panderers, frauds. Arturo thought so, too, but of course, Joan said, he'd been so unshakable, at least in terms of his confidence. That had been one of the things she'd liked so much about him in the first place, the way that nothing could sway him from believing in one of his own ideas. So when he'd suggested that she move to Spain to be with him, she was all for it, too eager perhaps, to escape the London scene, her Kensington flat, her routines, her friends. And by then she and Arturo had become inseparable, she said, cloyingly so. Everything about their time together was extreme—their meals, their wine, their fights, their reconciliations, their passion, their rage. And everyone should have a love like that at some point, too, Joan said. But ultimately, it's better to find love that's less volatile, she added, somewhat sadly. I told her that Keith was never volatile, that I was the volatile one. But you can't force it either, she said. You can't let your age or some silly preconceived notion back you into a corner. Is that what it looked to her like I was doing, I asked her, and she responded like Adele would have. No, no, of course not. She was only saying.

In Barcelona's Jewish quarter Joan took long walks in the afternoons, winding through narrow streets lined with crumbling stone structures, awed by the dexterity of tiny European cars, by windows that opened onto the street, by the minute mechanisms of an evolving historic city. Arturo usually stayed behind in his dark office, escaping the heat to work. One day Joan lit candles with a priest, having wandered into a square with a large basilica that she'd thought at first was empty because it was under extensive renovation. For some reason she'd stopped to peek inside. Then a man had smiled at her and beckoned for her to come in. There was scaffolding all over the place, she said, but it was still beautiful, with dark glossy panels of wood and delicate stained glass positioned high above the altar, so that colored rays of sunlight filtered throughout the vast room. For the rest of her time in Barcelona, she said, which was almost a year, she walked to that cathedral nearly every afternoon to light candles. Before she left she asked the priest why he'd invited her in that first day, why he'd allowed her to participate in a ritual that she didn't really believe in, or had no context for. It was because he knew that she'd needed to be there, he told her. He knew that she'd needed to come inside, and to feel God, even for just a moment. And maybe he was right, Joan said laughing. Because that was one of the things she missed most when she went back to London. She couldn't describe what it was she'd felt there, other than that something about it had seemed to her so emblematic of that perfect, magical city. She told me that if she hadn't loved Barcelona as much as she had, she probably would have ended things with Arturo sooner. Because eventually she'd found his volatile love to be too exhausting. She realized that his genius, his beautiful reckless spirit, was partly fed by conflict. Without it he was listless, sort of like a tired child, and once she faced that, she couldn't make herself stay.

Adele's written descriptions of Joan's life conveyed something entirely different. In her journals she described her daughter as headstrong, brilliant, a fearless single woman with limitless freedom. Joan's life abroad, she recounted meticulously, building on details likely described to Adele in letters and phone conversations. Her pride in her daughter's success was palpable, as was her envy and loneliness. It was also clear that Adele had had no clue that we'd all talked so much about her deli outburst or that it had defined, for my mother's people, the stark divide between the two families, at least for quite a while. There is no mention of it in her journals. At the time that it happened, along with her accounts of Joan living an idealized life of independent womanhood, she wrote most frequently, and very tenderly, about Henry, capturing the everyday moments of life with him, that he drank exactly one-and-a-half cups of coffee every day but insisted on pouring himself two, that he refused to use bookmarks, instead relying on his memory of the last page he'd read, a good habit, he said, something that young people hadn't the prudence and good sense to do. There was one mention of Howie, that Adele had attempted to establish boundaries with him. He'd apparently wanted to atone. That was the word she'd used. Though the sentences are cryptic, it was clear that she'd rebuffed, for years, his attempts to get to know his son. But this was a trivial thing, she seemed to be saying. Much more important was her daughter, out there conquering the world, or trying to.

Back in London Joan turned her energy to fixing up her apartment, finding work, reintegrating herself into the circles she'd only a few years before enthusiastically abandoned. But she couldn't gain momentum. Her work bored her. Her lectures, when she was asked to give them, fell flat. Adele wrote that she was certain that this could not be the case. Her daughter was far too intelligent to give a dull talk. Joan then began to travel by herself. Such a luxury, Adele wrote, recalling her time in Paris as a young mother. Joan visited Bombay, Marrakesh, Tangier, sending Adele postcards from each place. She stayed for almost a month in Edinburgh and then spent two weeks touring Serbia, which she'd loved. When she met Steven, her suitcases were still packed, stacked against the wall next to her closet. How ridiculous, Adele wrote, but oh what she would have done to have had those sorts of experiences too. How she had longed for an escape, to have been carefree, though there was a caveat. Adele was concerned about Joan's wandering. There was a restlessness to women these days that really was a bit much.

Then the entries stopped for a while, except for a few reports about Henry's failing health. Adele seemed to have wanted to focus on the good days, the days where Henry's movements resembled those of a healthy man, but her sense of hopelessness or impending doom permeated each page, affecting her interpretation of the world around her. She was furious, for example, that Joan had moved to South Africa. The country was a war zone, she wrote. How could Joan do such a thing. Even though she knew full well that Joan could do such a thing because this was the sort of thing that Joan had always done. Joan had arrived in Cape Town right before apartheid finally ended, when the whole country was whirling, and Adele recognized that this would be attractive to Joan, this tumult, just like the '60s, when she'd been so brash. And now she'd married a foreigner who was just like her, always chasing after something.

Joan had written to Adele that Steven had done a considerable amount of work with people who'd been imprisoned while the National Party was in power, and then released when Nelson Mandela was elected, but he wasn't sure what to do with his research. So they'd decided to work on a project together, cataloging and analyzing all the recordings he'd made. They found interesting trends in the ways that people talked about their imprisonment, how it factored into the way they saw themselves and their ability to connect to the political scene in South Africa. A lot of this Joan couldn't pick up on as easily as Steven could, she told Adele, because she was still getting used to the culture there. So the irreverent, hilarious anecdotes and the easy flowing sarcasm that was often interwoven within descriptions of traumatic, horrifying experiences seemed out of place to her, almost jarringly so. But Steven told her that what she was observing was a form of resistance, a way that people had learned to balance the agony of imprisonment with a sense of hope. Joan and Steven would sit together, she had written to Adele, on the floor of their new living room, the tape recorder between them, each taking notes. When he was killed, Adele wrote, they'd gotten through only about half of the eighty or so hours of recordings he'd made.

At this point Joan's voice grew faint. She closed the journal, her eyes filling with tears, and she pushed it away from her across the table. She began to shake her head. I got up, I think to hug her, but she reached out and pushed the journal farther, so that it fell to the floor, startling Roo. She told me that she didn't want to read anymore, she didn't want to remember it, and she didn't want to know what her mother had thought about it either. But when I bent over to pick up the journal, she pushed it further out of my reach with her foot. Don't you look either, she said. I told her that I'd been planning to put them all away, that I wouldn't read another page. She didn't say anything for a while. And then she began to tell me the story, much of which I already know, that she claimed she didn't want to remember.

Steven had picked up on a story in Zimbabwe. It had seemed beneath him, Joan said, and she'd told him that. It was just another weird skirmish, nothing of real substance. But he'd believed that that was how to figure out what was really going on, by paying attention to the minor acts that might seem disconnected and not part of a larger narrative. That was what he'd been doing by listening to the experiences of people who'd been imprisoned. He was right about the people in prison, Joan admitted, but she was right about

the skirmish. No one even talked about it after that, she recalled. It hadn't even made the news. No one said anything
about his truck having been held up by bandits, men who
were silly, violent nobodies. They weren't working for anyone and the attack wasn't political. Everything about it was
senseless.

About a year and a half later, Henry died. And because
Steven's death had been such a shock to Joan, Henry's death
felt that way too. She experienced them as one thing, she
told me, as if they'd occurred together. It was as if she'd entered a fog, she said. Time had stopped. There were weeks,
months even, that she couldn't quite account for. All she
knew was that she'd wanted nothing disrupted, nothing to
change. She told friends that she was waiting for some signal, a signal that never materialized of course. But the truth,
on some level, was that she didn't want to let go, to move on,
to dust surfaces again, to open windows. She tried to apologize to Adele on the telephone, for not having grasped how
sick Henry had been, even though she wasn't actually all that
concerned about whether she'd offended Adele or not. What
she felt was that she'd done something wrong, somehow
failed at something, and she couldn't manage the immensi-
ty of her grief alone. She wanted some sort of external pro-
nouncement, or punishment, something to unfurl her. Adele
had been a mess then, too, completely frantic, Joan told me.
On the telephone she'd made no sense, saying that the mist
from the sea had begun to penetrate her bones, that she was
worried that it was beginning to rot the house. She then had
said something about Howie. This was the first time Joan
remembers hearing his name. Joan had asked her to repeat
herself, and Adele had said, oh never mind, in an exasperated way, as if she'd been trying desperately to explain something that Joan had been refusing to hear.

Joan flew to Rhode Island for Henry's funeral, and
stayed longer than she'd planned to, in her childhood bedroom again at the back of the house. She was a wreck, she

said, sobbing at the drop of a hat. She dreamt of Steven almost every night, often waking up suddenly, images of his destroyed body flashing before her. Drinking coffee in the morning with Adele she felt drugged and sluggish, unable to maintain her end of the conversation, which Adele didn't seem to notice. Then at dinner one evening Adele spoke about Howie and Henry interchangeably, and at this point Joan began to wonder about the journals she'd taken after my father died. By then, she said, she'd almost forgotten about them. That night, waking from one of her feverish dreams, she heard something in the hall downstairs, so she'd walked to the landing and peered over the banister. Adele stood in front of the window, holding one of Henry's tweed jackets in one hand and what looked to be a single glove in the other. She was saying something. At least her lips were moving, and she kept shaking her head, as if she were trying to recite a poem the words of which she could no longer remember.

Joan didn't sleep well the entire time she was at the house. She'd become suddenly jittery when she'd lie down, unable to find a comfortable position. She realized, after a few nights, that she was angry, though the feeling was unfixed, not about one particular thing. It was about the loss of her father and everything he'd represented, and about Steven, too, that she had had to wait too long for him, and then he'd been taken from her, before they'd had the chance to settle at all. And she really had wanted to settle, she said. Everyone talked as if all she'd ever done was flee. But she'd never fled from Steven. She'd never even wanted to. Not once.

Adele wrote only a single sentence about Steven dying. And there was no mention at all of Henry's death besides the bulletin from his funeral that she'd stuck in between pages of her journal dated months afterwards. But she described in detail a conversation with Joan about the ghost, which Joan had no memory of, and seemed almost annoyed to read. She never would have said such a thing to Adele, Joan said, though she clearly had. She'd described that she'd turned on her side while lying in bed one night, so that she could face the window and see the waves crashing onto the shore, something that had comforted her as a child. The window was open and she'd reached forward, touching the windowsill, so that she could feel the dampness of the air outside. And then there was a stirring. She'd turned slightly, to see what it was, but saw only the gray silhouettes of her childhood bedroom at night, a dresser by the wall near the door, a wingback chair, a Guerlain trunk with Henry's initials on it. She'd felt suddenly certain that whatever she was feeling was the same thing that had moved the stones of the cemetery when she was a child, though she couldn't quite explain how or why. She awoke the next morning to heavy rain, dark clouds low on the horizon, and announced to Adele that she'd stayed long enough and was finally ready to return to her house in Cape Town.

Joan has only the faintest memory of the weeks that followed, really just disconnected snippets. She knows that she purchased a return flight and then packed her suitcase in a daze, and that the plane ride to Johannesburg felt interminable. She'd been unable to focus on whatever she was reading, but was too rattled or edgy to sleep. Then she became disoriented on the drive to her house and almost didn't recognize it because it seemed to her so startlingly untouched. She realized that she'd expected her seemingly never-ending grief and Steven's death to be visible in its architecture, boards collapsed, the roof caving in.

At first she felt like a stranger there, she said. She kept forgetting which one was the silverware drawer, where she'd stored the laundry detergent. She went days without sleeping. As Steven had, she found the sudden afternoon thunderstorms of summer soothing, the heat and the moisture and the smell of the earth a sort of tonic. She began to organize his papers. She contacted Cape Town University's oral history archives and offered to donate his research. She published two articles on their findings. She'd written them

quickly, distantly, early in the morning while still buzzing from too much coffee. In a subsequent issue of one of
the publications an anonymous reader wrote a dazzlingly
self-absorbed and brutal critique of one of her pieces. She
found it hilarious, she said, the whole system. The striving
for scholarly victories and the smug community such eru-
dite work is intended for. She then went back and reread
her articles. She couldn't determine whether she liked them
or not, or whether she agreed or disagreed with the critique.
She had no memory of having written them.

Alone in the house that had once symbolized all the happiness of a new beginning, she began to yearn for her father,
for his office with its books and polished wooden furniture,
vibrantly lit by the fire in the large stone fireplace. She felt
suddenly confident, capable of being in his formidable presence without losing her point of view. There was something
trite about this realization, she felt, something annoyingly cli-
chéd, that now that he was gone, she understood what she'd
been trying to grasp at all those years. She started talking to
a therapist. She explained to the therapist, while seated in
a black Eames chair, that she wanted to work through her
grief. She shouldn't be angry anymore. She certainly didn't
want to be, but she couldn't explain why or what she was getting at. She talked about Steven's goodness, the pureness of
it. She joked that he'd reminded her of my mother. People
like Steven and my mother lingered on the periphery, Joan
said. They didn't demand attention, but were content or willing to stay back, to chart their own paths. They were actually
stronger than the rest of us, maybe kinder, too, though that
sort of thing wasn't always immediately obvious.

One afternoon she told her therapist that she was terrified that she'd forget what Steven had looked like. She
started describing the face he made when he shaved, but
then somehow, remembered the dent in Henry's thumb-
nail, which as a child she'd assumed had something to do
with Germany and World War II though it had actually
happened in Gramercy Park when Henry was a child. He'd

spent most of his free time with his sister, wandering the neighborhood. They'd figured out how to travel seven blocks without touching the sidewalk by going through basements and over roofs. Henry got the dent in his thumb because his sister accidentally slammed the heavy iron door that led to the roof of a building six doors from theirs, before Henry let go of the frame where they balanced before jumping onto the stairs. Joan had learned this as a child, late one night when she'd been unable to sleep. When she woke that way, suddenly alert and too aware of the darkness, she'd walk to her parents' room and rouse Henry, but never Adele. Henry would put his fingers to his lips and she'd stand still, watching as he reached for his robe and slippers, and then they'd tiptoe down the hall lined with oriental runners, rugs that did nothing to diminish the creaking sounds of the old wooden floors. Back in her bedroom, Henry would pull the wingback chair a few feet closer to her bed and tell her stories about his childhood as she drifted back to sleep. Her favorite involved his waking up one night to the sound of heavy scraping, which turned out to be his father and a crew of men unloading crates of sugar from four parked cars in front of their building and carting them into the basement. Joan's grandfather had had a number of sugar plantations in Havana, and during prohibition he'd set up a hugely profitable bootlegging operation in the basement of his building and the three that surrounded it. Henry had explained to Joan that alcohol requires a good deal of sugar and that one of the ways the government clamped down on bootlegging was by monitoring the quantities of sugar that bigger companies imported into New York. But Henry's father didn't accurately report how much he was importing. Henry found the whole setup one day in the basement, huge vats of distilled alcohol that smelled sweet and heavy and medicinal. Then a few days later he discovered that the tunnel that he'd used to cross East 20th Street was blocked off, as were the rooftop doors and another side entrance to a building on East 18th, so he and his sister started playing outdoors, wandering the avenues or driving their father's car to the tip of Manhattan to throw rocks in the water.

Because I couldn't avoid it any longer I finally packed my duffle bag and returned to New York. Keith looked paler than usual, which he said had less to do with his actual pallor than my having a radiant tan, a result of my joblessness, a fair point. We had dinner at a new Vietnamese place and then made fervent love, the particulars of which I read too much into. I'd wanted to feel something undeniable, and maybe he did, too, but the truth is that the experience was an awful lot like being jostled through a car wash. That night I couldn't quell the knot in my stomach so I left him in bed and did a crossword puzzle in the bathroom while eating organic M&Ms.

The next morning I emailed my boss, Leon, about resuming work, and he responded by suggesting that we meet in person. Coffee, perhaps? We met two days later. We sat on the sidewalk of a café near the office and he admired Roo's mild manners, how not even the most trifling of pigeons seemed to bother her. He asked if I'd considered graduate school. I told him that I had not. We reviewed my work for him, and I talked at length about Jay, who I'd met at the women's facility, a real battle-axe. The extent of the project had entailed implementing six small farm gardens in prisons in upstate New York. My team had overseen operations in two locations, a men's medium-security prison and a women's facility, which already had gardens. On our first day Jay had given us a brief tour through the yard, pointing out the splintered wood and scrap metal fences that surrounded raised cinder block beds filled with rows of vegetables.

The first thing I had noticed about Jay was that she seemed abnormally centered, a straight-shouldered, average height woman, with black hair, graying in wisps near her temples that she slicked back in a tight bun. In marked contrast to my habits with men, I tend to collect women, having a knack for recognizing the good ones, and then I cling to them desperately, refusing to ever let go. Jay became a friend, and my confidante for the project, informing me about what was and wasn't working, the inner mechanisms of the facility, the secrets, the routines, the resentments, the injustices. One afternoon she walked me back and forth through a section of our most recent installation and pointed out that the idiosyncrasies of each woman were evident in her garden. Meesa's frightened, she'd told me, standing in front of a fragile looking tomato plant. She told me that she and her friends would jokingly call their gardens their bodegas. Did anyone want some lettuce, she'd yell. Okay. Hold on. I'll go to the bodega. I learned that she'd been in prison for twenty-six years for killing her abusive ex-boyfriend and then paying someone she'd trusted, who eventually ratted her out, to dump his body behind a shipping container in a factory lot in Queens. She had been unable to escape from him. He found her when she fled to her cousin's apartment, her parents' house, and a cheap hotel in New Jersey, where he re-broke her eye socket, cracked her femur, and shattered a part of her pelvis when he kicked her down a flight of stairs. She had a master's degree in psychology and had started a support group within the prison for victims of domestic violence. She'd survived breast cancer, a fractured jaw, two concussions, and the deaths of her parents, a sibling, three friends, and two cousins, while behind bars.

Throughout the years, Jay had become acquainted with a cadre of notable women who, for various reasons, had also wound up in prison. A few of the names I recognized from the rants I had paid so little attention to years ago when Isabella was just beginning to find herself intellectually in college, when she'd seemed to me off-puttingly paradoxical and severe. Because while she'd shrieked about the intellectual and physical valor of the radical women who marched and threw bombs and taunted the establishment, demanding respect, equality, and acknowledgement, Isabella herself had been shrinking, receding, a symbolic and physical silencing that affected her posture, her voice, her ability to defend herself. I told her recently, while seated on her kitchen counter, next to a wooden bowl of exactly five organic lemons, that for too long, I'd misjudged her, had written her off, had not fully grasped her nuanced and rather profound worldview. We'd been in the process of planning Consuelo's seventh birthday party, an afternoon that involved a visit to the dump and a local recycling station, as Consuelo is also an avid environmental justice activist. Consuelo had requested that we prepare a short speech to be delivered while the quinoa and avocado cake was being served. Not all of her friends recycle, she'd sighed, exactly the way Isabella did. When I'd first began to call Isabella, to report on all that I was learning at work and just how much it had begun to transform my thinking, she'd sighed in an aggrieved way, which I took to mean, I know all this, I've fucking been here all along, how could you have failed to see me. This was understandable, though it's also true that I really had come to see her.

Keith had little interest in or patience with the prison project, or my work in general. He teased me about it, always playfully, suggesting that I was unable to grasp the broader implications of my interests, that I viewed the affairs of the world through a narrow, simplistic lens. He laughed at my sincerity, my incredulity, my anguished horror and guilt. I threatened to punch him in the throat. I told him that he was a vapid asshole. I accused him of trying to dampen my spirit. But I didn't break up with him. Instead, I'd stomp from my apartment, Roo at my heels, to my favorite falafel vendor three blocks away. If the line wasn't too long, I'd order two—one for me and one for Roo—and then I'd rant, my mouth full of pita and breaded spiced chickpeas, into my cell phone to Isabella. I'd leave Keith in my apartment, stunned by the magnitude of my rage, as most people are when it happens, but not quite moved enough to chase me, which only enraged me further.

The farms my coworkers and I set up in the women's prison were much more successful than the ones in the men's prison, despite the fact that the men's prison had more participants, more space, and a larger allotment of our overall budget. One of my roles in the conclusion of the project was to determine why the outcomes in each facility were so vastly different without asking people insulting questions or blaming the staff, who'd already made it clear that they thought we were out-of-touch assholes, which, in a sense, we were. One afternoon I asked a man in his fifties, who read Baldwin and Ellison and Wright when he wasn't working on an appeal in the law library, about the impact the gardens were having. He worked diligently, weeding and planting, but it was clear that his thoughts were elsewhere. He told me that he liked touching the earth, and that he was grateful that we were there trying to help but he wanted to go home. He really just wanted to go home. Another guy told me that he'd gotten used to waking up at night convinced that he was having a heart attack, feeling as if his chest was both exploding and caving in. While he talked he pressed on his sternum, a gesture I saw him make often, subconsciously, even when he wasn't talking about the pain he experienced at night. He told me that he wasn't interested in the prison's medical services. He explained that it was just anxiety. He was overthinking things. He was going crazy because he'd been there so long. I told Jay about those conversations, while we sat in an open room near the cafeteria, a place that smelled sour and damp. Oh, and you think we don't want to go home, she asked me.

When I relayed my experiences to my mother she responded by telling me that for the sixteen years that she knew my father, she only saw him cry twice. This was an anecdote I'd heard often, though it wasn't until this conversation that I learned that what my mother was getting at was that she never saw him crying for himself, or even for us. He cried both times for strangers, for the young men who were wheeled into his operating room when he was doing his residency not long after I was born. The first time it happened he'd sat slumped in his chair with his hands covering his face, and my mother hadn't realized for quite some time how upset he was. The line of damaged bodies that night had seemed endless, he'd told her. He couldn't seem to make a dent in it no matter how tirelessly he worked. He talked at length about bullet holes, horrific wounds in otherwise healthy bodies. My mother wondered if something about his experience had forced him to either face or think differently about his own failing health, the cruel arbitrariness of it, but when she asked about it the next day he'd seemed not to understand her question.

He cried the second time a few weeks later because he felt guilty about the tactic he'd developed for the endless line of patients, which was to think of skin as cloth. He was methodically sewing pieces of cloth, not the bodies of young men, kids really. He told her that he couldn't bear to look into their eyes. He was certain that they were looking at him for reassurance. He could have nodded or smiled, he said to her. He could have tried harder to make those moments all right. But instead he froze, or he told himself that he was frozen, that he needed to focus on his work, and that's why he wouldn't look up. He'd let them down, he told my mother. They weren't even men yet and he'd let them down. My mother felt that she'd misunderstood my father this time too. She couldn't help but see his work in a broader political framework. She'd blamed the lines of bodies on the inanity of the drug war and the craze of conservatism, which he took to mean that she wasn't really listening, though she insists that she was. It was just that to her it was deeper. And then because she'd had a glass or two of wine, she started talking like her mother, about the suffering of people who've been gathered up and removed. Those lines that my father saw were filled with Lous, she said. Those lines were made up of the people who inhabited neighborhoods that formed after they'd been pushed to the outskirts, by highways and railroad tracks and plumes of smoke that poisoned the lungs of children.

Towards the end of the project Jay said that I could write to her if I wanted to stay in touch and then she invited me to a play that she and a number of women who were incarcerated with her had written, with the help of a graduate student, warning me that I would probably cry. By that time she'd seen me cry a number of times already. It turned out to be less of a play than a series of monologues about the women's lives, conveyed in a way that struck me as exploitative and sensationalistic, as if they'd been written by somebody else. Jay's girlfriend had the last monologue and she stood in the middle of the room and stared at her feet while she talked. She was crying and her nose was running and I couldn't help but focus on the fact that she didn't have a tissue, and that she was an adult woman with a runny nose, holding up her pain and despair for all of us to see, for nothing. She spoke softly and hurriedly about being molested by her older cousin's friends and then raped at age ten and then abused by every man she was involved with. Throughout the play I kept staring at the graduate student, hoping to make eye contact with her so that I could make it clear to her what a shit I thought she was. I pictured her in some dumb self-congratulatory seminar, gesturing with her hands while yapping in jargon about constructs. Afterwards she approached us and asked us what we thought and I told her that the play was really moving. She scrutinized my face while I talked. Really? How had it moved me, she wanted to know. Could I tell her more? I told her that the women were remarkable; that it was incredible how they'd thrived despite the trauma they'd been subjected to. She got tears in her eyes and shook her head and told me that the hardest thing for too many of the women was believing that their stories were worth hearing. I left feeling like a huge asshole.

Unlike Keith, my boss Leon understood why I was so moved by my brief experience with the prison project. He wasn't embarrassed about being emotional or admitting that he felt overwhelmed by both the magnitude of the problem and his shame at not having understood it sooner.

Even if he was privileged and white and male, even if he knew he would make idiotic misstep after idiotic misstep, he told me, he still wanted to do all that he could to make the world a better place. He leaned back, taking up a bit too much space, his trust fund confidence and healthy calm palpable. But at least he was trying, I thought, while eyeing his tan, not quite manly hands. I didn't feel great about it, but in all honesty, in that moment I had the urge to let down his man bun, and to throw my perfect body at him.

chose to chalk up my desire to sleep with a man other than the one I was in a committed relationship with both to my deep desire to escape the emotional heaviness of the women in my cabal and the general tumult of my life. The truth, however, is threefold: that I don't trust breezy women, that I hadn't shaved in a week and a half, and that I desperately wanted my job back and wasn't certain that my vagina was the appropriate avenue through which to achieve that goal. Curiously, when I described my carnal urges to Isabella on the telephone, she took control of the conversation, turning to her own sexual relations, which she insisted, fell well within the bounds of the moral high ground I was attempting to hold over her. I tried to correct her, as I did not jump my boss, even though I wanted to. Isabella, on the other hand, railed her coworker, though she did so, she absolutely insists, long after Jason had moved out.

What had spurred her urge, at least partly, was watching Jason attempt to get his shit together. He'd come by looking rather forlorn, with a few garbage bags hanging from his back pocket, which he planned to use to stuff with the belongings that he'd left in a closet, a relatively brainless task one might think. But it had clearly overwhelmed him. He'd seemed incapable of understanding basic physics, geometry, she'd noticed. He'd held an empty bag in one hand but couldn't manage to put a whole wadded up shirt inside of it, so clothing spilled to the floor. The bag split at its side. Was this the sturdy man I fell in love with so many years before, she thought, and had he always been this way. Towards the end Isabella had told her friends that she wanted to like Jason again, and that the only way to do that was to leave him. She'd said it jokingly, even though she'd been serious. But watching him then, the notion of whether or not she liked him felt almost bullying.

After Jason had made an ass of himself with the shirts and the bag, he'd sat down on the sofa and asked Isabella how she was doing and he'd seemed to be studying her face intensely. She became flustered, wondering if he somehow knew. She couldn't understand why she felt guilty. She hadn't done anything wrong. How could he still induce this sort of thing in her. She'd responded awkwardly in choppy self-deprecating sentences about her work, which she later regretted not only because it wasn't true.

Our mother watched Isabella's daughters on the nights she spent with Dean, which she loved. She developed rituals with them, making latkes in the morning, or cinnamon toast and milk with coffee syrup. She never asked Isabella any questions about her dating life, and was seemingly uninterested in what she was up to on her nights off, which Isabella found strange. She asked her about it once and our mother told her that she was trying to give her privacy. Isabella was entitled to a full life. That included a sex life. She didn't have to report back about it to anyone. Especially her mother. But a part of her, Isabella told me, had wanted to report back about it.

When our mother had begun to date after our father died she'd done so tentatively, as she'd been anxious about how my sisters and I would react, though we hadn't minded. It very rarely affected our lives, and when it did it usually meant a sleepover at Nana and Poppy's house or at Adele's. There had been a few men who she'd dated seriously, but she'd guarded her time and her space fiercely, because before she hadn't realized their value. Then she met Jacob, when she was in her fifties. He'd spotted her at a gallery.

He was jovial, tan, trim, confident. He'd done well in the private sector, well enough to have gotten what he needed from life, which is important for men, Joan pointed out, especially in terms of how they treat women. Isabella told me that she wondered if the secret to our mother's lasting relationship was distance, that she'd found someone who wasn't interested in pressing at her boundaries.

A few of my mother's paintings were being shown at the gallery. This was in a more experimental phase, where she used bolder colors, sometimes painting landscapes, which had previously never interested her. Jacob had wandered in, just to see what was going on. He'd been attending a meeting in a building nearby. He was retired by then, but was still on certain boards, as he's explained to me. He'd worn a suit that had reminded my mother of the sorts of things she'd seen in the windows of tailors' shops so many years ago in Florence, expertly engineered but not overly complicated. He'd stuck out in that crowd, she recalled. Most people had been dressed more casually, in draping things. She'd worn a linen sundress, something she'd had for years.

Nana liked Jacob immediately. At lunch one afternoon, pretty early on in their relationship, she went out of her way to laugh at one of his jokes, something silly, about crooked Rhode Island politics. Minutes before she'd happily accepted his advice on a glass of wine, even though she never drinks wine with lunch. Because she was so oddly taken with him, my mother had pointed out to her afterwards that, like Luke, Jacob wasn't Jewish either. He'd been raised Catholic, though he thought of himself as agnostic. Not that he really bothered to clarify how he identified about things like that. Nana said that she no longer worried about who was Jewish and who wasn't. She'd long ago given up that sort of thinking. Which was news to the rest of us.

I adore Jacob, and not only because he maintains a year-round tan, a deep red-brown color I've only seen in a particular kind of man in his late fifties or early sixties, the brown a result of exposure to the sun, the red of good health and resources. He slicks his hair back, the way all the Jewish men of Poppy's generation did. My mother noticed the same thing. When he approached her to ask about one of her paintings, bits of silver and black hair fell from the combed grooves that lined his head, just like it had with Poppy's hair. By the afternoon the slicked-back-ness was more of an idea or a reminder of what had been that morning. Many women, attuned to the Oedipal quagmire that this association implied, would have run to—or away from—him. My mother stayed where she was. Her first thought, she admitted, had been that he wasn't very bright, so neither threatening nor attractive. He'd asked her a leading question about art, to provoke a general conversation, and she could tell that he was used to winning people over quickly, his manner cool, slightly mischievous, his eyes twinkling. My mother's memory is that her response had been terse. He told us later that he'd found it sweet, though neither could remember what she'd actually said.

He ended up buying a painting, one she'd priced, somewhat arrogantly, she told us laughing, at a few thousand dollars. He hung it in the dining room of his summerhouse in Little Compton, he wrote to tell her in a thank you note that arrived at the house a few weeks after the show. She'd blushed while reading it, something about the ease of it, a quality she can't quite describe. He'd asked her to call him. He wanted another painting. She'd called him that evening. They talked baseball for over an hour and then he'd asked to take her to dinner. A few days later he brought her to one of the fanciest restaurants in Providence and ordered way more than they could eat, so that they could try everything that appealed to them as opposed to narrowing down their choices to only one entrée and an appetizer. That sort of thing had made our mother nervous at first, all the waste, the excess. But Jacob didn't see things that way. He was a self-made man, new money, so he had no qualms about enjoying the world and not taking things too seriously. They travelled together, to Portugal, Italy, and Spain, staying in beautiful luxury hotels. In Florence on one of their anniversaries he'd ordered an easel to be set up in their room facing the window because she'd told him about painting Santa Maria Novella through the window of Marcella's apartment so many years go.

Jacob had been married before, too, twice. One of his divorces had been amicable and the other bitter. He had two grown sons and he was close to both of them. He seemed to have learned from his previous relationships, my mother felt. Or she assumed as much because he was easygoing in a way most people aren't, almost always willing to listen. He held on to very little, she told Joan on the telephone, but Joan had pointed out that that sort of thing is easier for men. Men don't have to cling the way women do, because their concerns aren't constantly being picked apart.

When my mother had first described Jacob to Joan, five or so years ago, Joan had talked about the confidence that comes to women in their fifties. She thought that it made dating easier. She wanted to know if my mother planned to marry Jacob. My mother recalls being taken aback by the question. She hadn't really thought about it and she was shocked that Joan had. For the entire time my mother has known Joan, besides the years she was married to Steven, Joan has been adamant about her opposition to marriage, describing it as an antiquated institution designed to contain women. The day she called to tell my mother that she planned to get married, my mother had laughed out loud. She'd thought at first that it was a joke. Joan had sounded so silly, almost triumphant, and my mother could hear Steven in the background with his mellow South African intonation, calling to her about something. My mother explained that for her it wasn't about newfound confidence, though there was a sense of ease, because there wasn't a precedent for dating at her age, at least not that she knew of, so there were no standards to meet, no silly arbitrary rules she had to uphold. Their mothers certainly hadn't modeled this phase of dating for them, my mother told Joan. Nana and Leticia wouldn't have dreamed of beginning new relationships, and in fact, were vehement, almost proud, of their widowhood. And Adele had done whatever she'd done in secret, they'd agreed, whatever that meant.

The biggest concern my mother had had about dating Jacob, oddly enough, was how it would affect Adele, even though by then my father had been dead for years. But Nana told her not to concern herself with Adele's comfort about her personal life. She had no right to say a thing, Nana had said sharply, as if my mother had disagreed with her. Though Adele never said a word about it, my mother assumed that Adele would find Jacob ostentatious and lowbrow. He drove a Mercedes, after all, a new one, which my mother had alluded to once, in a strange and awkward attempt to introduce the idea of him to her and Adele had raised her eyebrows in a sort of mocking, laughing way, but had said nothing.

Though he gets along well with Isabella and Alessandra, Jacob and I clicked immediately and intensely. He is the kind of man I admire, sturdy, approachable, with a healthy drinking habit and an open mind. Not long before I left for South Africa I drank bottle after bottle of wine with him on my mother's sunporch and talked drunkenly until well after midnight about the ills of the world. My mother remained on the sofa, drifting off, interjecting every now and then. I'd described the play at the women's prison to him, railing about injustice and racism. I'd declared that the world had never been as bad as it currently is. My mother had roused herself enough to tell me that the '60s had been pretty intense too. Everything was going to shit, she'd said, because her generation had wanted to destroy the world and to save it at the same time. The statement hung in the air for a while. Most of the candles had by then gone out, extinguished by the breeze from the open windows. Then Jacob started talking about the old days, days he hadn't spent with my mother, but he talked as if he had. He was smiling, recalling moments of happiness, excitement at the thought of being at the brink of real change. My mother had started smiling, nodding, not at all interested in correcting him, reminding him that in those days they'd both been married to other people. My mother told me later that she'd been thinking of Jacob while we'd talked, but also about my father. She recalled their old fights, how she'd wanted to cling to the explosive power of the '60s and how he'd wanted to let go, to be a grown-up. Of course it was also that very authoritative confidence that drew her to him in the first place, she admitted, because being around somebody like him took the weight off of her. She didn't have to make the big decisions. He'd already figured it all out.

Jason had once provided Isabella with all the answers, too, and now, as a single woman she felt lost at times, without structure, even though it was also what she wanted. So she had tried to operate the way men do, as if her body and mind were separate, one not affecting the other. She had wanted to be oblivious, she said, like Jason had been. Dean's apartment was nondescript, with fewer books and less furniture than she'd expected, and neither clean or dirty. He'd fastened his bike to a rack on the wall as if it were artwork, like something a graduate student would do, which made sense. He was a graduate student, almost a decade Isabella's junior. The space he occupied, she told me, seemed to magnify his lack of certainty, his murkiness, his inability to provide the sort of stability she'd failed to cultivate in herself as an adult woman and sometimes craved.

The first time that she was in his bedroom, she told me, she felt both unsexy and unsafe. She suddenly didn't want to be there, she realized, but she stayed. She felt as if she were watching herself from above, the crudeness of her situation too visible. She played her role with ease, she told me, which wasn't his fault. She was just too used to playing roles by then, falling into them too easily. But instead of finding this notion only depressing, she said that it also enabled her to feel more empathetic. Thinking of Jason then, while in bed with another man, a kind of sadness washed over her. Recalling his struggle to put his shirts in a bag, she said she could feel her old anger receding. He wasn't to blame for all of it anyway.

Lying there that way began to feel ridiculous to her. She started to cry, feeling as if she'd once again abandoned herself, allowed herself to get invaded by something not entirely un-dangerous. Dean had attempted to comfort her, very kindly. She pulled herself together after a while and tried to laugh about it. He told her that he understood. Afterwards she drove to our mother's house. She'd meant to drive home, she told me. She'd wanted to be in her own bed, to try to make sense of what had happened, but she found herself staring up at our mother's window. The light was still on, and Isabella idled in the street before going inside, quietly unlocking the front door and pushing it softly, as it often made a deep, creaking sound. Our mother had called out nervously when she heard the noise, because Isabella hadn't told her where she'd be sleeping, or when she'd pick the girls up. Isabella ended up lying down at the foot of our mother's bed. Our mother asked her if she'd been crying and she'd nodded but didn't explain herself. Then she fell asleep and woke up to the sound of her daughters in the kitchen downstairs, and the smell of coffee. Our mother was crouched on the floor at the end of the bed facing her. She handed Isabella a cup of coffee and then began to talk about our father, which annoyed Isabella at first. Because our mother had been so adamant about not equating Isabella's divorce with my mother's experience of losing her husband to illness. But then so often, she seemed to do just that.

Isabella informed her that she was not depressed, if that was what she was getting at. She was simply a grown woman who'd fallen asleep, while trying not to cry, at the foot of her mother's bed. There was nothing more to it, she'd said. Our mother had smoothed her hair and nodded, and continued to talk about our father. She told Isabella about Adele having us bring him blackberries on the last day of his life, which she obviously knew already. Adele had made such a production of it, our mother said, as if it were something that he'd wanted, or that had been asked of her. They'd talked briefly on the phone the day before, but Adele had refused to acknowledge how dire the situation was. My mother had tried to relay to her a conversation she'd had with his doctor. Adele had responded by telling her that she planned to make a tart, the dessert that my father had loved as a child, something she'd discovered in France. My mother told her that our father wasn't eating much, which she'd said before and Adele knew already.

When Adele arrived at the hospital with the blackberries her face was so flat that it irritated our mother, she said. She had wanted Adele to cry. She wanted to see Adele feeling as ragged as she did. But Adele just pursed her lips, and sat cross-legged on the metal chair next to our father's bed, barely looking at him. She faced our mother instead, and laughed about how I'd thrown such a fit that she hadn't had time to make the tart. But so as not to come empty-handed, she'd brought the berries my sisters had picked in a china serving bowl covered in plastic wrap. My mother remembered this part of the conversation afterwards. At the time she was too dazed to comment on the ridiculousness of Adele worrying about coming empty-handed, as if she'd been invited to some sort of garden party and not her son's deathbed.

My sisters and I were there, too, though all of our memories of these last moments are different. My mother told Isabella that I'd stood stone-faced next to her, something that I have no memory of. I only recall staring at the catheter tube, feeling embarrassed, or confused, a series of feelings I couldn't quite understand. I still don't. As Adele talked, I'd gently removed the blackberries from the bowl and lined them up in rows, my mother says. She remembers the beautiful dark purple of the berries, almost black, on my father's starched white hospital sheets. Alessandra remembers this, too, and that I'd dropped a few of the berries, clumsily, and that she'd picked them up, but had been unsure what to do with them. Putting them back in the bowl made no sense, and she knew not to hand me the dirty berries that she'd retrieved, that they shouldn't be put on the bed with someone who was dying. So she'd held them, her small warm fists slowly squishing them so that their juice dripped between her fingers. Isabella remembers guiding her to the bathroom and throwing the berries in a large metal waste basket and helping Alessandra to wash her hands with potent antibacterial soap.

Our mother had tried to prevent Adele from leaving, she recalled to Isabella, not because she wanted her company, but because she didn't want to be left alone. She was no longer thinking clearly, she said, but attempting to stave off what she knew full well was coming by aligning herself with Adele's intractable denial. But somehow Adele left without my mother's realizing it, and then it was just the two of them, our parents, alone again in that awful room. Our father grew restless. He began to cough, great wheezing movements that rattled his whole body. Our mother brought him water but he shook his head when she offered it to him. She used his old tactic, and tried not to look at his face, turning every which way to avoid his gaze. After a while he told her in a rasping, tired tone how much he loved her. She raised her head. She'd been slouched in her chair. He was smiling at her strangely, drugged looking. He told her that he thought that it was happening, that this was the moment he was dying. She ignored him. Or she tried to. Because she didn't know how to respond. She couldn't bear the thought of it. She tried to change the subject but he cut her off, telling her that he had loved her from the first time he saw her. She started crying, drained by her attempts at vigilance. He began to apologize, saying again that he loved her and that he was sorry. She felt dizzy and her heart began to race, the sterile, antiseptic odors of the hospital burning her nose and throat. Images of their years together rushed at her, she said. Distant memories, strange and out of sequence, scrolled past, like clips on a movie reel. In that desperate moment, she told Isabella, a part of her had tried to figure out if it had all been worth it. Meeting him, marrying him, trying to save him, all the fights with her mother. How cutthroat she was, she remembers thinking. Who looks at their life this way, as if it's some undeviating progression, black and white.

So she got up and sat on the edge of our father's bed, taking his hands in both of hers. He shut his eyes, which made the room feel unbearably empty. She thought about the day in Italy when she'd walked to Santa Maria Novella a few days after learning that he was sick. She'd had a headache. Marcella told her that it was because of the tolling of the bells from the church. They drove Marcella crazy, but they never bothered our mother. Marcella brought her a glass of some kind of dark liquor and told her to lie down on the sofa with her feet up. Our mother had tried to, but she was too agitated, and whatever Marcella had given had been bitter, irritating her throat. After a while she left the apartment and walked around the neighborhood. She sat down on a bench outside of a café a few blocks away and ordered a glass of wine but only took a few sips of it. She remembers thinking that she had to figure it all out right then. As if she would never have a chance to rethink anything. But she can't remember what her logic was about this, what her calculations were. After a while she'd gotten up to walk back to Marcella's apartment and somehow along the way she decided that she would go back. She would go home to Rhode Island. She would marry him. She felt certain, she said, because she thought then that she had to be.

In the hospital, on that last day with our father, with the sound of his strained breathing filling the room, she told Isabella, she started wondering what it would have been like if she'd done something else. Maybe it wouldn't have ended up all that differently, she'd thought. Maybe she would have finished the seminar without rushing home. Or stayed on in Italy forever the way she'd sometimes wanted to. When they'd first met, our father had told her that it was silly to assume one could know the outcome of the path that wasn't taken, and she'd loved that he thought that way. So she told him that she loved him, too, but that there had been times when loving him had crushed her. She could hear the anger in her voice, and she had wanted him to take it with him. She wanted it erased from the world that she'd ever felt that way. He told her that he understood, that he'd never meant to do that to her. Tears streamed down her face, blurring her vision. She remembers struggling to figure out what it all meant, what exactly they were talking about, whether it was even the same thing. She wondered if he would have said those things or eventually changed how he was if he'd never gotten sick. If he had remained king of the world, she said to Isabella, would it have occurred to him to see her differently.

By then he was almost yellow, our mother told her. The golden undertones of his skin had grayed and he was so gaunt that the angles of his face made him look like a caricature of himself. She'd clasped his hand, too tightly, thinking of the way he'd slumped in his chair late at night after work, trying so hard to fight his feelings of hopelessness. She saw him as a young boy, passed back and forth between Adele and Henry, both coddled and neglected, in a stark, regal house, haunted by ghosts. She saw him fumbling, his hand shaking, the plaintive face he'd made when he'd asked her to marry him. She'd wondered how it all looked to him, if it all felt worth it, if it was true or not that there's some sort of clarity achieved at the approach of death. And then, holding his hand that way, in his last minutes, she'd realized that it didn't matter, and that for her, it had been worth it. Because she hadn't really been after the happy ending. Not that she didn't want one. But that hadn't been what it was about for her. She wasn't going to bother wondering about the path she hadn't taken.

A nurse came in at some point and fiddled with our father's IV but neither he nor my mother moved. When the nurse left our father had stared at the door for a while and then asked our mother if she forgave him. Then he shut his eyes and she stared at his face and squinted, so that she could see again the man she'd met so long ago, the man with the face that was so unlike any she'd ever seen, and she told him that yes, she forgave him. And then he died. And for a long time, she told Isabella, she couldn't see him at all. Years went by. And then she finally saw him again. In our faces, she sees him.

Later that day, at home in her shower, Isabella started thinking about Jason, how different one man was from another. She wondered if he'd been with someone, too, something her friends had warned her about. Men move on so easily, they'd said. There are too many eager women out there. She wondered if Jason would deplete this phantom, eager woman, too, if she would also get to a point where she no longer liked him, and would have to leave him so she could like him again. And then my mother's memories came to her mind and Isabella remembered how Jason had seemed to her when she'd first seen him, so balanced and open-minded and kind. She'd begun to see him that way again, not entirely but somewhat. She could see the positives again, the brilliance, that despite all his faults, he would never watch her at a party feeling a bitter urge to expose her for what she truly is.

She realized after a while that she was crying. She wondered at first if it was that she missed him, though she knew that it was really that she didn't miss him. It was something about the emptiness of the shower, her shower, Jason's old shower, a small place in their world that had once held his things, a particular brand of soap that he'd liked, shampoo that smelled like cedar. Something about the experience magnified for her the sadness of falling out of love. For so long it had seemed impossible, the aching, overwhelming, relentless love and admiration she'd felt so deeply for him had seemed too solid to ever break down. It hadn't occurred to her how powerful and toxic accumulated resentments can be—that despite what she had told herself, how she viewed herself, pushed herself—she wasn't immune to them.

She then had the feeling that she'd had in Dean's apartment, she told me. She pictured encountering herself, or someone like her, in a similar position, in a movie or a book. It occurred to her that she probably wouldn't like or relate to the woman she saw, but would see her as a nuisance, would find her complaints irritating. Stop being so difficult, she'd think, just as her friends likely did. Look at how wonderful he can be. Why are you harping, wallowing. She began to plead with herself, she told me, with the detractors in her head, but lost her way. She found their arguments too tempting. They were her own. She'd been constructing them for years. She stood still, her fingertips pruned, her chest red. A wave of self-hatred washed over her. Her own privilege, her undeniable good fortune, her luck, compared to so many woman, to most women, to most people, made her circumstances seem trite, spoiled, another hideous example of privilege. She turned the water off. Consuelo and Vanessa were standing on the bath mat outside the shower staring at her. Vanessa handed her a towel. Isabella apologized for taking so long. Vanessa reached up and pressed on her chest, leaving tiny blotches of white fingerprints that quickly reddened again. There was no sense to be made of any of it, Isabella told me. That's what our mother had been trying to tell her.

A few weeks later Jason dropped the girls off after a weekend away. They seemed happy to be home, Isabella had thought, but not relieved, which she found reassuring. The mess of the divorce was real, but her daughters were all right. Jason had lost weight, she noted, and had a coating of stubble, which she'd always liked. He'd looked tired, but somehow sweet. The girls scampered off somewhere and Isabella had leaned against the door frame that led to the living room while Jason told her about their weekend. His sentences were light and easy, and his demeanor pleasant. He made funny self-deprecating jokes about his helplessness without her. At one point he became sheepish. She'd looked away, almost tearful, unable to not see all his good.

She watched him leave. He pulled on the light windbreaker he wore if there was even the slightest chance of rain and lowered his sunglasses, which had been resting on his head. There were bins overflowing with recycling on the front porch. Consuelo had organized it all, including what the city wouldn't take. Every couple of weeks she and the girls carted the ink cartridges, batteries, certain types of plastic and Styrofoam to a recycling center outside Providence. As Jason stepped off the porch his foot caught one of the bins, toppling it. Glass jars, aluminum cans, bits of paper, and wine corks bounced down the front steps. Debris spread across the porch floor and rolled onto the sidewalk. He'd paused to look down at a jar that was almost entirely rinsed of peanut butter that he'd stopped with his foot. He then wedged it against a large clay planter, preventing it from rolling further away. He stood there for a while, keys in hand, looking at the glass jar on the ground, and then he stepped over a newspaper section, an empty egg carton, the lid of a yogurt carton, and got into his Saab and drove away.

CHAPTER THIRTEEN

I t was Alessandra, who, through despair and deductive reasoning, had determined that it had been Howie who'd found Adele's body, and not Raul, as we'd originally thought. Howie had told Raul, a remarkably agile young man from North Dakota of all places, who'd dropped out of college to move to Newport so that he could apprentice at the hands of a builder of wooden sailboats, vessels he'd fantasized about as a child. Years ago Raul had sold a boat to Adele, a small wooden sloop, which she'd sailed twice, leaving its maintenance to Raul, who was happy to take on such a task. He was then asked to look after the other members of the fleet, equally unused, a larger sailboat, a Boston whaler, something else, too, I believe. Raul had given Howie, whose history he knew nothing of, our mother's phone number, but Howie told him that he didn't feel comfortable making such a phone call. So it had been Raul's report that we all heard, as described to him by Howie, unbeknownst to us.

Howie had worried about Adele, all alone in that great big house. He'd stopped by, as he'd been doing, also unbeknownst to us, by then pretty regularly. He found the heavy inner kitchen door wide open, and the screen door rattling back and forth in the wind, periodically slamming against the house and then back in its frame. He'd looked through the rooms of the house, calling to Adele, growing more and more frightened. Then he'd found a flashlight in the coatroom, hanging on its hook, because the sun had set by then, and he set out for the cemetery, certain that that was where she was. He found her halfway up the path, the blood thick, a vibrant red, matting the golden white of her hair. He fell to the ground next to her, shook her, yelled her name, but she didn't respond, her hand still clenching the bundle of wildflowers she'd picked for Henry. Howie told Raul that the sight of the flowers relieved him, that a profound and cathartic sense of absolution had washed over him, not because he wasn't sad about the loss of her, but because he knew then, in a way he hadn't ever before, that what he'd done to her hadn't destroyed her. Raul chalked up this response to the horror of seeing a dead body. Of course, Howie would experience a kind of guilt, or something strange at least. Raul only remembered this detail when he was pressed about it, and we assumed that it was his stable Midwestern upbringing that prevented him from understanding the swirl of pathos within which he'd inadvertently found himself. Alessandra had called him, suddenly desperate for the kind of closure that's impossible to attain. He'd walked her through the interaction a number of times, very politely, she said, though also clearly taken aback by her tearful persistence.

When Alessandra relayed all of this to me back in New York she was no longer tearful, though she seemed for the duration of our conversation at the brink of total collapse. We'd planned to meet for dinner, which she'd tried to wiggle her way out of, so I'd marched to her apartment, expecting to find her lying in bed sobbing, or somehow as vulnerable as she'd appeared while telling us about Seth a few weeks before in Adele's kitchen. But she was seated at her desk, which she'd moved since I'd last been there, so that it now faced the window. She asked if I wanted wine and then began to uncork a bottle from the fridge before I'd said anything. She started rambling about her book, which she'd alluded to over the years, but that I'd forgotten about. I told her that she seemed frenzied and she laughed at me. Eventually we sat down on the floor in the kitchen. She said that she was having trouble organizing her thoughts. I asked if she was still going to the group that had been so helpful and she nodded emphatically, robotically.

We continued to talk about Adele and then we drifted, or she drifted. I got the sense that she was trying to reset on some level, that she wanted to change whatever perception of her life she'd left me with, though she couldn't come out and say so. A part of me, I must admit, wanted the same thing. Her revelation had rattled me almost as much as Adele's death had, and the two instances seemed to feed off of each other in my mind. Or maybe it was that Adele's death and the mystery she left behind colored my thinking. Isabella said repeatedly that none of it mattered anyway, meaning that whatever the truth might be about our father's father, and Adele's relationship to him, that our sense of her and our world and family should remain as it had always been. It had been Adele's story to tell, after all, and she'd chosen not to tell it. So we ought to just leave it at that.

Alessandra agreed with this in theory, though she pointed out that of course it was much more complicated than that. She seemed eager to continue dissecting, which surprised me. I would have thought she'd be more aligned with Joan, creating some opaque academic argument about the power of narrative and the historical record, to keep from probing too much into territory that was beyond her control. But, shockingly, I was wrong. I was wrong, in fact, about all of our reactions to Adele's journal revelations, including, in some ways, my own. But with Alessandra at least, there were reasons for this. She was awash in her own secrets, and like Adele, she'd been revealing them all along. In her own way, of course, which is to say that she wasn't really revealing much of anything. Perhaps this is what had bonded the two of them so deeply during the last year of Adele's life. Adele gave Alessandra the distance she needed, never bothering to poke through the fog she surrounded herself with, understanding that she had to go somewhere with her story, the way we all do. Adele always said that every woman has a story to tell, a story that gets told, even if the story is that no one is to tell it.

Rather provocatively, Alessandra declared that she'd hidden nothing, that she'd been open actually, with all the details of her life, which I didn't quite know what to make of. It was true that we'd all known about Seth's promotion, which included a substantial raise and a move to Munich, though only Adele understood what that had meant for Alessandra. After the first announcement I heard nothing more about it. At least that's how I remember it now.

Alessandra had been unable to make up her mind about whether or not she'd go with him. She'd waffled about it for weeks, her indecision substantiating his assumptions about her, justifying his rage and contempt and frustration. She was holding him back, he told her, holding both of them back. One minute she wanted to go and the next she became evasive, and he told her, very cruel. She couldn't make sense of it herself, she'd told Adele. Because in the moments that she loved him, she felt a pulsing need to be near him, his ruggedness, his brilliant, analytical mind. She worried that without him she'd never again experience passion. But in the moments that she hated him and didn't want to go, she couldn't bear what had become of her life, her principles. That these two trains of thought existed at the same time somehow affirmed the claims he made, the ones that landed so firmly when she was vulnerable and confused. She was manipulative, the one who held the reins. Her feelings could change without warning or provocation. She was the one who was hurting him.

She miscarried in her first trimester. She told herself on the plane back from Munich, that it had been that sensation, the searing pain, and the blood, that had jostled her and set her head straight. But it wasn't. Or it was. But it was more than that too. She'd begun to feel psychologically unreliable, the roots of her nervous system deadened, her ability to reason no longer dependable. But she'd told Seth that it was the miscarriage, because unlike everything else, the miscarriage was a tangible, concrete thing that she could point to. He'd done this to her, she'd said. He'd brought this on. When she talked that way he only nodded, humbled suddenly, and she'd straighten her back, her anger rising. He'd lost his temper the night it happened, after they'd fallen into one of their usual arguments. He'd broken her lamp, slamming it on the ground after yanking it from the table, the cord thrashing as it ripped from the outlet. He'd held the tops of her arms and shaken her. She was sobbing by then, staring at the lines in his face that seemed to her in that moment repulsive, manifestations of ignorance. Later that night the bleeding started. He'd held his head in his hands, slouched at the side of the bed. She was inconsolable, she told me. She couldn't speak in full sentences. She went to the emergency room alone.

Had she told all of this to Adele, I'd wanted to know, but Alessandra wouldn't really say. Instead she responded as if I'd asked a question that required a long and multifaceted response, which she also didn't give me. She just made the face she'd made as a child when Henry read aloud to us from one of the tattered copies of *Winnie the Pooh* that had belonged to our father. Alessandra knew every word, because she'd read them numerous times herself. But her face always conveyed an expression of pleased relief, of ah yes, I'd hoped that this next part was coming.

A few days after her miscarriage, she said, the meanness started. She spoke harshly to a man at a bodega. She was incensed, but she can't remember why. A wave of nausea washed over her an hour or so afterwards as she'd recalled the interaction. The man had stammered, kindly, apologetically, trying to fix whatever she'd decided was problematic. She'd been completely apathetic, emotionless. Incidents like that accumulated, she told me, and then she turned on Seth. But it wasn't like the taunting she'd danced around before, when she'd simultaneously tried to temper his anger while baiting him. This was calculating and precise. She said horrible things to him because she wanted to hurt him, and she knew how. The women at the group in Washington Heights told her that her anger had the potential to provoke more violence from Seth, that she was now in a particularly precarious place. Her rage was empowering her. But if he sensed that and felt threatened by it, he could become dangerous. She was pushed to think more seriously about ways to extricate herself from the relationship, conversations she hated, that never quite seemed to square with the reality of her life with him, at least her perception of it.

Seth's firm had set him up with an apartment for his first year in Munich. He showed Alessandra pictures of it that had been emailed to him by a colleague, a gleaming metal kitchen and a living room with a black square sofa and a wall of windows. She agreed to go with him, for only a few days, to help him settle in, though she backed out of that at least twice, too, she said. She made excuses about work, family. He threatened to end things with her, which he'd done before. A few times he'd refused her calls, once for almost a month, which she'd found unbearable. She was unable to picture a life without him. How were days structured, how are things managed, she'd wondered, even though her terror both of him and of what a life with him meant was there too. She recalled the feeling of being lost in the maze that Henry had cut for her as a child. Nothing was straightforward. Straight lines, on closer inspection, had been slightly curved. Openings were dead ends. It was ostensibly a game, but it hadn't felt like one.

A few days before they were scheduled to leave, Seth softened. He told her that he understood why the trip felt stressful, why it all felt stressful. One morning he held her in what felt like a plaintive way. She was in her bathrobe waiting for the coffee to brew and he'd clasped his arms around her tightly, like a frightened child. He told her that he was terrified of losing her. He didn't know how to think about a life in Munich without her. She couldn't help but be moved by this sudden vulnerability. It suggested redemption to her. She could still fix all of this, she told herself. She could heal them both. They talked about the miscarriage, what it had meant, although she of course lied to him, she said, blatantly.

On a few nights they dabbled in learning to speak German, fantasizing about their life there, their fresh start. They used podcasts and apps and flash cards. Her accent was horrible. Seth struggled to memorize basic vocabulary.

Somehow she got the idea that she wanted to go back to Dachau. She told Seth that it was about her book, the one she hadn't written, the one she hadn't even started, that she kept telling people, including him, that she was writing. The lie was one of many that justified her rigidity, she said, her insistence on certain boundaries, but that also plagued her with guilt and anxiety, partly because she had no trouble maintaining it. She had actually started to believe that it was true, that she really was writing a book about her college thesis. When she had a night to herself she'd pull out her old notebooks and pore over sketches and notes she'd taken years before. She could remember vividly the lucidity of her thinking, the feeling of satisfaction she'd experienced at the way the disconnected puzzle pieces she'd fixated on, pulled from an assortment of courses, had suddenly assembled before her in a cogent argument. But looking back on it, alone in her apartment, she could no longer make sense of it. She couldn't follow her own trains of thought, why she'd associated one thing with another. Her notes felt hurried and remote, and her ideas not fully developed.

The built environment is a result of culture, language, societal standards, she'd written in one notebook. It often encompasses the subconscious, the aspirational, a vision for the future. She'd made two lists. One titled: It matters who is building what and why. Another: It matters how such projects get funded, followed by pages of buildings and builders. In another notebook she'd written: Angles and lines are rarely arbitrary. Prison yards are the new plantations, prisons the new concentration camps. Innovations in architecture and engineering give structures permanence. Forever visible but unseen evidence of the depth of collective human evil.

Her old thinking, that had once brought her such confidence, that she'd once believed had defined her, struck her then, sitting alone on the floor of her studio in a nightgown, as juvenile, embarrassingly simplistic. So she'd hurriedly stuff the notebooks back into the drawer where she'd stored them, flushed and mortified. Then later at night she'd jerk awake and recall a sentence, wondering if it was really so bad, so unredeemable. So on some level at least, she told me, seeing Dachau again was about standing on the same ground she'd stood on before, a lifetime before, it felt to her then, where Henry had once stood, too, where her thoughts had been her own.

But when she and Seth finally got there, she felt nothing like what she'd felt when she'd first seen it all with Isabella. This time she walked around stiffly, somewhat frightened, eerily indifferent to her surroundings. Something about the experience was energizing, galvanizing somehow, but not the way she'd hoped it would be. They passed the place where she imagined Henry had seen the piles of bodies, and the place where he saw the dying man marching past him, smiling. Seth had reached for her hand and she knew absolutely, without a doubt that she didn't want to take it. She suddenly didn't want to be touched by him. She shivered. Her thinking cleared. They were just far enough away from each other that she was able to avoid his reach without it seeming like she'd done it on purpose. She backed away, her arms folded tightly in front of her, inching closer to the wall, and pretended to be reading a plaque.

That night as darkness enveloped their hotel room she became nervous, her certainty of the afternoon subsiding. Seth lay next to her on his back, sleeping deeply, his mouth open slightly. She leaned closer to him, resting her face on his chest so that she could hear his heartbeat. Because of the way she was situated, with her ear flattened to his body, it sounded thunderous and violent. Her teeth began to rattle. She wondered if they were breaking, if she'd choke, swallowing them, as his body shook hers. So she pulled away. She sat up and inched to the edge of the bed. The room was quiet. She could hear only the sounds of her rattling teeth.

So she put her hand on her chest and felt her own heart, which wasn't loud. But it was steady. She tried to recall how to say heart in German. It was herz, she thought. Herz, herz, herz. Or was that soul. Was that the direct translation. Was it her soul beating or her heart.

They spent the next day wandering around Munich. Seth was to report to work the day after, and Alessandra would return to New York, ostensibly to pack up her things to move to Munich. She had their cab driver wind through certain neighborhoods that she'd photocopied from the maps and blueprints she'd found in her old notebooks. She pointed out a street to Seth, telling him that it was the street where Nana's cousins had lived. Look, she'd said, that building on the corner. On the third floor. Even though it wasn't true. Or maybe it was but she hadn't known that. She hadn't looked into where our family had lived before they'd ended up at Dachau. She could tell that he knew she was lying but he said nothing and just nodded back at her.

She called him from the airport and told him that she wouldn't be coming back. She stood only a few feet from the entrance to the plane, staring out the window at a landscape she was determined to never see again. For weeks after that he called her at all hours. First he threatened her. He said he'd come get her. He'd find her, no matter where she went. Then his tone changed. They even had some nice conversations. Days passed where she heard nothing. Then he told her that he'd found someone else, someone who wasn't as complicated and demanding as she was, and though she knew that she needed to be away from him, she couldn't stomach the thought of his moving on, or that she'd been so easily replaced. She cried for days. She even started trying to contact him. At first he took her calls, but he eventually stopped. She couldn't sleep. She pictured a strange woman, beautiful and soft, selfless in ways she'd failed to be, somehow able to save him from himself. She pictured her body, her hair. She felt dirty thinking that way, repulsed by the images she concocted, but still continued to do it. She began to wonder if she was losing her mind. She heard echoes of Seth's voice on the subway. She had nightmares that he was back in New York. She'd hear him banging on the door of her apartment or he'd show up at her work furious, both things he'd actually done. During their last conversation he'd said that the way she'd treated him on her last day in Germany had made him fall out of love with her. It's what she'd wanted, he told her. And she always got her way.

Finally the nightmares stopped. At first they got less frequent. Then one afternoon, walking home from work, she realized that it had been twelve days since she'd dreamt of him. The realization startled her. She even tried to conjure his voice, but all she could hear was the din of Manhattan traffic. She threw herself into her work. She continued going to the group in Washington Heights. Sometimes she went twice a week. There were new people almost every meeting. One woman, Alice, handed out pamphlets and recommended books, none of which she read. Rafaela ended up in the hospital. She was gone for almost a month and then came back for one meeting before disappearing again. Alessandra listened to German podcasts when she couldn't sleep, perfecting her accent by speaking out loud at night in the dark stillness of her apartment. Weeks passed, and then months. She cut her hair. She cleaned her apartment, donating old clothes and throwing out expired canned goods. Then she abandoned the place completely for the larger space with the better kitchen, where she lives now.

That's when she started calling Adele in the evening, she told me. She can't recall what prompted the first call, only that Adele had talked about Henry. The next night Alessandra told her that she was learning to speak German and that she was going to write a book. Adele told her about a German novel she'd just read, something about a woman who commits a murder because the press went after her, destroying her reputation, after she'd spent the night with a criminal. Heinrich Boll, the author was. A very good German man, Adele said. A Nobel Prize winner. They talked about Alessandra's childhood, about all of us. A few times Adele made her laugh out loud. At some point Alessandra realized that she'd begun to think about Seth the way Adele would have. That whole period of her life, she began to see as if it were a movie, one that had had a huge impact on her but that she could only recall in snippets. Sometimes it felt to her like the sensation that occurs when you narrowly dodge something physically dangerous, like when you catch yourself before falling or barely avoid colliding with another car on the road after getting distracted. Often she and Adele talked well into the night. Adele used the cordless phone in her dressing room, and Alessandra could hear her pouring her vinegar, the clinking of the cap on the bottle, and the bottle on the marbled glass goblet.

Had it ever occurred to her, I wanted to know, that she could have talked to me, to Isabella, our mother, Joan, that maybe she should have. Only in moments, she told me, shrugging. Everything felt strange then. One of the women at her group had outlined symptoms of PTSD, which Alessandra recognized immediately. The sudden terror she experienced in the aisle of her neighborhood market when she saw a certain kind of shoulders, a particular cut of overcoat. Smells that she associated with men, nothing she could really describe, that she often encountered outdoors, she found overwhelming. More than once she thought she'd vomit, but ended up hyperventilating instead. Once she had to brace herself on the ledge of a set of stone steps leading to a brownstone a few blocks from her apartment. She'd stood there panting, aware how odd she must have looked, but unable to do anything else until the feeling passed. One evening she'd gotten so anxious on her walk home that she'd begun to run, first a jog and then a sprint. When she'd reached her building she was sweating, dizzy, the hair on the back of her neck wet and heavy. She convinced herself that each landing of the staircase had the potential to be harrowing, dangerous. As she neared each one a wave of terror washed over her, propelling her to the next flight. In her new apartment she sat on the floor at the foot of her bed, rocking slowly back and forth.

Sitting there panting she recalled a fight she'd had with Isabella sometime in high school. It had started because she'd taken one of Isabella's sweaters, though Isabella had asked her not to. The sweater had some special meaning for her, which Alessandra had laughed about, in a mean way, she told me. And Isabella had wanted to wear it for some reason, a date or an event. Alessandra had assumed that she'd be able to put it back before Isabella needed it, but of course she'd lost it. The degree of Isabella's sadness about the loss of the sweater Alessandra had found off-putting. She felt guilty but refused to be cowed by her melodrama. Their argument escalated. They said terrible things to each other, both wanting to win, wanting to hurt the other. At one point Isabella told her that she'd get hurt someday. That someday someone would hurt Alessandra the way she hurt everyone else. She would then finally see what it feels like to be around her. And she would have no one.

I'd drained my wine by this time. Alessandra had as well, refilling her own glass, but not mine, not to be rude, but because she was focused so intensely on our conversation. She said that Adele dying when she did, just as she was starting to feel like herself again, felt like a kind of punishment, inflected more severely on her than the rest of us. This is not true, she knows, but she feels this way all the same. I searched for something to say but came up with nothing. She was looking past me, at the wall behind me with her messy bookshelf. She recalled that I'd wanted to know what she'd done to make it stop. I'd asked her about it at Adele's house. Did I still want to know? I did, in a sense, so I nodded. It was our mother's silly story about learning German, she told me. How our mother had wanted so badly for us to understand what it had meant for Poppy to have said to her in the '50s that she had better learn German if she planned to be a scientist.

CHAPTER FOURTEEN

Before I'd left Adele's house, Joan had talked at me about the merits of work while cooking probably the stupidest egg I've ever seen, which I'd eaten only to be polite. I hadn't realized what a God-awful cook she was, though I should have. Nana has warned me repeatedly of the culinary habits of the goyim what with their artificial butter sprays and overcooked, unseasoned meat, the sorts of people who wouldn't know an eggplant if they were hit in the head with it. Joan had watched me eat, sipping her coffee thoughtfully. I asked how she'd learned to cook an egg and she told me that she had not learned, and that what she'd slopped on my plate was one of maybe seven she'd made in her entire life. I looked mournfully out the window for a bit and when I turned back to face Joan I could tell that she felt sorry for me, but not because of the abomination she'd served me. She pities women who seem lost, she told me, which upset me incredibly, as I'm not at all fond of inciting pity. I asked about her kitchen in Cape Town, which had appeared to be the sort of kitchen in which eggs are prepared properly. I recalled the glass jars filled with spices that had lined the counter next to the stove, and the heavy cast-iron pans, sleek and oily with use, that hung from a steel rack over the island. I told her that it had actually seemed like a real cook's kitchen, and she said that it was. Steven had been a wonderful cook, Joan told me, and since his death she's tried not to change much. She also encourages her friends to come over and use it, which is one of the more brilliant ways I've heard of to throw a dinner party.

I said so and then was about to say something about not really being lost just as it occurred to her that she'd almost always been drawn to men who cook. Just like my mother, she said, laughing. How absurd. Anyway, she said, I was welcome to stay as long as I wanted. Far be it from her to tell another woman what to do with her life. But then she told me exactly what to do with my life. Go get your job back, she said. Go be with your sisters because they need you. And with this boyfriend, shit or get off the pot, but for God's sake stop complaining about it.

Joan then prattled away while I packed my suitcase, covering her travels, her affairs, the importance of her work, which she claimed has always provided her deep spiritual solace no matter her surroundings or circumstances, a blatant falsehood, but I didn't say so. In her forties, she told me, she'd been able to write for hours without interruption. It was like church, she said, like praying. She'd set her alarm for a few minutes before sunrise, drink two cups of strong coffee, read the paper in its entirety, and then write, sometimes until four in the afternoon. Working that way is good for the self-esteem, she said. After she quit smoking though, she could only write until noon. Maybe until one if she was lucky. And then a few years after Steven died, when his absence began to feel to her as normal as it ever would, she'd sit down to write, but find herself suddenly someplace else. Hours would pass. She thought about anything and everything. The London archives. Old railroad ledgers. Her parents. Political violence. Barcelona. You never know in the moment when you're in the midst of real change, she said, because that sort of thing is only clear in retrospect. Which is to say that despite her grief, her distractibility, and her age, which even she, she wanted me to know, sometimes grappled with, she still got on with her life, which, I think, was her way of telling me about getting back in touch with Arturo, her black-eyed, volatile love.

Joan and Arturo had gone a few years without hearing much from each other, she said, and then they began talking again, at first about work. He'd write to her asking if she'd review something. She'd recommend a book. By then he'd been married three times. His most recent wife had thrown a cast-iron pan at him before she left him. He said he'd watched it sail through the air towards him and it was in that moment that he knew he needed to change. He wrote Joan very funny letters about the agony of a third divorce. She wrote him about Steven's death. He called her and invited her back to Barcelona. They could argue again, he said, and drink good wine.

She stayed in a hotel near the apartment she'd rented over fifteen years before. She took long walks, as she had then, trying to familiarize herself with a now-strange city she'd once known so well. The second day she was there she found the cathedral where she'd lit candles with the priest before she'd returned to London. The façade's restoration had by then been completed, probably years before. It had begun to age again and appeared weathered, the stone-work clean but graying, and the arched doorway mottled with small cracks. She stood across the street from it for a while, and then approached the massive open door, the clean smell of damp clay and incense drifting towards her. She recalled the feeling she'd had when she'd first seen the place, lost and vulnerable, stuck and uncertain. She looked down at her feet. She'd gotten a pedicure a few days before in Cape Town, dark red, the same color she'd always worn, just like Adele. She remembers wondering if it had all been a dream. London again. South Africa. Steven. Had she actually just been there this whole time? Right there on that decaying stone step.

She had agreed to meet Arturo where their favorite café had once been, now an upscale home goods store. Standing there waiting for him, she became nervous. She wondered if he'd find her appearance startling. When she'd turned forty she remembers feeling strangely confident, thinking that she looked better than she had in her thirties when she was with him. She thinks it was really that she liked herself better then. Or that she understood how she worked in a way she couldn't have when she was younger. When he saw her his eyes lit up, she said. He said her name a few times and told her that she was still so beautiful, and she realized that she was the one who was startled by the way he looked. He'd gained weight and his eyes were heavy and tired, puffy, and smaller than she'd remembered.

They walked to a restaurant a few blocks away and sat at a table outside. Because she wasn't worried about loving him or being loved by him she found that she could appreciate him or see him in a way she had been unable to do when they'd been together so many years before. She found herself wondering if he felt the same way about her. He told her the story that he'd written about in his letter to her, about the pan flying through the air at him, and she laughed until tears streamed down her face. He told her that his ex-wife had been aiming for his head but that she was too small to get enough power to launch it that high. He would never touch a small woman again, he told her, laughing. Small women were far too dangerous. Joan told him that this small woman sounded wonderful. He stared at her for a while, his eyes soft, and then he told her that she must be heartbroken, to have lost the person who she'd loved so much, meaning Steven. The world is just too cruel, he supposed, and then he'd gazed into his wine the way he had years ago when they'd argued, but his face had grown kinder with age, and more playful. She told him that she wasn't heartbroken and he'd laughed, shaking his head. She laughed, too, and then insisted that really, she was not heartbroken, that that was not what she felt. She told him that she was grateful to have had what she'd had, because not many people get to experience that sort of thing, and that she knew that she would never be the same, that there were things she'd likely never feel again. But she had felt them. She really had. So no, the world was not cruel and she was not heartbroken. She was all right. Joan hadn't realized, she told me, that she felt that way until that minute, and that if she hadn't gone back to stand on that spot on the steps of the cathedral she may never have known it. Must they always argue, Arturo had wanted to know. Couldn't she just drink her wine and agree with him for once?

Joan started travelling again after that. She had wanted my mother to go with her. But my mother was too nervous about being away from my sisters and me, and Nana. So once more Joan set out alone. Thailand, Indonesia, Australia. She came home for a few weeks and then flew to Brazil, then Guatemala, and then she stayed for a few weeks with an old friend in Mexico City. When she got home she was able to write again. First on subjects she was already familiar with, and then she started looking through old notebooks from her London years and even earlier, back to the days when she'd kept lists of the things she hoped to someday write about. In one she came across a paragraph about her grandmother. Her grandmother had described playing with Morning, the woman whose name she later forgot. They'd made dolls out of cornhusks. Morning had let her grandmother climb trees, which her parents had forbidden her from doing. Joan had tried to transcribe exactly what her grandmother had said, the phrasing and the pauses. She read a few sentences out loud to Adele on the phone one afternoon, something about how Morning had covered her mouth constantly, as if she were apologizing. Adele had laughed and said something about her mother's fickleness, and that she'd always had a terrible memory.

One of the objectives of Joan's diatribe about women needing to just get on with it, I eventually gathered, was to let me know that despite it all, we'd all known very little about the depth of Joan's relationship to her mother. The truth was that by the time Adele died, she and Joan had developed something of a friendship. Joan had lost the urge to dredge up old anger, to throw it at Adele, to make Adele resolve it for her. Of course Adele was still caustic, secretive, self-absorbed, Joan said, but her life had started to look less

and less in her control, something that hadn't occurred to
Joan when she was younger. Joan began to sympathize with
Adele, she told me. She'd even begun to like hearing her
voice, the way she verbalized things. Joan especially liked
the way she talked about Henry. There was no formalness,
no snobby propriety or forced sentiment. There were only
frank descriptions of a person, a man who'd been lonely,
scrupulous, who probably drank too much, who had liked to
rake and shovel and make meticulous lists. Adele told Joan
a funny story about one of his tirades about toothpaste.
Why blue? Why sparkly? He found it disgusting, a cartoon
substance. But he thought the all-natural versions were
much more offensive. He had apparently really liked Janet
Jackson. He found her fascinating. He read a profile of her
somewhere and then bought a few cassette tapes and then
played them constantly in the Corolla. When Adele cried,
he'd held her hand. He promised to always protect her, to
defend her, but he refused to go to church with her.

Joan was shocked to learn that during those years her
mother had concurrently developed a relatively deep
friendship with Leticia. A few days before I'd arrived Leticia
had called the landline at Adele's house and had talked to
Joan about it for over an hour. Joan had sat in the wingback
chair in the den, her feet resting on the coffee table, the way
she'd sat sullenly as a teenager. Her immediate reaction to
this news was childish, she admitted, a pang of sadness at
the idea of the world existing, thriving without her. How
long had this been going on? How had she not known? How
close had they actually been?

Leticia told her that she'd been appalled that Adele had
never learned to bake anything besides that silly tart, which
Leticia had explained wasn't really a tart, but a strange
French pastry. Joan was fascinated by Leticia's portrayal
of their friendship. The woman Leticia described sounded
decidedly unlike Adele, open, silly, easy to talk to. One afternoon Leticia had tried to teach Adele how to bake something, scones or some kind of pie, she told Joan. Adele had

sat at the kitchen table sipping wine. Leticia drank some, too, which she rarely did. Adele had been distracted or uninterested, babbling about other things while Leticia set up a baking station at the trestle table. But they'd both eventually gotten too tipsy to do much and decided to give up the project, so they'd held hands and teetered to the living room. They'd laughed at first but then the conversation became sad and serious when they talked about the sons they'd lost.

I was aware that Joan believed that she was being helpful. I gleaned that I was to be taking from her something profound, about growth and forgiveness, albeit with a touch of that brittle WASP sensibility that Adele had had plenty of too. I began to feel like my mother had as a young woman, at a table full of grand old WASPs, listening to their convivial banter and having no clue what was going on. I actually even thought Joan had somehow gotten the story wrong. I couldn't really picture Leticia and Adele talking to each other the way she'd described it as happening. And I couldn't picture Leticia talking to Joan that way either, though the reasons for this are hard to articulate. But it was the truth, Nana told me, when I called her from the car on my way back to New York. The two had really connected. The night that they'd gotten drunk, Nana said, it was like being in the presence of two teenage girls, with the slurring and the silliness. But then Leticia had started to cry. She told Adele that sometimes, in the middle of what should be a mindless happy moment, she'd think of Darren. And then she'd start to feel sick with guilt because he was gone, locked up, because too much time had passed and too much had changed even though he was still the boy she'd raised, even though she could still smell his baby smell. She could still remember, as if were yesterday, the way his mouth had looked when she breast-fed him, how he'd made a tiny fist with one hand, how he'd drifted off to sleep, furrowing his tiny eyebrows. But he was a grown man now, a man who was in some ways a stranger, and in other ways not a stranger, but when she looked into his eyes in those horrible visiting rooms, she often thought of his perfect baby face and of that deep love that words simply can't capture that mothers feel for their babies, and all she could do to keep from crying was hold her mouth in a tight straight line. Leticia had looked at Adele and said, Oh but why am I crying like this now. Why am I acting this way. And Adele told her that she was acting just fine and that crying that way was fine too. And then she told Leticia about a time when she was sitting in the back of a car with her son Luke, my father, when he was a child, maybe five or six. She can't remember the car, who it had belonged to, or if anyone else was there. All she remembers is that my father had a piece of candy that was wrapped in wax paper and that he'd unwrapped it so carefully, the depth and purity of his excitement palpable in a way that had struck her as terrifying. She'd wanted to tell him, hide that happiness. Don't show the world how much you want that piece of candy, how much it matters to you. Wasn't that an awful way to react to the joy of one's child, she'd said to Leticia. But Nana can't remember how Leticia had responded, only that they'd sat there next to each other for quite a while, crying every now and then, until one of them got hungry, but she can't remember who.

Nana told me that the night before Adele's funeral she couldn't get an image out of her head of Adele with a gray skeletal face. She'd called Leticia to tell her about it a few hours after it had happened and then she mentioned it again the morning of the burial. Nana thought the image was coming to her because Adele had died sad and that she'd been sad for a long time, but Leticia thought it had something to do with the spirits Adele always talked about, the spirits that roamed her looming dark home. Leticia had seen a ghost there herself one of the nights they'd stayed with Adele. Nana didn't believe her at first. She'd thought Leticia must have been dreaming, but she insisted that she was wide awake. She said she'd only just turned out the light. She'd been reading a biography of Arthur Miller. She said she was still sitting or propped up, because there were always a lot of pillows on the beds at Adele's house. She'd turned to her side to move a few of the pillows but heard something behind her. She said it sounded like a door opening but that wasn't where the door was. Then she saw a woman, or the hazy form of a woman. The woman was putting linens away in the large wooden armoire across the room. Leticia said she was terrified but she didn't do a thing. She just sat there frozen. And then the woman was gone but Leticia couldn't remember seeing her leave, if she'd opened the door and walked into the hall or simply disappeared.

The last time Leticia and Nana had dinner with Adele, Adele told them that she brought flowers to Henry's grave almost every day. She said that she got so sad missing him that she'd start arguing with him. Out loud. She laughed recalling this, Nana assumed, because she no longer cared about keeping up appearances with them. Adele said that she wanted to be next to Henry again. She was tired of being alone, without him. She told them how practical he'd been, what a reasonable thinker he'd been, that he was all sorts of things, but that he'd never been mean to her. Then she shook her head and said that that probably wasn't true, but that it felt that way then, after so many years without him. All she could remember now was that she loved him.

Before I left, I'd stood with Joan on the stone steps that separated the patio off the kitchen from the path towards the garden by the driveway, my weekend bags stacked next to me. Roo was sniffing about, refusing to pee, in order to prolong our stay. Joan was silent for a while and then had sat down and pretended that she knew how to weed by sort of tugging at herbs in a raised bed. All morning I'd wanted to ask her what she planned to do with the journals and I don't know why I didn't. So I sat down next to her and said something about the view because we could see the water from where we sat. Being alone isn't so bad, she said after a while. I told her that I didn't have a problem being alone and she laughed and told me that everybody says that, even though everybody has a problem being alone. Even Adele, she said, had told her, sort of insistently, that she'd really come to enjoy her time alone. This had been their last conversation. Joan hadn't known this at the time, of course, but she had been struck by the comment, because in her mind at least, Adele had never been truly alone. She'd always had people looking after her or the house. Though it was true that she went to sleep alone, that she drank her morning coffee alone, that she took her late afternoon walks alone. Adele had told Joan that she'd taken to visiting Henry's grave and her voice, Joan recalled, had been light and sarcastic. Henry had been certain that there was no God, no hauntings or spirits, no reincarnations. This was something they'd argued about, Adele told her. Henry had told her that his physical self would slowly turn to dust and that his soul would very likely go with it, if anything remained of it. Speaking that way to Adele was how he'd teased her. Or Joan had always assumed that it was. But Adele seemed to see it differently. To Adele it was a result of Henry having been broken, damaged irreparably by his experience in Germany. It was her job, she felt, to prove him wrong. So she'd visited his grave every day, bringing him flowers in the spring and candied oranges in the winter. She spoke out loud to him, looking directly at his gravestone. She told Joan that Henry had promised to save her, long ago, and that she'd always assumed that he hadn't, and that it wasn't until he was gone that she realized that he had.

CHAPTER FIFTEEN

Ａnd so life went on. Or it tried to. Or I tried to. It's hard to know really. Back in New York at the end of the summer when the city is drained of most of its inhabitants but filled with a humid smog so oppressive that even the streams of dirty water that trickle from air conditioning units are a welcome respite from the heat, I'd attempted, as Joan had suggested, to just get on with it. Leon had agreed to let me come back to work and Roo had been accepted into a program that would enable her to be a service dog, though I was told that she would have to work on her penchant for naps. Service dogs were to be docile, but to actually fall asleep while "on duty" was not acceptable. Keith and I worked past our obvious issues by not talking about them. Instead, we resumed old patterns. I forced myself to un-see things about Keith and myself, a cursed skill, and one that my gender excels at. I made lists in my head of his good qualities, insisting on their value, in the hope that I might combat the torrent of thoughts that came at me when I couldn't sleep, the kind I fought so desperately each time they surfaced, and so often pretended not to have. The unchecked boxes, the conventions that I abhorred and shunned and so desperately wanted to participate in, to be validated by, lined up in rows, marching through my mind, like asshole automaton sheep. I was at war with myself, knowing full well what was best for me but finding myself suddenly stuck, alone in the morass of adult womanhood. On the telephone Isabella asked me why I was trying so hard to make something work that wasn't working, as if she didn't know the answer, as if she didn't do the exact same thing herself, the way we all do, even the very best of us, the warriors.

Jay was granted parole a few weeks before I returned from South Africa, and she was the first person I spoke to after learning that Adele had died. I'd often described Adele to her in letters. She'd responded by comparing Adele to Rapunzel, a strange and tortured woman, trapped in the high tower of a castle, which I thought was hilarious at first, but then later, when I thought back on it, found rather apt. Before her release, Jay sent me a packet of short stories that she'd written during her incarceration, which I read while on my layover at Heathrow. One of them was about all the apartments she could see from the roof of the Brooklyn building where she'd lived as a teenager. Through a square, doubled-paned window she saw a daughter being molested by a father figure, two floors below. On the ninth floor, a woman was rolling out tortillas on the counter. She'd taken the burner off the two-burner stove and was cooking them in a cast-iron pan. The images in the stories were so vivid that I assumed Jay really had seen those things, that they'd really happened. But they hadn't. On the telephone after I got home, Jay explained that remnants of truth probably existed in all of her writing, and that she had sat smoking on the roof of her building when she was younger, but that she'd always faced the other way, towards the gleaming lights of Manhattan.

Through the help of an advocacy organization, she'd gotten work doing something described as janitorial, although what she actually did every day sounded more like engineering. She used the skills she'd developed in prison, and displayed a kind of manual competency that exceeded that of her coworkers, a union of men who never explicitly complained about the quality of her work but made it clear to her that she was unwelcome, somehow tainted. She told me one day that she was surprised by the depth of her loneliness. She explained that though she didn't want to go back to prison, she'd believed, or had desperately hoped, that all the hard work she'd done there, and the reputation and relationships she'd built there, would have been more transferrable to her life outside. Now all that time, all that work and expended energy, felt futile to her. One night on the phone, she broke down in tears describing the obstacles she faced as she attempted even the most basic tasks, trying to set up a bank account, to establish credit, to begin the process of trying to find health insurance—which she needed as a cancer survivor—after having been in prison for so long.

Feeling ignored, and in keeping with the most petty characteristics of his gender, Keith began to question my honor, suggesting that my relationship with Jay was something other than platonic. First it was a joke. Then the jokes grew pointed, and not at all funny, his behavior a result of his feeling that he wasn't getting the attention he was certain that he deserved. He resented my time being taken up, by a woman no less, particularly a woman like Jay. He expressed his frustration in phrasing laden with misogyny and racism, but he did so subtly, the heinousness of it shrouded by the impenetrability of a tall white man expressing himself, so that I felt compelled, at least at first, to put his feelings before my own. I attempted to disentangle his logic, to point out where he was being unjust and unkind, to defend Jay, who'd done nothing wrong, and to present him with my point of view. But instead I ended up crying, exhausted by the impossibility of attempting to articulate the simplest of concepts to someone who'd decided, long ago, not to hear them. He sneered at me, the kind of behavior I rarely saw, that only emerged when he felt he was being criticized unfairly. This was so typical of me, to rage and then to cry, he practically spat, which only made the argument feel more hopeless, though I kept at it, long after it made sense to.

At some point, I remember blinking, and the vision of the woman I saw from the train outside of Johannesburg returned, somewhat blurred. At first it surprised me, that she'd surfaced, once again for reasons I couldn't quite grasp, at least not right away. But I had time to think, as Keith was by then lecturing vehemently, in the hopes of unsteadying me, distancing me from my own point of view. Sitting there then, some weeks removed from the incident, on the floor of my apartment with my pit bull in my lap and the sounds of Manhattan summer traffic swirling about the room, it dawned on me rather suddenly why that woman who I both knew and didn't know had once again come to mind. It was because she'd brought back to me, that fateful day on the train, the ghosts of my childhood, the images and stories I'd been told, the hazy conceptions of the world I'd formed, the childish but vital and authentic promises I'd made to myself, back when it was still inconceivable to me that I'd grow up and begin to break them. Momentarily stunned by this insight, I remained, for a time, uncharacteristically quiet and still. Clarity and composure returned to me. And then, Reader, I let his dumb ass go.

His initial response was to argue me out of it. He began by framing the parameters for our discussion, demanding a detailed explanation for what he saw as my about-face. I fell for this tactic at first, until it grew too tiring. He then told me that I was bitter and cruel. I told him that he was becoming emotional. When it dawned on him that I was not to be deterred, he began to plead with me, begging me to change my mind, to give him another chance, reversing old declarations, claiming that I simply didn't understand how much he loved me. Obviously I was moved by this, but not quite enough. He then told me that I was being childish, that I didn't understand what I was doing, that by leaving him I was forever giving up the privilege of having a man who understood me, and who would put up with my shit and not be an asshole about it, an outright lie, of course. He was absolutely an asshole about it, and if history or Adele had taught me anything, it was that there would certainly be more men in my future upon whom I could heap shit. This was not, I told him, my first rodeo.

After he'd fully exhausted both of us and finally left, I finished my wine, cried a bit more, examined my reflection in the mirror, and then called Isabella. She was appropriately sympathetic, though clearly struggling with issues of her own. She was distraught, plagued by the anxieties of re-acclimating, after so many years, to the single life, but not only that. There was a hideous sense of stasis, a "now what" kind of feeling. The separation had happened, the consumptive, energizing aspect of it had now subsided, and she couldn't quite make sense of this new path that lay ahead of her. I told her that I was certain that she'd be fine, that the problem all along had been the dead weight she'd been carrying around. Now she was free so the world would brighten. She told me that all of that was true, but that there was also so much else, so many other things she was grappling with, so that the brightness she'd hoped for and sometimes felt was so often overshadowed. As I'd attempted with Alessandra, days before in her apartment, I offered encouragement, lofty sayings and such. But I couldn't quite manage to lift her spirits. At a loss I asked if Isabella had sought the assistance of our mother, Nana, or Leticia. She had. Each had been perfectly wonderful, she told me, but somehow she was still stuck, by what she couldn't quite explain. It was at that moment that the glaring, awful permanence of Adele's absence set in, for both us, which is precisely why we began to bawl together in despair on the phone. To be clear, we were under no illusion that Adele would have had a solution for any of us, but that was far from the point. Because she would have had wine, a gourmet meal, a plush bed with high thread count sheets, ironed to perfection, in a bedroom that faced the water. She would have listened, raised her eyebrows at the approach of theatrics, recommended restraint and more wine, offered a joke, an anecdote, a playful saying that conveyed everything and nothing at all, which is to say quite simply that she would somehow have made everything better.

I could think of nothing more fitting then than for me and my sisters to return to her house, to be once again in the presence of the soothing, contradictory, painstakingly curated world she'd spent so many years creating. Isabella agreed. So I called Alessandra after I hung up with Isabella and ordered her to immediately pack her bag. She told me that she had a job, but would be happy to join us that weekend. Isabella and I left our respective cities a few days later. I brought an assortment of groceries, and while Consuelo and Vanessa played outside, the three of us cooked together in Adele's kitchen, which felt fine. I think I'd been expecting it not to, that our personal struggles would overtake us, that we'd break down constantly. But we didn't, though this is not to say that no tears were shed, because they certainly were. But we laughed a lot, too, teasing each other about Isabella's divorce, Alessandra's rigidity, my catastrophic and unsurprising breakup. Then it dawned on me that we'd become the women my mother had always wanted us to be, women who laugh and cry together at night.

After dinner, at my suggestion, Isabella and I took the girls down to the water, while Alessandra stayed at the house to take a bath even though I'd asked her not to. I'd wanted to continue to bond. I'd had a vision, back in my apartment, imagining an evening stroll bringing us all a sense of closure, renewal, and peace. I'd pictured the three of us ambling down to the shore together, prancing about the rocks, finding spiritual solace in the waves as they crashed about us. But it had been a gray day and the fading sunset was muted. Only the faintest traces of dull gold and peach remained, streaking a slate-colored sky, which dampened our moods, despite my best efforts. I clambered about for a bit, in an attempt to induce a sense of excitement in the girls at least, though they were decidedly unmoved, telling me that it was cold and dark and actually sort of dangerous really. Even Roo refused to join in my efforts at merriment, remaining curled on the chaise in the living room. Isabella was probably the biggest pill of all. She stood stiffly, making it clear that she had no interest in being there, explaining that she'd only come because I'd insisted on it, that she was cold and tired and had never been one for evening strolls the way I was. The whole thing was rather dismal, I finally had to admit, so I relented, and together, in a little clump, we traipsed back to the house.

I was abandoned quickly, Isabella and her daughters each marching off to their quarters with a book, a glass of milk, a section from the day's paper. Isabella had appeared to brighten as we approached the house. She'd announced that she, too, planned to take a bubble bath, a long one. She'd use the lavender bath salts Adele left in porcelain bowls in all the bathrooms with bathtubs. Minutes later I could hear her humming through the open windows, a Blondie song. My nightly ablutions were a protracted affair. I dawdled in the bathroom, washing and toning my face, applying heavy creams and filing my nails, while Roo snored audibly at the foot of the bed, half burrowed in a quilt. When there was nothing left to clip or smooth or pluck or moisturize, I slipped under the covers and attempted to further distract myself with a collection of novels I'd already read, piled on the nightstand, *Tess of the D'Urbervilles*, *Middlemarch*, *Song of Solomon*, but my thoughts wandered. So here I am again, I thought, in this bed, with Roo, thirty years old, a horrid temper, an unquenchable neediness, a burning desire for freedom, a biological pressure to reproduce, a cultural pressure to do so quickly, all compounded with a deep visceral need to complicate just about everything, simply because, it often seemed. I turned off the lamp and lay down. And so this is it, I suppose, I said smiling, to no one. Or maybe I just thought it.

As I drifted in and out of sleep, I heard someone or something on the stairs, whispering something I couldn't quite make out. I sat up, rubbing my eyes, still quite groggy. Moonlight bore into the room, illuminating the droplets of dew that dotted the windowsill and the floor below it, so that the room appeared to sparkle, like a fairy-tale structure, crystalline and ethereal. There were the sounds of footsteps that stopped suddenly at the landing. I rose, shivering in the damp night air, and tiptoed down the dark hall. And then I saw her. A stark, willowy form, standing rigid at the top of the stairs by the large open window, framed by the curtains that flapped violently at her sides. She wasn't looking at me but I recognized her face, the squinting eyes, the soft lines. Her hand, also lined, she held so that it covered her mouth.

The hall felt cold and enormous, a cavernous wind tunnel, the colors of night all dulled to a spectrum of gray. I felt an urge, deep and visceral, to move towards her. I wanted to touch her. I wanted to hear her story, to call out to Adele that she was definitely there, that I absolutely saw her, but I knew that I couldn't, that if I tried to she'd disappear. So I simply waited. The wind howled, and the sounds of the waves crashing against the rocks on the shore echoed throughout the room. Finally she moved her hand, letting her arm drop down by her side so that I could see her mouth, regal and bold, her lips slightly curled. I strained to hear her. Right before she disappeared I realized what she'd been saying. My name is Adele.

ACKNOWLEDGMENTS

Endless thanks to my team at Bold Story Press, Emily Barrosse, Karen Gulliver, Julianna Scott Fein, and Laurie Entringer. My thanks also go to Corrine Pritchett, Elysse Wagner, Marissa DeCuir, and everyone at Books Forward. I am profoundly grateful to my friends and early readers, particularly Betsy Pattullo, Amanda Coulombe, and Georgia Fan Shaw, and to my wonderful family for all their love and support. My mom and siblings provided invaluable insight, and Jack, Lydia, Quinn, and Naomi made the entire experience one filled with laughter and love. Most of all, thank you to my husband, Jess Manolo Torres. I don't know what I'd do without you.

Bold Story Press is a curated, woman-owned hybrid publishing company with a mission of publishing well-written stories by women. If your book is chosen for publication, our team of expert editors and designers will work with you to publish a professionally edited and designed book. Every woman has a story to tell. If you have written yours and want to explore publishing with Bold Story Press, contact us at https://boldstorypress.com.

BOLD STORY PRESS

The Bold Story Press logo, designed by Grace Arsenault, was inspired by the nom de plume, or pen name, a sad necessity at one time for female authors who wanted to publish. The woman's face hidden in the quill is the profile of Virginia Woolf, who, in addition to being an early feminist writer, founded and ran her own publishing company, Hogarth Press.